PRAISE FOR

TALES OF THE FROG PRINCESS

"High-spirited romantic comedy. . . . Fans of Gail
Carson Levine's 'Princess Tales' should leap for it."
—*Kirkus Reviews* on *The Frog Princess*

"Quests, tests, hearts won and broken, encounters
with dragons, and plenty of magic . . .
As tasty as its prequel."
—*School Library Journal* on *Dragon's Breath*

"Baker's . . . vividly imagined fantasy world . . .
[is] irresistible and loaded with humor."
—*VOYA* on *Once Upon a Curse*

"Kids will get a kick out of the hip *Shrek* vibe . . .
in this updated fairy tale."
—*School Library Journal* on *No Place for Magic*

"An entertaining prequel. . . . An engaging main
character . . . , sibling rivalries, and a romantic love
interest combine in this appealing choice."
—*Booklist* on *The Salamander Spell*

BOOKS BY E. D. BAKER

Dragon Kiss

Book Seven in the Tales of the Frog Princess

E. D. BAKER

BLOOMSBURY
NEW YORK   LONDON   NEW DELHI   SYDNEY

First published in the United States of America in September 2009
by Bloomsbury Children's Books
Paperback edition published in August 2010
New edition published in February 2015
www.bloomsbury.com

Bloomsbury is a registered trademark of Bloomsbury Publishing Plc

For information about permission to reproduce selections from this book, write to
Permissions, Bloomsbury Children's Books, 1385 Broadway, New York, New York 10018
Bloomsbury books may be purchased for business or promotional use. For information
on bulk purchases please contact Macmillan Corporate and Premium Sales Department at
specialmarkets@macmillan.com

The Library of Congress has cataloged the hardcover edition as follows:
Baker, E. D.
Dragon kiss / by E.D. Baker. — 1st U.S. ed.
p.   cm. — (Tales of the frog princess ; bk. 7)
Summary: Despite obstacles, an ice dragon named Audun pursues the love of his life—
a human girl who can transform into a dragon using magic.
ISBN-13: 978-1-59990-348-4 • ISBN-10: 1-59990-348-2 (hardcover)
[1. Fairy tales. 2. Dragons—Fiction. 3. Love—Fiction. 4. Courtship—Fiction.
5. Human-animal relationships—Fiction. 6. Magic—Fiction. 7. Humorous stories.] I. Title.
PZ8.B173Dn 2009   [Fic]—dc22   2008055131

ISBN 978-1-61963-623-1 (new edition) • ISBN 978-1-59990-583-9 (e-book)

Typeset by Westchester Book Composition
Printed and bound in the U.S.A. by Thomson-Shore Inc., Dexter, Michigan
2   4   6   8   10   9   7   5   3   1

All papers used by Bloomsbury Publishing, Inc., are natural, recyclable products
made from wood grown in well-managed forests. The manufacturing processes
conform to the environmental regulations of the country of origin.

This book is dedicated to Ellie, my first reader and a marvelous author in her own right; to Kim, my horse expert and the one who makes my Web site possible; to Victoria, from whom I've learned so much; and to my wonderful fans, who are so encouraging.

One

What do you mean, you're going after that girl?" demanded Audun's grandmother. She set the sack she'd been carrying beside the pile of the family's belongings waiting at the mouth of the cave and turned to look at the fifteen-year-old dragon. "You know she's really a human!"

Audun looked at her in surprise. After everything that Millie had done for them, he hadn't expected anyone to object to his plans.

"I thought all of you liked her," he said, glancing from his grandmother to the rest of his family.

"We do," said his mother while his father nodded. His grandfather just shrugged and looked apologetic.

"Liking her has nothing to do with this," his grandmother, Song of the Glacier, replied.

"You can't have forgotten that she saved our lives!" protested Audun.

"We know what she did," said his grandmother. "And we appreciate it, but that doesn't change the fact that she isn't a dragon. Just because she has magic doesn't make her one of us."

Audun shook his head. "I don't understand why that's a problem. I mean, I've heard about dragons that can change into humans. What's wrong with a human who can turn into a dragon?"

"I'm not arguing with you about this, Audun," said the elderly dragoness, "and I'm not giving you my permission to run after that girl like some lovesick albatross. Now go help your grandfather gather the rest of the sacks. We'll be leaving in a few minutes."

"Then you'll be going without me," Audun declared. "I love Millie and I don't want to live my life without her!"

Audun's mother, Moon Dancer, gasped and gave her son a horrified look. In the dragon world the elderly were revered, especially the dragonesses; no one ever talked back to them.

"I can't believe you spoke to your grandmother that way!" exclaimed Audun's father, Speedwell. "Please accept his apology, Mother. He's young and foolish."

Dragons were honest at heart and found it nearly impossible to lie. Once in a while, however, Audun wished that he could lie, just a little. "I didn't mean to be disrespectful, Grandmother," said Audun, "but I can't apologize when I don't mean it." He stepped to the ledge that fronted the cave they called home and turned to look at her once more. "I just wanted to tell you where I was going before I left. I thought you would understand, but I guess I was wrong. Safe travels." When Song didn't respond with a similar farewell, Audun spread his wings and leaped into the frigid mountain air.

He tried not to look back, but he couldn't help himself. Swooping one last time around the mountain-ringed valley, Audun glanced down at the ledge as he worked to gain altitude. Only his parents had remained outside to watch him go. Seeing the sad curve of their necks even from a distance made him wonder, for just a moment, if he was doing the right thing. But then he thought of Millie and how much she meant to him. She had left only the day before, yet it already seemed like an eternity. His parents would understand with time; it was Millie he had to go see now.

Since the hour he was hatched, the only time Audun had been separated from his family for longer than a few days was when they were trapped in the walls of a witch's ice castle. It was Millie who had set them free. Audun had been fascinated by the lovely green dragon from the moment he first saw her, and had fallen in love when he discovered how sweet and good and brave she was, despite the fact that she was really a human. Dragons often fell in love at first sight. His parents had done it and so had the parents of some of his friends. It was usually with someone the dragon king had chosen for them, but it was true love, regardless. However it happened, once dragons fell in love, it was for the rest of their lives.

Audun's grandmother often accused him of acting without thinking first. He admitted to himself that he might have been hasty in leaving his family the way he had, but he already knew that Millie was right for him. It was true that she was a human part of the time and a dragon only when her magic changed her, but she was the most beautiful human Audun had ever seen and she wasn't at all what he'd expected of a creature with only two feet. Brought up to believe that humans lied, cheated, stole, and thought only of themselves, he'd been delighted to meet Millie, who was as honest as a dragon and even more caring.

Audun was certain that all he had to do was encourage Millie and his grandmother to spend some time together and the two of them would get along. Two such wonderful females would have to like each other, wouldn't they?

❧

Dragons have an unerring sense of direction, and more acute senses than humans, especially their vision and sense of smell, so it wasn't hard for Audun to locate Millie's trail. Every dragon's scent was unique, but Millie's was more unusual than most. Part smoky musk of a dragon and part flavorful undertones of a human, her scent varied according to whatever form she was in. Because she'd been a dragon when she flew south, Audun smelled more of her dragon than of her human scent.

Starting out the day before would have been better for tracking her scent on the air currents between the mountains, but he hadn't wanted to leave without spending some time with his family after their experience in the witch's castle. Audun's long neck wove from side to side as he followed Millie's scent between the mountains and over the pass leading to the foothills beyond. He circled above a large outcropping of rock where he thought he detected the smell she'd given off when she was a human, but the scent was old and the storm that had scoured the mountains the day after Millie arrived had nearly erased it. A short distance away he spotted a snow leopard, which ran in fear at Audun's approaching shadow.

Picking up her dragon odor again, he followed it above the foothills and across the lush forests and rolling grasslands that made up much of the Kingdom of Bullrush. The countryside was lovely, although Audun preferred the glittering ice and pristine snow of the Icy North. The air was warmer here, too, and uncomfortable for a dragon from a land where the ice never thawed and the snow never melted. When Audun noticed a river flowing beneath him, he didn't think twice about landing at the water's edge.

Drawing his wings to his sides, he curved his neck to the river and hunched down to gulp gallon after gallon of cool, fresh water. He closed his eyes in pleasure, dunking his head until he was submerged all the way to his shoulders, and didn't open his eyes until a change in the current told him that something large was close by.

A pale face with wide-open, staring eyes engulfed in a cloud of some sort of green weed drifted toward him. Audun jerked his head back, certain it was a drowned human. Although he didn't want to touch it, he thought he should take it out of the water in case someone was looking for it. The current was carrying it past quickly, so he grimaced with distaste and reached out with one clawed foot, pulling it from the river to the soft mud of the shore.

Audun jumped back in surprise when the body jumped to its feet and shouted, "What do you think you're doing, you brute?"

"Sorry!" said Audun. "I thought you were dead."

"How dare you!" exclaimed the young woman, flicking the dripping strands of her long, green hair over her shoulder. "That has to be the rudest thing anyone has ever said to me!"

Audun didn't know what to do when the woman hurled a clump of mud at him before bursting into tears.

"I know I've been looking a little pasty lately and I have taken to floating aimlessly, but still . . ."

"I said I was sorry," said Audun. "I don't know very many humans. I've never seen one with green hair before and the way you were staring at me—"

The woman stopped crying to give him a nasty look.

"Haven't you insulted me enough already? I'm not a lowly, smelly human. I'm a water nymph and this is my river!"

"I didn't realize . . ."

"It's not your fault. I haven't been myself ever since that horrible troll ate two of my favorite fish. What is the world coming to? Trolls stomping across river bottoms, stirring up my nice silt and polluting my lovely, clean water with their awful stench as they devour my little darlings! Then humans clutter my riverbank with rafts . . ."

Audun didn't hear the rest of the nymph's complaints once she gestured to a raft lying on the shore only a dozen yards upriver. Raising his head to sniff, the dragon smiled as he recognized Millie's human scent. He was sure he would have noticed it sooner if he hadn't been so distracted. The nymph was still talking when he turned away and trotted to the raft. Although the logs were old and battered, the vine holding them together looked fresh.

Audun bent down to give the raft a thorough sniff, paying special attention to the side Millie had touched. He also found the scent of the boy, Francis, as well as that of the obnoxious troll. The nymph was right about the troll's stench.

"I've been talking to you!" shrilled the nymph, who had followed him to the raft.

"Right . . . ," Audun replied, still not paying attention to her. He was pleased to have found the raft. It was a connection to Millie, something she had touched and used.

"I've got to go," he said, as he spread his wings. Although he'd known he was on the right track, it was good to have the knowledge confirmed. She seemed that much closer now; his search might almost be over.

Audun took to the air and recaptured Millie's dragon scent. It took him across the river to a land of scrubby grass and rolling hills that grew taller with each passing mile until they became mountains. These were different from the mountains that he was used to; they weren't as high, and there was snow only on the tops of the very tallest, but even there the air flowing past them seemed warm and gentle.

He almost lost the scent at times, and had to cast back and forth for it, but when he reached one of the mountains farthest to the south it became so strong that it seemed to fill his nostrils. Following the curve of the mountainside, Audun began to see signs of humans: a rough path zigzagged down the side of the mountain, following its contours to a village on one side, and a castle perched on a pinnacle of rock on the other. Millie's scent was strongest near the castle, both as a human and as a dragon, so he descended, hoping to see her.

He was flying over one of the squat, sturdy towers when a shout went up and arrows began to whiz past him. Dodging the arrows was easy at first, but then the archers' assault intensified and he had to fly higher to get out of range.

"Millie!" he roared, turning this way and that as he struggled to avoid the flood of arrows. "Millie, are you there?"

A figure seated on a broom shot from the top of the tower, and Audun was certain that it was Millie. But then another figure joined it and the two of them steered their brooms toward Audun. They were talking to each other as they flew and he could hear what they were saying even before they reached him.

"Hey, Ratinki! Will you look at that!" said the younger of the two witches in a voice so loud that Audun thought they could probably hear her back in the castle. "I've never seen a white dragon before. Have you?"

The old witch shook her head and replied in a raspy voice, "Nope. He's a good looker, though. I wonder what he wants with our Millie."

"He was calling her name. He must want to talk to her," said the younger witch.

Ratinki looked exasperated. "You're such a ninny-head, Klorine! Of course he wants to talk to her. Maybe we can find out why." Using one hand to shade her eyes from the sun, the old witch shouted, "You there!" and flew higher until she was facing Audun. "What do you want with Millie? None of your dragon tricks now. We're powerful witches and can turn you into a flea in the blink of an eye."

"I just need to see her. Is she here?"

"Maybe she is and maybe she isn't. We're not telling you a thing until you tell us why you want her. Go on, you can tell us. We're friends of the family."

"I'm not telling you anything," said Audun. "It's personal."

Klorine eyed him as she flew up to join them. "She met you on her adventure, didn't she? We were dying of curiosity, but she wasn't here long enough to tell us anything. Her parents whisked her away right after she got back."

"You simpleton!" snapped Ratinki. "I was going to make him tell us all about it. Now we'll never know what happened!"

"Maybe Millie will tell us the next time we see her, although I don't expect that to be for a good long time. I've never seen Emma and Eadric so upset."

"If she were my daughter, I'd lock her in a tower and throw away the key," said Ratinki.

"If she were your daughter," said Klorine, "she would have locked herself in the tower and thrown away the key."

Audun couldn't wait any longer. "Where did they take her?"

"Home, I suppose," said Klorine.

The old witch snorted with disgust. "You're going to blab everything, aren't you? So much for keeping secrets from the enemy!"

"I'm not your enemy," said Audun. "I love Millie. I

would never hurt her. If you could just tell me where she lives . . ."

"Greater Greensward, of course."

"Klorine!" shouted Ratinki. "Don't tell him that! Who knows what he has in mind."

"Don't be silly, Ratinki. He said he loves her. I think true love is so romantic!"

"Between humans! But he's a dragon. For all we know he might want to eat Millie!"

Klorine pursed her mouth in disgust. "Now who's being a ninny-head? This is a nice young dragon, not some ravening beast. Don't pay her any mind," she said, turning back to Audun. "Just head south over the forest and the river. Millie's mother is the Green Witch and a Dragon Friend. Any dragon can tell you how to find the castle. There are lots of dragons in Greater Greensward. You'll feel right at home there."

"I doubt it, but thanks, anyway," said Audun.

Two

When it began to rain, Audun searched until he found a cave where he could spend the night. He finally found one that was big enough, but was disappointed to see that a family of wolves already occupied it. Fortunately, after he went in to look around, the wolves decided to go somewhere else to sleep, and he spent the night undisturbed. Even so, he had trouble falling asleep. All he could think about was Millie. He'd never met anyone like her before.

Every time he was ready to drift off, Audun saw Millie's face. He remembered how her eyes had lit up when she smiled at him, and how frightened she had looked when she'd found him frozen in the ice with his own noxious gas swirling around him. He remembered how she'd melted the ice with her dragon fire and had taken the flames into herself when his ice-dragon gas exploded. After she had saved his life, fire had nearly consumed her and she'd had to dive into a valley filled with snow to put it out. The snow had melted and she was sinking in the water when he dove in after her. Audun rubbed his forelimbs, remembering what it had been like to carry her. He wished he could touch her again, if only for a moment, and he went to sleep only after he'd promised himself that he'd be with her very soon.

The sky was clear the next morning except for a scattering of clouds in the distance. He had no trouble finding Millie's scent again, but he hadn't flown far before he lost it. This didn't worry him at first. Turning on a wing tip, he retraced his flight path, returning to the spot where he'd last smelled her. He continued on, more carefully this time, and lost the odor at exactly the same place. Audun tried again and again, each time becoming more agitated as well as more determined not to give up.

Eventually, he caught the faintest whiff of another familiar scent, one he had smelled for the first time in the castle near his home. It had been the Blue Witch's castle, and although his family had been trapped in the walls, it hadn't been the witch's doing; she had been a prisoner as well. He couldn't remember the old woman's name, but he did know that she and Millie had become friends of sorts. It was possible that she might even know Millie's whereabouts.

Following the new scent, Audun flew toward a part of the forest where the trees were older and taller. As he passed over a clearing, he glanced down and saw a nymph with long, green hair paddling in a small pond, while a unicorn drank from the shallower water. At Audun's approach, the nymph slipped into the depths of the pond. The unicorn snorted, shook its mane, and turned to run.

The dragon flew on and soon the old witch's scent drew Audun to a clearing where nodding bluebells surrounded a small, well-kept cottage with a newly thatched roof and a gently puffing chimney. Three white-haired women sat in the shade of the only tree in the clearing, sipping from cups shaped like half-opened tulips. Not wanting to startle them, Audun landed at the edge of the forest. He was about to call out a greeting when the woman in the muddy-colored gown glanced over her shoulder and said to her friends, "Don't look now, but there's a dragon sneaking up on us."

The woman in gray lowered her cup. "If you won't let us look, Mudine, you'll have to do the looking for us. Is it anyone we know?"

Mudine shook her head. "I've never seen a dragon like this before. He's white."

" 'Never trust a dragon you don't know,' my old mother used to say," said the woman in gray.

"Don't be ridiculous, Oculura," snapped the smallest woman. "I had the same mother as you and I never heard her say such a thing! She wouldn't have trusted any dragon, living or dead!"

"You're older than I am, Dyspepsia. You left home years before I did. I had to listen to a lot of mother's adages before she choked to death on that fried radish."

14

"Can you two stop arguing long enough for us to deal with this dragon?" asked Mudine.

"That's easy enough," said Oculura. "A wall of flame should chase him off. It worked on my last husband when he wouldn't stop coming around."

"That's even more ridiculous!" said Dyspepsia. "This is a dragon we're talking about. They love flames! Why don't we try something like this . . ."

Rising to her feet, the little old witch swept her arm in a grand gesture while muttering under her breath. With a rumble and a *whoosh!* a torrent of stones rose out of the ground and flung themselves at Audun's head.

Befuddled, Audun half-turned, lifted his tail, and swatted the stones aside. He hadn't done anything to provoke these humans, yet they were attacking him. All he wanted to do was talk to the Blue Witch about Millie. Maybe they didn't understand . . .

"Excuse me!" he called, taking two steps closer to the old women. "I just wanted to . . ."

"Well, that didn't do a bit of good," said Oculura. "The beast is still coming to get us. Maybe if I do this . . ." Speaking under her breath, the witch held her hands in front of her, then thrust them apart as if she were trying to move something heavy.

Audun yelped as the ground opened beneath his feet. He spread his wings and was about to fly away when Mudine said, "And I'll do this!" Smiling with glee, the old woman fluttered her fingers at his feet and said something Audun couldn't quite hear. Vines erupted from the hole in the ground and wrapped themselves around Audun. "Go ahead and use your fire on those, dragon!" she shouted. "Those asbesta vines will never burn!"

The white dragon roared in surprise, jerking at his trapped feet and flapping his wings. Suddenly the door to the cottage burst open and a fourth white-haired lady stepped out, blinking at the sunshine. "What's this racket about?" she demanded. "I thought you were going to let me take a nap."

Taking a deep breath, Audun exhaled onto the vines, which immediately turned a sickly shade of yellow and shriveled. Free again, he rose into the air and cupped his wings so he could stay in place. He would have flown away if he hadn't recognized the woman who had just stepped outside as the witch he had come to see. It was plain that she recognized him at the same time, because her eyes grew wide in surprise.

"What are you doing here?" she asked. "I never thought I'd see you again."

"I'm looking for Millie," said Audun. "Do you know where I might find her?"

"Why?" the witch asked, sounding suspicious.

"Because I love her," he replied. "I don't want to live without her."

The Blue Witch snorted and said, "You sound like you want to propose."

"I do," said Audun. "I want her as my mate. I want to spend the rest of my life with her."

Slapping her knee, the Blue Witch chortled. "Now if that doesn't beat all! That's got to be the funniest thing I've ever heard."

"I wasn't joking," Audun said, giving her the sternest look he could muster.

"Then you're in for a big disappointment," said the witch, sounding a lot less cheerful. "Her family would never let her marry a dragon! You'd have to be a human before you'd get even a glimmer of a chance."

The crest on the back of Audun's neck wilted. "So you're saying there's no hope for me?"

"I didn't say that," said the Blue Witch. "Dragons can do lots of things, some that come naturally, and some that have to be taught. Your elders figure they'll teach you what you need to know once you're old enough and smart enough to handle it. If you're serious about Millie, go talk to your king and his dragon council. They're the only ones who can help you."

"I'll do that if I have to, but I want to talk to Millie first. Do you know where she went? I was following her scent until I lost it over the forest."

"You won't be able to find her. Millie's mother used

magic to whisk her away to someplace where they could talk with no one interrupting them. Even I couldn't follow them if I wanted to. I doubt Millie would want to see you now, anyway. She's in a lot of trouble and having you there would just make it worse. Nope, your best bet is to see your dragon council. If you're lucky, the members might have a soft spot for true love—if you really love her, that is. You do, don't you? I'll be angry if I helped you like this and you weren't sincere."

The Blue Witch wouldn't let Audun go until she was convinced that he meant what he'd said. After that, she made her friends apologize to him for attacking him with their magic, and by then they were all declaring how hungry they were and made him stay to eat. While they shared a meal of leftover stew (giving Audun all the meat), the Blue Witch began to reminisce about life in the Icy North, making the white dragon tell her friends about it as well. It wasn't until late afternoon that she finally let him go with a sack of dried fish and the good wishes of four white-haired witches.

❧

Audun's wings were heavy as he flew away from the witches' cottage. He had been so looking forward to seeing Millie again that he hadn't allowed himself to consider the fact that she might not be findable. Dipping one wing, he started to turn in the direction of the Icy North, but changed his mind. Although he might not be able to see Millie, at least he could see the castle where she'd grown up. Even that much contact with something of hers might ease the ache in his chest.

The castle wasn't hard to find once he left the forest where the witches lived. Scanning the horizon, he soon saw green pennants snapping in the wind atop the tall, slender towers of a castle. With the sun at his back, he sped toward the castle and landed in the courtyard. A stable boy was nearly dragged off his feet when the horse he was walking saw Audun. Screaming, the horse fought to get away, but the boy held on and got the animal under control long enough to get it out of sight of the dragon.

Audun was wondering if he should leave when an older woman with gray-streaked auburn hair swooped out of the sky on a magic carpet and landed in the courtyard beside him. "May I help you?" she asked.

"I wanted to see Millie," said Audun. "I'm a friend of hers."

The woman's lips widened in a warm smile. "I'm her great-aunt Grassina. Wait just a minute and I'll see if she's here."

A flicker of hope lit up Audun's eyes. "Do you mean she's home?"

"A little bird told me that she got back a few hours ago," Grassina said over her shoulder as she headed for the door. "She might be resting, though. I'll just go up and—"

The door flew open and Millie came racing out, shrieking, "Audun!" Dashing across the cobblestones, she threw her arms around the dragon's neck and clung to him.

Audun smiled, curved his neck around her, and said, "I told you that you couldn't keep me away." Millie turned her head and he saw that her lovely green eyes were red from crying and her cheeks were streaked with tears.

Two other women appeared in the doorway, neither of whom was smiling. The older woman had golden hair like Millie's, but it was sprinkled with white. She was beautiful, despite the cross expression she was wearing. "It's that dragon, the one she was telling us about. He shouldn't be here, not after all the horrid things Millie said."

"I didn't say anything horrid, Grandmother," Millie cried, before turning back to Audun. "I just told them how much I care about you," she said, looking into his eyes.

"No human should love a dragon," said her grandmother. "It isn't right."

"That isn't fair, Mother," said the other woman. "Eadric loves me whether I'm a human or a dragon, just as I love him no matter what I am. I simply don't understand how Millie could feel so strongly about Audun after such a short time. Unless it's her dragon side . . . Flame Snorter swears she fell in love with Grumble Belly the first time she saw him."

This woman looked remarkably like Millie and it occurred to Audun that this had to be Millie's mother, who was not only a princess, but also a witch and a Dragon

20

Friend. Audun squinted his eyes and could see a rosy glow around her, the fabled sign of a true friend to dragons.

"I'm honored to meet you, Dragon Friend," he said, bowing his head. "I've come to court your daughter."

Millie's grandmother's hand flew to her forehead and she swayed as if she'd been struck. "This is worse than I thought," she said in a strained voice. "We can't let this happen. We'll be the laughingstock of all the kingdoms. Or worse yet, the object of their hatred. If we let dragons marry into the family all the neighboring kingdoms will consider us unsuitable to rule. We'll have armies marching on us from every direction."

Millie's mother sighed. "I wouldn't go that far, Mother. No one has complained about my dragon side. However, Millie, we can't let you marry a dragon just because you're attracted to him. I'm sure you think you love him," she said, holding up her hand when Millie started to speak, "but you hardly know him. You can't truly love someone you don't really know."

"That's not true, Mother. Audun and I have been through so much together! I know him enough to know that I do love him!"

At Millie's words, Audun felt a warmth growing inside him like he'd never experienced before. While he'd known that he loved Millie, he hadn't been sure that she felt the same way about him. Now that he was sure of her feelings, he knew that nothing in the world could keep them apart.

"I'm sure you think you love him, darling, but there's only one way to know for certain. Give it time and see if you both still feel the same way."

"Oh, we will," Millie said.

"Did I forget to mention that the test works better when you aren't together?" her mother asked. Dust began to swirl around Millie's legs, tugging at the hem of her gown.

"No, Mother, don't do this!" Millie exclaimed, looking at her mother in horror.

"It's for your own good," her mother's voice said over the rising wind. She was standing only a few yards away, yet she sounded as if she were a long way off. "You'll appreciate what I've done someday."

"Millie!" Audun shouted, as he felt her being pulled away. And then both she and her mother were gone, leaving Audun with Grassina and Millie's grandmother.

"Don't look at me that way," the older woman told Audun. "It's for the best. You never should have come here. Now go back to wherever it is you're from and leave my granddaughter alone." Turning abruptly, she strode back to the castle door. "I'll see you inside, Grassina," she added, then firmly closed the door behind her.

Audun felt as if a giant had swatted him out of the sky into the side of a mountain. He turned toward Millie's great-aunt, certain that she was waiting to tell him how his love for her niece was hopeless and that he should leave and never come back. She was wrestling with her magic carpet, however, and was more intent on shaking off the dust that had covered it when the wind had carried Millie away than she was in telling Audun anything.

"Let me help," said Audun.

Grassina stepped aside as the dragon picked up the edge of the carpet with his talons and flapped it until the dust puffed free and drifted across the courtyard. "Thanks," she said, nodding her approval. "You know, you don't have to listen to everything Millie's grandmother says. My sister, Chartreuse, is a very negative person and can never see the good in anything. My husband is a wonderful man. He was an otter for many years, although I fell in love with him when he was human," she said, half to herself. "Chartreuse still doesn't like him and is always making unnecessary comments about smelly otters and how she expects him to lick his fur. He hasn't done that in years—at least, not in public. All I wanted to say was that if you really love each other, you shouldn't let anything stand between you. If you want to be with Millie, I'm sure you'll find a way."

Three

*I*t took Audun three days to reach the part of the Icy Sea where King's Isle was located. On the final day he'd flown above frigid, choppy waters where jagged glaciers provided the only places to land. A storm chased him for the last few hours, catching up with him shortly before he reached the island. Fighting against the buffeting wind and freezing rain, he saw little of his goal in the stormy darkness and would have flown past it if a flash of lightning hadn't reflected off the island's icy crags. He didn't notice the dragon sentries who flew out to meet him until their wings actually touched his. Flying wing tip to wing tip, they guided him to the only opening into the home of the ice-dragon king, leaving Audun at the highest spire.

With ice-coated wings and aching muscles, Audun was so tired that he staggered as his claws finally touched the ground. When the door opened and another dragon appeared to escort him to a place where he could rest, Audun could only nod his thanks and stumble after him to an empty chamber where a ledge along the wall served as a bed. Curling up on the ledge, he slept the rest of that day and well into the next, too tired to open his eyes when dragons came to check on him. He dreamed of Millie and of what their lives would be like once they were together. When he finally woke, it was to the sound of the door creaking open and talons clicking across the floor.

Raising his head, Audun blinked in surprise at the pair of young dragons who stood by the door, watching him. They were both females, one was probably nine or ten years old and the other's age was closer to his own.

"He's awake!" the younger dragoness whispered to the other.

The older dragoness had been staring at Audun in a way that made him want to squirm. "Welcome to King's Isle," she said, giving him a radiant smile.

Although Audun had never visited King's Isle before, he knew quite a bit about it. It was the stronghold of the king of the ice dragons from the day he was chosen to rule until the day he died. Dragons lived for a very long time, so the selection of a new king happened once every few hundred years. The current king had been selected nineteen years before, after the death of the previous ruler, who had been so old that his scales were dull and brittle and his teeth worn down to nubs. The stronghold was also the home of the king's councillors, as well as of the dragons and dragonesses who made up his court.

Because far fewer female dragons than males were born, females were treasured and treated with great care. At the age of eight, dragonesses were brought to the court of the dragon king to be raised until they were old enough to start a family with their own mates. It was the responsibility of the king to select their mates as well as to see to the education of the dragonesses. Both Audun's mother and his grandmother had spent their formative years living on the island. Audun was sorry he had ignored most of their stories. It would have helped if he'd learned what the dragons on the island did, especially those like the dragoness eyeing Audun.

"My name is Hildie," she announced, letting her eyelids droop in an odd sort of way. "I'm glad you're awake. Dragons our age rarely visit the island. Have you come to petition the king for a mate? Say you have. All the others who have come are so old. I'd hate to end up with one of them."

Audun shook his head, saying, "I'm here to ask the king and his councillors for their help. I'm not looking for a mate."

"That's too bad," she replied, turning so that her tail rubbed against his leg. Wetting her lips with her tongue, she looked him up and down, her gaze lingering on the muscles in his legs and the ridge along his back. "The king is very busy now," she said. "One of the old councillors died and King Stormclaw has been meeting with her replacement. You probably won't get an appointment for days."

"Is there anywhere that I can—," Audun began.

The door slammed open and a burly dragon, over twice Audun's height, ducked his head and squeezed through the doorway. There was a silvery tinge to his scales, and he had a ridge as sharp as dagger blades and the longest talons Audun had ever seen. Audun stepped back from the anger flashing in the huge dragon's eyes; Hildie just looked disgusted.

"What do you think you're doing here?" the dragon growled at her. "I leave my post for two minutes to help Iceworthy and you sneak past."

"We were waiting in line for our turn on the ice chute when we heard that *he* was here," the younger dragoness announced, pointing at Audun. "Hildie wanted to come see him up close before any of the other dragonesses could. She thinks if she meets him first, she'll have first claim on him. She shouldn't be here, though, should she, Frosty-breath?"

Hildie turned on her companion and scowled. "Be quiet, Loolee. No one asked you."

Loolee smiled sweetly at Audun and skipped out the door. Frostybreath growled at Hildie until she started to leave as well. "You'll have to forgive Loolee," she said, pausing in front of Audun so she could tilt her head, making her neck look long and slender. "She's just a child and doesn't know what she's talking about."

"Hildie!" snapped Frostybreath.

The dragoness made an exasperated face and smiled at Audun one last time before she, too, left the room. Frosty-breath squeezed through the doorway again, shaking his head and muttering to himself.

The door shut with a click. Audun sighed. He'd been about to ask if there was somewhere he could go to get something to drink, but he hadn't had the chance. Thinking that he would look for a drink himself, he opened the door and was halfway out when a deep growl made the ridge along his spine rise.

"Get back in there, squirt," said Frostybreath, baring his fangs.

"I was just—"

"I don't care what you were doing," said the dragon. "You're not going anywhere until I say you can."

Audun was puzzled. Although he hadn't known what to expect when he'd arrived at the island, it had never occurred to him that he'd be treated like a prisoner. "I really just want—"

"Yeah, yeah. That's what they all say. Then the next thing I know you'll be flying off with Hildie or another young dragoness and I'll have to go out in the wind and rain to haul you both back. I don't like the rain, boy, so don't even think about it. Now go in that room and don't come out until I say you can."

Frostybreath took a menacing step toward Audun and the young dragon backed into his room and shut the door.

He was studying one of the walls of ice, wondering what would happen if he licked it, when the door opened and an elderly, narrow-faced dragon official, wearing rings on every talon and a medallion in the shape of the king's head, stepped inside. The dragon carried a stylus in one set of talons and a stiffened parchment in the other. Peering down his long, thin nose at Audun, he said, "My name is Iceworthy. I understand that you want to ask the king and his councillors for help. What, precisely, is the nature of your request?"

"It's personal," said Audun.

"I see," murmured the dragon as he wrote. "P-e-r-s-o-n-a-l. And what exactly is this personal request?"

"I'd prefer to ask the king."

The dragon raised a brow ridge and twitched his tail. "You would, would you? Apparently you don't understand how things work here. King Stormclaw is a very important dragon and cannot talk to just anyone. My job is to make sure he isn't bothered by minor nuisances like you. Nothing gets to King Stormclaw without my approval. You either tell me now, or I'll have Frostybreath throw you off the island. Which shall it be, hmmm?"

It was obvious from his expression that the old dragon wasn't going to give in. The young dragon sighed. "I want to ask how to become a human. I was told that I should go to the king and his council for help."

"Human, eh? Well, I'm sure you have your reasons, although no one in his right mind . . . Ah, well, that's neither here nor there. What is your name, young dragon? I'll have to write my report, then turn it in. You should hear back from the council in a few days. A week at most."

Audun sighed. "I'm Audun, son of Moon Dancer and Speedwell, grandson of Song of the Glacier and High Flier and—"

The dragon grunted and gave Audun a peculiar look. "Enough!" he said, lowering his stylus.

The old dragon's bones creaked as he turned around. Audun followed him to the door, saying, "Please, sir, before you go, if you could just tell me where—"

The door shut in Audun's face, leaving him even more puzzled than before.

Although the young dragon tried to distract himself in the empty room by counting the number of his reflections he could see on the ice walls and finding cracks in the ice that looked like animal faces, it wasn't long before all he could think about was how thirsty he was. Rather than lick the wall and risk getting his tongue frozen to it, Audun used his talons to gouge out a piece of ice. He was just about to place it in his mouth when the door opened and Frostybreath came in, carrying a platter of newly caught fish and a jug of fresh water.

Seeing the ice in Audun's talons, the guard shook his massive head, saying, "I wouldn't eat that if I were you. An old sorcerer used magic on it to keep it frozen for as long as there are dragon kings. Put it in a closed vessel and it

30

will freeze any liquid around it. You wouldn't want to see what it would do to your blood if you ate it."

Audun dropped the chunk of ice. Frostybreath smiled and set the platter and jug on the floor. "Eat hearty, squirt. You're meeting with the king and his councillors in the morning. I'd get a good night's sleep, too, if I were you. You'll need your wits about you tomorrow."

After the guard had gone, Audun squatted on the floor beside the platter, drained the jug of water into his mouth, then picked up the chilled fish and dropped them onto his tongue, one at a time. He thought the whole thing was too confusing. First he was a prisoner, then he was about to be kicked off the island, now he was getting just what he wanted sooner than he'd thought possible. *If only I could get someone to tell me what's going on,* he thought, yawning until his jaw made a cracking sound. *If only I'd listened more when Mother and Grandmother told me about living on the island.* He picked up the empty jug and shook it. *If only I still had some water left!*

He was settling down on the ledge when he bumped the piece of ice he'd broken off the wall. It skittered a few inches, but Audun reached out and caught it before it could fall off the ledge. *Magical ice might come in handy,* he thought, and tucked it into the pouch that all ice dragons have under a flap of skin between the base of their wings and their back.

Although Audun didn't think he'd be able to sleep that night after having slept most of the day, he lay down to

31

rest and didn't wake up until Frostybreath brought him more fish in the morning. The dragon guard grunted a greeting, and handed Audun a platter and another jug, saying, "Hurry up and eat. I'm supposed to take you to the council chambers right away, but I don't want you fainting from hunger at the king's feet."

While Audun ate his breakfast, Frostybreath stood by, tapping his talons impatiently against the ice. Audun was licking the last fish scale from his lips when the dragon beckoned him to the door. "Come along. The sooner I have you delivered to the council, the sooner I can get back to my real job."

"I thought guarding newcomers like me *was* your real job," said Audun, as he trailed Frostybreath out the door.

The big dragon shook his massive head. "Not at all. I'm just filling in for a friend who had to get a broken fang fixed. My real job makes use of my talent. I can freeze things just by blowing on them. I'll show you. Spit."

"What?" said Audun. "Here, you mean . . . now?"

"Right here. Don't worry. No one will mind."

Audun shrugged. "If you say so." Gathering moisture in his mouth, he spit at the wall in front of him. Just as the fluid left Audun's mouth, Frostybreath exhaled. The air crackled and shimmered; a small chunk of ice hit the wall with a *thunk!* "Wow!" said Audun. "That's some talent."

Frostybreath looked pleased by the compliment, but he shrugged as he lumbered down the corridor. "That's nothing compared to what the king and his councillors can do. King Stormclaw can call up storms—"

"I've heard that," said Audun.

"Here we go. We'll take this ramp down to the lower levels. See how much brighter it is now? The storm must have stopped."

Audun had not seen any windows, but the ice was translucent and let in daylight when the sun was out. The walls that had seemed gray and dismal the day before now looked as bright as the ice on the mountains back home. The ramp was wide enough for two ordinary-sized dragons to walk side by side, but Frostybreath was far bigger than average. Audun had to follow him down the ramp, staying well back to avoid the other dragon's swinging tail.

"And one of his councillors, Frostweaver, can make intricate patterns out of frost," Frostybreath continued. "They say that the newest councillor . . . Hey, watch where you're going!" the big dragon shouted, as a pack of giggling young dragonesses raced past in the opposite direction.

Audun thought he saw Hildie and Loolee in the group, but they were gone before he got a good look. "Where are they headed?"

"To the top of the ice. They'll take turns riding down the chute that winds around the outside of the stronghold. You wouldn't have seen it, coming in when there was a storm the way you did, but it is pretty impressive if I do say so myself. Took me nearly a year of my days off to make it."

"You made it by yourself?" Audun asked.

"The little ones needed something to do when the weather is bad, seeing that it's bad most days. Ice floe tag isn't safe for the youngest during a storm. Sliding down the chute has become their favorite game. Ah, look, I was talking so much that I didn't realize we were almost there. You go right through that door and wait for the councillors to send for you. Shouldn't be long now."

"Thank you," Audun called, as the bigger dragon continued down the ramp.

"My pleasure!" Frostybreath rumbled over his shoulder.

Four

Following Frostybreath's directions, Audun closed the door behind him and took a seat on a ledge. He was curling up to rest his chin on his foot when a door opened and a dragoness who wasn't much older than he was peeked into the room. Gesturing for him to follow, she stepped aside as he slipped through the door.

"What do I do now?" Audun whispered. He had entered the largest chamber he had ever seen. A hundred dragons could have spread their wings and still had room to move around. At the far end of the room five great slabs of stone rose from the floor in a half circle with the open side facing Audun. The center slab was higher than Audun's head, with the rest only a foot or so shorter. Carvings of dragons in flight covered the slabs and each slab supported a life-sized statue of a dragon.

"Answer their questions," said the dragoness, and she disappeared into the room he'd just left, pulling the door shut behind her.

Audun looked around the room. It was more dimly lit than the antechamber had been, and encased in so much ice that the sunlight didn't penetrate as well as it had at the upper levels. He assumed that another door, near the slabs, was the entrance for the king and his councillors. Keeping his ears perked for the sound of approaching feet, he padded across the stone floor, trying to see what famous dragons the statues might depict. Audun was only a dozen yards away when the statue in the center moved.

"That's close enough, young dragon," boomed a voice that seemed to make the walls shake.

Suddenly the torches on the walls flamed brighter and Audun realized that the shapes on top of the slabs weren't carvings at all, but real dragons. And if they were real, then the one in the center must be King Stormclaw and the other four could only be his councillors.

Uncertain how to act before the king, Audun bowed so that his forelegs were bent and his chin almost touched the ground.

"You may rise," said the king.

Audun glanced up. He'd heard that the king was always chosen from among the older dragons, but he didn't think that King Stormclaw looked that old. His neck still supported his head proudly, his back was still straight, and his wings showed no tears or gaps; the only evidence of age was the dullness of his blue-white scales and the shortness of his fangs. He was an imposing dragon and must have been exceedingly handsome when he was young.

Audun dropped his gaze when he realized that the king was studying him just as carefully. Finally, Stormclaw spoke, although he wasn't talking to Audun. "So, Song, I finally get to meet your grandson. He looks a lot like you, although I can see High Flier in him as well."

Startled, Audun looked up and let his gaze follow that of the king. Two elderly dragonesses were seated to the right of King Stormclaw. One of them was a stranger to Audun. The other was his grandmother.

Audun was confused. When he'd last seen his grandmother, she'd been with the rest of his family on the way to their cave overlooking the sea. No one had mentioned that they were going to visit the king. He couldn't imagine what might have happened to bring them here. Before he could ask, however, King Stormclaw turned to him and said, "I've been asking your grandmother to join my council for years, but she's only just relented. You should be very proud of her. She's a remarkable dragoness. A talent like hers is rare."

Audun nodded, but the king wasn't finished yet.

"Young dragon, why have you come to see me? Are you here to make sure that I'm treating your grandmother well? As one of my councillors, she'll be among the most respected dragons in the kingdom."

It took Audun a moment to realize that the king

was waiting for him to say something. The problem was, Audun wasn't sure quite how to phrase his request. Although the other councillors were watching him with interest, his grandmother's gaze was as impassive as if *she* were the stranger. He had a feeling that he wasn't going to get any help from her.

Audun was still trying to think of what to say when the pale gray and white dragoness seated beside the king leaned toward Stormclaw and whispered something.

"Ah, yes," said the king, nodding. "I remember now. Iceworthy mentioned something about your wanting our help. Something about becoming a human, as I recall."

"That's right, Your Majesty," said Audun.

King Stormclaw frowned. "A peculiar request, and one I'm not often asked. Why do you want to be a human, boy? Isn't being a dragon good enough for you?"

"Being a dragon is the best thing in the world!" said Audun. "I don't want to give up being a dragon altogether. It's just that, well, there's this girl . . ."

"Ah, I see," said the king, the furrow in his brow relaxing. "You met a dragoness and you want to impress her. I can understand that, but there are far better ways to impress a girl than by turning into a human."

"That's just it," said Audun. "The girl is a human, or at least part of the time. She can also be a dragon and when she is, she's the most beautiful shade of green—"

The king snorted and twitched his tail. "There's no

such thing as a green dragon, and even if there were, no human could possibly turn into one without . . ."

Song of the Glacier leaned toward the dragoness beside her and whispered into her pointed ear. The two councillors carried on a short, whispered conversation before they both turned to the king.

"Do you have something to tell me, Song?" said King Stormclaw.

Song nodded. "I've seen the girl myself, Your Majesty. She can indeed turn into a green dragon. You were right in that no natural dragon is green, but she is a dragon through magic, which might explain her . . . unusual color."

The king's brow ridge rose in surprise. "A human who could do that must be able to harness some powerful magic! Why have I never heard of such a one before?"

"She isn't from the Icy North," said Audun. "I followed her trail south to a kingdom called Greater Greensward. She is a princess of royal blood as well as the daughter of a powerful witch who is a Dragon Friend." The hiss of indrawn dragon breath nearly drowned out Audun's next words. "Whether a human or a dragoness, she is a brave and true friend and . . . more than that, to me. I love her, Your Majesty, and I've learned that the only way I can ever be with her is if I can be a human just as she can be a dragon. I've been told that you might be able to help me. Can you, Your Majesty?"

King Stormclaw scowled even more fiercely than before, but it wasn't Audun who received the first taste of his anger. "Did you know of this, Song of the Glacier? Did you know that your grandson is enamored of the Green Witch's daughter? She is the only human living who dares to call herself Dragon Friend and if she is friend to the fire-breathers, she is no friend of ours. You have sorely neglected your grandson's education if he doesn't know of the enmity between us."

Song of the Glacier raised her head and looked directly at the king. "What happened between our kind and theirs took place long ago. Few living today feel as you do about the fire-breathers, Your Majesty. I did not teach my grandson such a lesson because it is not a bias that I would want a young dragon to learn."

The dragon king narrowed his eyes in anger and the other members of the council gasped as the crest on top of his skull rose. Only Song of the Glacier didn't seem intimidated by his aggressive stance. "You would not say such things if the fire-breathers had killed members of your own family," growled King Stormclaw.

"But they did!" exclaimed Audun's grandmother.

Glancing at the others in the chamber, the king shook his head. "We will talk of this another time." He took a deep breath and his crest relaxed, making him seem less formidable. Turning to Audun, King Stormclaw said, "You ask for something I will not give. You may spend one more night in the stronghold, and leave in the morning. Now go, before my temper rises again."

Audun felt as if someone had stuck an icicle into his innards and twisted it. He toyed with the idea of fleeing the island to go find Millie before King Stormclaw could stop him, but then he saw a peculiar look pass between the king and Song of the Glacier. Apparently something was going on here that he couldn't understand.

Worried and upset, Audun left the antechamber. He had no sooner stepped onto the ramp when a gaggle of young dragonesses rushing up the slanted floor surrounded him and carried him along with them.

"Wait!" he said, trying to work his way through the crowd. "I have to—"

Someone nudged him back into the middle of the group of dragonesses. "You have to go with us!" Hildie announced from beside him. "We want you to try the chute. You've never seen anything like it."

"But I'm really not in the mood for—"

"Then we'll put you in the mood," said Hildie.

Loolee danced around him, nimbly avoiding the other dragons' feet. "You have to come with us, Audun! Please?"

"All right. I'll do it for you, Loolee," Audun replied, smiling down at the little dragoness.

The dragonesses' enthusiasm was so contagious that by the time they reached the top of the ramp, Audun was nearly as excited as they were. They had passed countless corridors on the way up, but there was nothing at the highest point of the ramp except a level platform and a smooth tunnel angled steeply down.

"I'm going first this time!" Loolee shouted, as she ran to the edge of the platform. Amid a storm of protest from the other dragonesses, the little dragon girl carefully tucked her wings to her sides and hopped off the platform and into the tunnel. "Hoowee!" she shouted, as she disappeared from sight.

"Audun is next!" Hildie cried. She shoved him to the front of the still-forming line.

"What should I do?" he asked, teetering on the lip of the platform.

"Go!" shouted all the dragonesses. Half a dozen of them pushed him from behind.

Audun stumbled off the edge . . . and fell. "No!" he shouted. His heart seemed to climb into his throat, but the ice that formed the twisting, turning chute was so smooth that he couldn't have stopped, no matter what. Opening his wings was out of the question—there wasn't enough room. He raised his head once, bumping it sharply against the ceiling of the chute. After that he remained crouched as he hurtled down the incline on all fours, using his tail to keep his balance.

The chute wound steeply around the island, doubling back and looping through the center at least twice. There was no way out until the bottom, but soon the drop that had been terrifying became exhilarating and Audun didn't want it to end. Finally, the ice-filtered daylight gave way to the absolute darkness of stone, and his ride was over. Sliding out of the chute onto a smooth stone floor, Audun glanced up at the wavering torches and saw Loolee waiting for him in the long, narrow room.

"Did you like it?" the little dragoness asked, her eyes bright.

"That was great!" said Audun.

Loolee grabbed his arm and pulled. "Come on, then. We can do it again, but we have to get to the top before anyone else or they'll make us go to the end of the line."

Audun stood on wobbling legs and said, "Lead the way." Loolee grinned, and Audun grinned back. He looked around as he followed the little dragoness up the ramp and was surprised by how deep into the heart of the island the chute had carried them. "What's down here?" he asked, as they passed the first of the corridors.

"Not much," she replied. "King Stormclaw's lair is one level below this, but you can't get there from here. Even if you could, it's off-limits to just about everybody. They say he keeps his treasure in a pit below his lair and it's filled with precious gems. His councillors all have their rooms on this floor. They have meeting rooms and stuff on the floors above this. The audience chamber is on the floor above those. I don't like it down here. It's too dark even with the torches. I like the ice levels better. It's always brighter up there, except during the really bad storms."

"Are the councillors' chambers off-limits, too?" asked Audun.

Loolee shrugged. "I suppose not, but nobody ever wants to go there. Why do you want to know?"

"Because my grandmother is the king's newest councillor," Audun said. "I'd like to go see her if I can."

"You're related to a councillor! That's so chilled! I wish I was!"

Audun chuckled at the little dragoness's enthusiasm. "So," he said, "if I wanted to see my grandmother, which way should I go?"

"That's easy. Go back to that hallway," Loolee said, pointing to the corridor they had just passed, "and turn right. You'll know you're almost there when you run into the guards. But I've got to go if I want to be first again. See ya!"

While the little dragoness ran up the ramp, Audun followed her directions and went the other way. The corridor was wide, and it made abrupt changes in direction that soon had him completely disoriented. He slowed when he heard voices ahead, one of which was familiar.

"And then I told her, 'Of course my feet are cold. I'm an ice dragon, aren't I?'"

Audun recognized Frostybreath's voice and wondered if the rough laughter that followed his joke belonged to the guards Loolee had mentioned. Rounding the next corner, Audun found Frostybreath talking to two equally huge dragons wearing medallions bearing the insignia of the king's guards.

"Halt!" cried one of the guards, the smile on his face changing to a scowl as he arched his neck and spread his wings to make himself look even bigger and more intimidating. "What business have you here, young dragon?"

"I've come to see my grandmother," Audun replied. "I heard her rooms are on this level."

"That depends," said the other guard. "Who is your grandmother?"

"Her name is Song of the Glacier," said Audun, looking from one guard to the other.

"It's true," Frostybreath said, when the two guards looked skeptical. "Iceworthy told me so this morning."

"Then you're in luck, young dragon," said the first guard, as he lowered his wings. "Your grandmother returned to her rooms not ten minutes ago. Someone will have to escort you to her, however, and we're not allowed to leave our posts." The dragon gave Frostybreath a meaningful look.

The big dragon sighed. "I suppose I can take him. But you owe me for this, Tailshaker, just like you owe me for guarding him while you had your fang repaired."

"I'll pay you back next week." The guard laughed. "You can count on it."

Audun was impressed by the size of his grandmother's rooms. There were three of them and each was bigger than the largest room in his family's cave. The first two rooms were furnished with dark woods and rich fabrics that rivaled the colors of his grandfather's jewels. The bathing pool in the third room was big enough to fit his entire family at once and still would have left room for guests. Even so, what he noticed most as his grandmother gave him a tour was the stiff way she held herself and the cool tone of her voice; it was clear that she wasn't pleased with him.

"Why did you come to see me, Audun?" she asked. "You can't think that I'm going to help you by influencing the king's decision."

"I must admit that I was hoping you would," said Audun, "but the real reason I came is to find out why you're here. At first I thought Grandfather might be with you, but I haven't smelled him or seen any of his things in your rooms."

There was sadness in Song of the Glacier's eyes. "No," she said, "he didn't come with me. The king asked me to come to the island and didn't include my mate in the invitation."

"How did you become one of the king's councillors?" Audun asked.

"King Stormclaw wasn't exaggerating when he said that he'd been asking me for years. I'd turned him down every time because I never felt that he really needed me until now. Even so, when I heard that one of his councillors was dying and that he'd need a replacement soon, I'd hoped to avoid coming here by taking our family and fleeing the Icy North, but after what happened in that witch's castle, I knew that I couldn't put you, your parents, or High Flier in danger just because I wanted us to be together. You left before I could explain what I had to do."

Audun nodded, but there was still something he didn't understand. "Did you know Stormclaw before you came here?"

His grandmother sighed. "I met him the first time I came to the island. His father was in charge of the guards and his mother had died in a storm just the year before. Stormclaw had nowhere else to go, so the old king let him live here. We became friends and later . . . more than friends."

"When did you meet Grandfather?"

"Old King Bent Tooth had chosen your grandfather, High Flier, for me. Dragonesses must marry whomever the king chooses, and my parents made it clear that I would be no exception. You must understand, I care for your grandfather, but back then I loved Stormclaw and I still do."

"So they made you leave Stormclaw and marry Grandfather."

His grandmother nodded. "We hadn't spoken in years because I thought it would be too painful. When he was

47

chosen as the new king and first asked me to be one of his councillors, I didn't want to come because I wasn't sure what would happen if I saw him again. I've spent most of my life trying to be a good mate to your grandfather, while knowing that someone else was my true love. It's hard for someone your age to understand, but I hope you will, someday."

"I think I already do," said Audun. "It's why I need the king's help. It's why I need your help, too, Grandmother."

Song of the Glacier twitched her tail in agitation. She began to pace in front of him, her scales making a swooshing sound. "Ordinarily, I would do whatever I could to help you, but a human and the daughter of the Green Witch? Are you sure it's really love, Audun, and not infatuation? Any dragon would be attracted to someone who saved his life, but that doesn't mean you have to spend your entire life with her. Humans aren't like us. I've told you many times that they lie, cheat, steal, and think only of themselves. They can be cruel to members of their own species and twice as cruel to species they regard as animals, including us."

"But Millie isn't like that. She put her own life in danger to help us. And she's honest and caring ... I love her, Grandmother, and it isn't just because she saved our lives. She is the one I want to share my life with. I will never love another dragoness the way I love her."

"Perhaps not, Audun, but have you really thought this

48

through? I've seen what living among humans can do to dragons. If you get your wish and learn how to change your form into that of a human, you will always have to hide who you really are and what you can do. You'll live in constant fear of discovery."

"It wouldn't be like that for me," said Audun. "Millie is already a dragon part of the time and the people in her kingdom accept her the way she is. Her mother is a Dragon Friend, which means that members of our own kind accept and respect her."

"Fire-breathing dragons, perhaps, but you heard what King Stormclaw said. Our kind may not revile her as he does, but neither would they accept her. It's true that the feud between us is old and mostly forgotten, but the king could make trouble for you should you even desire to remain friends with the girl. If you pursue this relationship without his approval, King Stormclaw will banish you at the very least."

"What happened between the fire-breathers and us, Grandmother? No one ever told me."

"It happened hundreds of years before I was born, so I don't know precisely, but apparently, by chance, the ice dragons discovered a cave rich in gems. Considering the love of jewels that all dragons feel, this was a marvelous find. Although the cave was in a distant land, we mined it for years undisturbed, bringing the jewels here to the stronghold, and enriching our kingdom's treasury. When the human king of the distant land discovered what we were doing, he threatened to bring the wrath of all humans down on us. Instead, we made a pact with him wherein we would continue to mine the gems, and he would receive a share.

"Once again, all was well, until the fire-breathing dragons learned of our pact with the human king. They tried to find the cave, forcing us to take ever greater measures to hide its location. One day they managed to waylay the dragons bringing the gems to the stronghold and stole a vast number of them. There was a great battle and many were injured on both sides. It happened so long ago that most families have recovered from their loss. But some, like the family of King Stormclaw, hold too tightly to their grudges."

"And that's why he hates Millie's mother?"

Audun's grandmother nodded. "He's a good dragon, but he can be rash at times as can most dragon kings. That is why they have councillors, like me. You do realize, Audun, that even if you lived in a kingdom where you wouldn't be persecuted for what you are, you would be throwing away a promising future among dragon kind. I'd always hoped that someday you might aspire to a high position, perhaps even the central platform in the audience chamber."

"I don't want to be king, Grandmother. I just want to choose my own mate. Is that really too much to ask?"

"You sound like I once did, more's the pity. No," she said, sighing again. "I don't think it's too much to ask. But what about your talent? I know you haven't learned what it is yet, and you may not for many years, but what if your talent is something you can use only in the Icy North or that you can't use around humans? If I didn't live among glaciers, I would never have known that I can hear them speak."

"That's true, Grandmother, but a lot of ice dragons have talents that have nothing to do with where they live. Grandfather can fly high wherever he is and Mother's graceful all the time. I bet Frostybreath could freeze things even if he was someplace hot. I just hope my talent is a good one, but whether it is or not, it will have nothing to do with Millie."

Song of the Glacier stopped pacing and turned to face him again. "If you truly love Millie, there is one other thing you need to consider. Dragons live for hundreds of years while humans have a much shorter life span. We never have more than one mate. Are you sure you want your mate to be someone who will not live as long as you will? If you marry her, you will do so knowing that you will outlive her and have to endure many years of grieving once she is gone."

"I understand that, Grandmother. It is a price I am willing to pay if it means I can have even a few years with Millie."

"Then I hope she loves you as much as you love her, my dear grandson."

"Will you talk to the king and the other councillors for me?" Audun asked.

Song of the Glacier sighed. "You're very persuasive, Audun. I'll do whatever I can to help you."

Five

Once more it was Frostybreath who came to tell Audun that the king had summoned him. "But I thought he didn't want to see me again," said Audun, rubbing sleep from his eyes.

"A king can change his mind, just like everyone else," the big dragon replied. "But be careful what you say. He seemed mighty worked up about something."

"I hope he *has* changed his mind," Audun said, suddenly feeling much more hopeful. "Why did you come for me? Still filling in for your friend?"

"I was on my way to the top," said Frostybreath. "So I told my friends that I'd save them the trouble. I'm adding a curlicue to the first part of the chute. I thought an extra flourish would be fun."

"I went down your chute with Loolee yesterday. I don't think I've ever had so much fun before. It's great that you can use your talent to make other dragons happy," said Audun.

Frostybreath grunted. "I do what I can. It seems to me that a talent isn't worth much if you can't use it to help others."

Audun waved good-bye to the dragon as they parted ways. He hadn't discovered his own talent yet, but then few dragons did until they reached their twentieth year. Although he wasn't worried, he hoped that his talent would be something worthwhile. His grandfather could fly higher than anyone else. His father could fly faster. His mother was as graceful as a drifting snowflake. But his grandmother's talent was so subtle that she didn't seem to do anything except sit with her eyes closed, so that she almost appeared to be asleep. When she finally opened her eyes, she would tell Audun and his parents what the glaciers were saying deep in their depths. Sometimes she said they talked about the changes in temperature or what was in the water around them. Sometimes it was about the creatures that lived in the sea nearby. When two or more glaciers bumped into one another, regardless of whether they thundered or whispered, they usually talked about one another.

As a little dragon there had been times when Audun thought that his grandmother didn't really have a talent and that she was making it up, but everyone else seemed to believe her and she always did know when a glacier was about to move or when there were new fish in the area. Sometimes dragons came to ask his grandmother for advice and she would go off by herself to listen to a glacier. Eventually, Audun came to understand that she really was special, but it had never occurred to him that the king might think so as well. The more he thought about it, however, the more sense it made that a talent like his grandmother's could be valuable to anyone who watched out for the welfare of dragons who lived on and around glaciers.

Audun had almost reached the audience room when he began to wonder what talents the other councillors might have. He'd been so concerned with getting the king to agree to help him that it hadn't occurred to him to ask his grandmother about the other dragonesses. Although most dragons knew about the king's history, little was generally known about the dragonesses who advised him. Audun hadn't paid much attention to them the last time he was in their presence, but he did seem to recall that they were older than Song of the Glacier, and at least one of them had looked at him with kind eyes. Perhaps she would help Song of the Glacier change the dragon king's mind.

Audun was about to enter the chamber when a dragon wearing the satchels of a messenger strapped to his back emerged, looking harried and tired. He nodded at Audun who waited until the exterior door had closed before opening the door to the audience chamber.

King Stormclaw wasn't seated on his stone pillar as he'd been during their last interview. Instead, he was pacing the length of the room, his tail twitching in agitation. The king stopped when he spotted Audun waiting nervously by the door. "Come in, young dragon. No need to stand there looking like I'm about to rip off your head. You'll be pleased to hear that I've reconsidered. At first I thought you were crazy for wanting to learn how to turn into a human so you could be with a human who can turn into a dragoness. I'd never heard such a thing! And knowing who the dragoness is, I must tell you that I was tempted to lock you away for your own good. However, out of regard for your grandmother, I have reconsidered your request and am willing to give you the opportunity to show me that you deserve to be taught how to turn into a human. You will have to complete five tasks to prove your worth." He gestured toward the dragoness seated farthest from Song of the Glacier. "Frostweaver will tell you what you must do."

Audun turned to the dragoness and bowed, so excited at the good news that he couldn't help but grin. The old dragoness was smiling at him when he looked up, and he could see that at least two of her fangs were missing. The flesh on her jaws was lined with wrinkles and her white scales were dull and yellowed with age. Her blue eyes bore a filmy cast but, even so, he saw excitement gleaming in their depths. Frostweaver looked so fragile that he couldn't help but wonder if she could still fly.

"Good day to you, Audun, grandson of my new friend, Song of the Glacier. It gives me great pleasure to tell you of your task and to set you on the road to achieving your goal." When the old dragoness waved a talon before her face, Audun thought she was about to fall over. It took a moment before he realized that she was using frost to draw a map in the air as if she were writing on ice. The frost shimmered and grew more solid, until he thought he could almost reach out and touch it.

"Far from here," said Frostweaver, "lies the kingdom of Aridia. In the southern half of the kingdom you will find the Arid Desert. Although many believe that the shifting sands harbor no life, we dragons know that is not true. You must fly to the Arid Desert and look for the rarest of all birds, which can be found only in the driest of lands." With a swipe of her talons, the map faded away, and the picture of a bird replaced it. The bird was ugly, with a bald head and small, piercing eyes. It looked scrawny at first, but as Audun watched, its body filled out until it looked like a different bird entirely. "You may find the desicca bird in either of its phases, but it is not the bird itself that you seek. Locate the bird and follow it to its nest, buried deep within the burning sands. Retrieve one of the eggs and bring it back here. If you are to succeed at your task, you must ensure that the egg remains intact and that the chick inside lives. Upon successful completion of this test, you shall receive your next task."

Audun nodded, relieved that the task was so simple. Find a bird and bring back its egg. Yes, he could do that.

He studied the picture as it faded, then bowed once more to the old dragoness, and turned to leave.

"Just a moment, young dragon," called Frostweaver. "You will need to take this with you." Audun glanced back to see the old dragoness weaving strands of frost in the air in front of her, creating a band of silver and white. The band grew, becoming a square as wide as her wings could reach. When she finished, she tapped the center of the square and it shrank until it was no bigger than the span of the outspread talons of one foot. Pinching the square between two talons, she handed it to Audun, saying, "This will keep the wearer whatever temperature he needs to be and will grow or shrink to the necessary size. Remember what I said about the egg. I'll be looking forward to your return. Dragonspeed!"

Audun took the square from Frostweaver and bowed once more. He was tucking it into his wing pouch as Song of the Glacier came forward. "I wish you well, Audun. Be careful in the desert and don't eat any spoiled meat. Safe travels!"

It was the farewell he had longed to hear when he left his family only days before.

❧

The young dragon was on his way up the ramp when Hildie ran after him, calling his name. "Is it true you're leaving?"

she asked, coming so close that the scales of their legs brushed together as she matched her pace to his.

Although Audun had had plenty of friends while growing up at the edge of the Icy Sea, they had all been boy dragons. All the dragonesses he'd ever known had been adults, so he wasn't sure how to react when Hildie persisted in touching him. It made Audun feel uncomfortable and he moved aside to give her more room. She followed him, staying just as close until he was bumping against the far wall.

"Where did you hear that I'm leaving?" he asked, picking up speed as he tried to put space between them. "I only just learned it myself. Does your talent allow you to see into the future?"

Although he was half-joking, Hildie seemed to take him seriously. "Actually, I don't have my talent yet. Frosty-breath told me that you were leaving. A dragon charged with cleaning your room for the next visitor told him so."

"Things move quickly around here," said Audun.

Hildie shrugged. "They usually do, although I wish they hadn't moved so quickly this time."

"Audun, do you really have to go?" cried a voice, as a small dragon launched herself onto his back.

"I do, short stuff," Audun said, laughing as he spread his wings. The little dragoness slid down just as she would the chute. "There's something important that I have to do."

"Will I ever see you again, Audun?" Loolee asked, but Audun could see that Hildie was waiting for his answer, too.

"I'll be back before you know it, little one. This shouldn't take long at all."

Six

Audun decided that Frostweaver must have done something special to the map; he could recall the way to the Arid Desert as if it were etched on the air in front of him even as he flew, and his memory wasn't usually so precise. The sun had been shining when he left the island, but the sky darkened only a few miles out and rain began to fall. Fighting his way through a vicious squall that lashed the southernmost shoreline of the Icy Sea, he followed the curve of the land until he reached the range of mountains that defined the western edge of the Kingdom of Bullrush. He skirted the mountains and went inland, turning west again before reaching the mountains of Upper Montevista. It took him two days to get that far. Another day of flying carried him across the desert of East Aridia where it was so hot that he began to sweat with his tongue and from the bottoms of his feet.

It was night when he passed over the castle in the center of a huge city. The castle was wide, with tall spires and pennants flying everywhere. Row upon row of soldiers were lined up around the inside perimeter of an enormous courtyard in the middle of the castle grounds. Bright torches edging the courtyard showed that a mosaic depicting an older man with flowing, white hair covered the very center. A man with a shining bald head stood at the edge of the mosaic beside a man who looked remarkably like the one pictured. When the bald-headed man raised his arms, the crowd grew quiet. He paused, as if for effect, then performed an intricate gesture with his hands. Audun realized that the man must be a wizard when the mosaic seemed to come to life, blinking and opening its mouth to speak. The man in the mosaic talked about the bravery of his army and congratulated the officers who had led the soldiers into battle. He spoke of the conquest of another kingdom and of how much the subjects in East Aridia would benefit. Audun thought that the man who looked like the mosaic might be doing the actual talking, but he couldn't tell for sure without going closer.

As Audun circled overhead, the face in the mosaic stopped talking and grew still and lifeless once again. The soldiers cheered, saluting the man with the flowing hair. They held their spears aloft and shook them; the glint of metal in the torchlight reminded Audun of the soldiers who had shot arrows at him in Upper Montevista, so he turned once more and headed back over the open desert.

On the fourth day he reached Aridia. A dry, hot wind

was blowing, slowly moving dunes of golden sand across the land below him. Growing up in the Icy North, he had seen countless snowdrifts, but none so wide that they stretched as far as he could see. The heat radiating off the dunes parched his throat and made him wish for the rain that he'd battled only days before.

Audun closed his inner lids to protect his eyes from the biting, wind-carried sand, but even though he flew high above the ground, he could hear the sand hissing against his scales and feel it scouring away the grime he'd acquired while traveling. By dusk he still had not found any birds, let alone the desicca bird he'd seen in Frostweaver's image.

Audun stayed aloft until long after the sun had set and the searing heat of the sand had cooled enough that he could land. Settling on the ground, he welcomed the night chill that enveloped the desert, and fell into a fitful sleep where images of Millie crying as her mother whisked her away made him growl and twitch his wings.

The heat returned with the morning and once again Audun took to the air. He hadn't gone far before he saw an enormous bird flying far off in the distance. Even in the Icy North, dragons had heard of rocs, but it was the first time Audun had ever seen one. He wondered what other kinds of creatures might live in the desert and was surprised when a short time later he glanced down and saw the ground moving. Drawing closer, he spotted a horde of insects with daggerlike stingers arched over their backs scuttling across the sand. As he passed over wind-eroded ruins, he saw an enormous snake with an arrow-shaped head investigating the remains of a collapsed wall.

A little farther on, he watched as a huge cat nearly the color of the sand slunk along the ground, stalking its prey. He would have thought nothing more of it if he hadn't seen what the cat was hunting. Three human children were shuffling across the sand, looking forlorn and bedraggled. The boys, who weren't very big, were half-carrying, half-dragging a girl even smaller than themselves. Audun might have continued on if the little girl hadn't glanced up just as he flew overhead. She looked terrified, but what made Audun want to stop and help them was the girl's blond hair and the shape of her face: the little girl looked much the way Millie must have when she was very young.

Audun was too far away to hear what the girl said when she pointed up at him, but he could see the frightened looks on the boys' faces. The older boy dropped the little girl's hand and reached into his waistband for a forked stick. Audun didn't know what he was going to do with it until the boy set a stone on a leather strap tied to the prongs of the stick. He was pulling back on the strap when the big cat wiggled its rump and charged. Not wanting to see what happened when the cat reached the children, Audun tucked his wings close to his body and aimed for the beast. The younger children began to scream just as Audun opened his mouth and roared. The boy let the leather sling go as the dragon flew over their heads and the stone bounced off Audun's neck. The young dragon barely felt it as he flew past them and landed in the big cat's path. With its fur bristling, the cat pulled up short. Faced with an angry dragon three times its size, the animal turned and ran.

To Audun's surprise, the boy turned to him and bowed, saying, "Thank you most kindly, gracious dragon. I apologize for thinking you meant us harm when you were really defending us from that horrid lion. I never thought I'd see a dragon here. My name is Galen and these two are my brother Samuel and my sister, Shanna."

All three children had straight hair bleached to a pale blond, but while Galen had blue eyes, the other children's were a warm brown. With their straight noses and squared chins, Audun would have known they were siblings even if Galen hadn't told him so.

"You are most welcome, young sir," said Audun. "I am Audun of the Icy North. If I may ask, how is it that you can talk to dragons?"

The little boy shrugged. "We had a tutor who had some magic. He taught us many things."

"Where is your tutor now? Why are you here without an adult to protect you?"

Shanna pulled a piece of cloth from her sleeve and clutched it to her chest. Audun noticed that it had a wooden head and was roughly shaped like a human. "We ran away," she said, and popped her thumb into her mouth.

"We had to," said Galen. "We lived in Desidaria, the city that surrounds the royal castle of King Cadmus, although the castle no longer belongs to him. He was killed in the war."

"There's been a war?" Audun remembered the throngs of armed people he'd seen in the courtyard in East Aridia.

Galen nodded. "It ended just a few days ago. King Beltran of East Aridia sent his soldiers to attack Desidaria. They defeated our soldiers and ransacked the city. A lot of people were killed, including our king. His brother, Dolon, swore fealty to King Beltran. Dolon sits on the throne of Aridia now."

Shanna pulled her thumb out of her mouth to tug at her brother's sleeve. "What about Owen? Can the dragon help us get Owen back?"

"We have to go," said Samuel. "Owen could be hurt."

"Who is Owen?" asked Audun.

Galen rubbed the side of his head and frowned. "He's our older brother. After King Beltran left, there were a lot of orphans and nobody knew what to do with them. Dolon said that they could all come live in the palace. He put us with them until Owen was able to sneak away from where he'd been in training and come for us."

"Owen rescued us!" said Shanna. "He was very brave!"

"Owen helped us get out of the city," said Samuel. "He was taking us to our aunt's home on the other side of the desert when the roc came."

"It came down, *whoosh*!" Shanna said, demonstrating with her hand. "And took Owen away."

"We were going after him when you found us," said Galen. "It's what he would have done if one of us had been carried off."

"Do you think he's all right?" Shanna asked, her brown eyes big and round.

"I'm sure he is," Galen said, but he didn't sound very convincing.

"We have a problem, though," said Samuel.

Audun raised a brow ridge. "Only one?"

"He means we're lost," said Shanna.

"Owen was the one who knew the way," explained Galen. "I thought I knew which way the roc took him, but I've been getting all turned around . . ."

Shanna rubbed her eyes with a grubby hand, wiping away a tear. "I want to go home, Galen!"

"I know, Shanna," said her older brother, as he put his arm around her. "That's what we all want. But we can't go back to Desidaria now."

"I can take you to your aunt's home," said the dragon, "as long as you can tell me where it is."

Samuel shook his head. "We have to get Owen first. We can't go anywhere without him!"

"Could you help us find him?" asked Galen. "We could find him faster if you were looking for him, too."

"You have wings!" Shanna said through her tears.

"We'd go with you," said Samuel. "If we were all looking—"

"I can't take you with me. You'd be in the way. And I can't leave you here. It isn't safe. I'll take you to your aunt and come back and look for Owen."

"No!" cried Samuel. "He's *our* brother. *We* have to go rescue him!"

"Take my help the way I offer it, or don't get it at all. It's up to you. I have my own task ahead of me, so if you don't want my help . . ."

"But we do!" Galen said. "You and I could take Shanna and Samuel to our aunt's home, then I could go with you."

"Galen!" shouted his brother and sister in unison.

"That wasn't what I offered," said Audun.

"Then we accept your offer as it was given," said Galen through stiff lips. Audun thought he looked as if he wanted to cry.

Audun crouched down and bent his neck so the children could climb on more easily. "We'd better hurry," he said. "I have a lot of flying to do."

With the map that Frostweaver had shown him set in his mind, Audun was able to use the children's scanty memories of the way to their aunt's home to head in the right direction. It took him longer to find the town than it had to cross the desert, but when he did he landed on the outskirts and refused to go into the town itself. Although the children assured him that their aunt would want to thank him, Audun couldn't help but remember the reception he'd gotten from other humans.

"Do you know the way to your aunt's home from here?" Audun asked as the children clambered down.

Galen nodded. "I came to visit her last year. I know right where she lives."

"You're going back for Owen, aren't you?" Samuel asked, his brow creased with worry.

"I'm going to start looking for him now," said Audun. Dipping his head to the children, he spread his wings, pausing only long enough to say, "I'll bring him back if it's at all possible."

"Are you sure I can't go with you?" asked Galen. "Two pairs of eyes can see more than one."

"That's true," said Audun. "But dragon eyes can see farther than human eyes. And trying to take something away from a roc won't be easy or safe. If you go with me, I'll have to worry about you as well as your brother. You don't want me to be distracted when I'm trying to rescue him, do you?"

The little boy looked at the ground and muttered, "I guess not."

"Besides, your brother and sister need you to take them to your aunt. Someone bigger and stronger than them has to show them the way. Samuel and Shanna are depending on you."

"That's true," Galen said, glancing at the smaller children. Shanna was rubbing her eyes again and it was obvious that she was having a hard time keeping them open. Aside from two bright red spots on his cheeks, Samuel looked pale and shaky.

"Take care of each other," Audun said, backing away so he could flap his wings without knocking the children over.

"Thank you!" Galen shouted as the dragon took off.

◦⟋

Audun didn't know much about rocs, other than that they were big. He'd heard that they might fight dragons if provoked, but no one he knew had ever fought one and he didn't want to be the first. If rocs were as territorial as a lot of other birds he knew, there probably wouldn't be too many in one area, which meant that the bird he had seen before might be the very one he had to find now. With the wind shifting the sand, it wasn't easy to find a certain spot in the desert, but Audun was sure he had come pretty close. He flew in the direction that he thought the roc had gone, looking for any sort of sign that a big bird had passed that way.

It was late in the day when he saw the first droppings. Something big had created the huge black and white speckled piles that littered the desert floor like half-melted globs of snow. The enormous feather resting on the sand beside them was as long as his wings were wide.

A penetrating scent grew stronger as he flew on. The ground below him began to change. Instead of sand, he saw rocky outcroppings with occasional withered plants growing in the cracks. The outcroppings became taller and more misshapen the farther he went, until a bizarre garden of weirdly shaped formations lay before him. Having been blasted by wind and sand for many years, the stones had taken on outlines unlike anything else in nature. Fantastic protuberances, curves, and spires stood sentinel, casting their shadows on the land as the sun prepared to set.

Still following the scent of the roc, Audun eventually came upon a tall spire with a nest made of entire trees stacked and woven together on top. Vines as big around as a human man's waist helped to hold it together. Audun was impressed by the enormous distances the roc must have flown to bring such big trees to build a nest. He was even more impressed as he drew closer and could see the nest's actual size. A dozen dragons could have slept in the nest without any one touching another.

At first the nest appeared to be empty, but then he saw movement: a down-covered baby roc three times the size of a baby dragon waddled from one side to the other. Audun had flown close enough to spot another fledgling when he heard a loud squawk and saw a shadow pass overhead. The mother roc was back, bringing food for her babies. With the enormous bird approaching, Audun didn't have much of a choice; he could hide or fly away and hope she hadn't seen how close he had been to her nest. Because he still didn't know if Owen was there, hiding seemed like the better choice.

Audun put on a burst of speed and flew under the nest to latch on to one of the tree trunks with his talons. Hanging upside down beneath the nest, he turned his head to the side as rotting bark became dislodged, pattering around him as it fell. There was another painfully loud squawk and the entire nest dipped down when the adult roc landed. The nest continued to shake while she walked across it, chirruping softly to her babies. Audun tried not to make a sound as he fought to hold on.

Something heavy hit the nest as the roc dropped whatever she had brought to her babies. There was more thrashing only feet above Audun's head, making more debris rain through the cracks. Peering through the gaps in the interwoven trees, the young dragon could just make out the patterns of a two-foot-thick snake that reared up when one of the babies pecked it.

With the snake hissing just above his head, Audun moved to the other side of the nest, looking for something to indicate that the boy, Owen, had been there. He was halfway to the outer edge when both babies attacked the snake at once and the mother joined in to help them, making the nest bounce and shake.

Stopping to peer up through the tree trunks every few feet, Audun eventually reached the far side of the nest and began to move along its rim. He was working his way around a thicker cluster of branches, trying to see through some still-attached foliage, when a face appeared and two vivid blue eyes blinked at him. The face was that of a human boy about the same age as Millie and her friends, and his hair was the same shade of yellow as that of the three children Audun had just met.

Audun hadn't expected to find the boy as easily as this. "Are you Owen?" he whispered.

The boy looked stunned. He drew back, but the branches wouldn't allow him to go far. "How do you know my name?" he asked.

"Your brothers and sister sent me to find you. I'm here to take you to them."

Hope lit the boy's eyes. In his excitement, his voice was louder than before. "You've seen them? Are they all right?"

"Shh!" said Audun. "Not so loud or the birds will come looking. Galen and the others are fine. They're just worried about you. Is there any way down from there?"

"You mean a hole through the bottom? I don't think so. I was looking for one, but this is all I've found. It's sort of a pocket between the trunks. The little ones can't reach me, but I won't stand a chance if a big one comes looking for me. There are two adults. The one that brought me has been gone for a while. I thought I could wait until night and climb down if I could find a gap big enough to let me through."

Audun turned his head and stretched his neck to see what was below him. The nest was on a pedestal of stone with sheer drops on every side. Unless the boy was a very good climber, he wouldn't have made it, especially in the dark.

"I wouldn't recommend it," Audun whispered to the boy. "I can't get to you from here, but if you climb onto the nest I can carry you away."

"Why should I trust you? How do I know you really helped my brothers and sister?"

"I didn't come to steal you from a roc's nest so I could eat you, if that's what you're thinking. Do you want my help or not?"

A tree trunk groaned as the adult roc settled her weight on it. The sun was going down. Although Audun was looking forward to the cool of the night, he wasn't so sure how well a human would fare. The other roc would probably be back soon, making it that much harder for Owen to sneak out of the nest.

"If I draw the adult roc away, do you think you could climb out and hang on to the bottom of the nest until I come back to get you? I'll be as fast as I can, but we should do this now."

"I think I can," said Owen. "I used a branch to keep them off me before. How will you draw the big one away?"

"That," said Audun, "will be the easy part."

Audun's talons wouldn't let go at first, after having gripped so tightly for so long. When he could finally move them, they were stiff, but he was able to work his way to a spot where there weren't any protruding branches to get in his way. Finding a clear space below him, Audun let go of the nest and fell, opening his wings with a snap. Gliding out from under the nest, he beat his wings when he was past the edge and rose up so that he could look inside. The two babies lay beside their mother, their bellies full and rounded. At the sound of Audun's wings, the adult bird opened her eyes and looked him full in the face. "Awk!" she cried, nearly deafening Audun.

Throwing his head back, Audun roared, the sound of his voice almost as loud. Then, before the roc could react, he flew straight at her head, slapping it with his tail as he flew up and over her.

The nest tipped abruptly as the adult roc launched herself into the air. She came after Audun as if her tail were on fire, her shrill screams echoing off the rock in front of him. Audun angled his wings and began to climb. The roc was right behind him, her heavy wings pounding the air with a *whump! whump!* Veering this way and that around the bizarrely shaped spires, Audun led the giant bird away from her nest. Miles of ground sped by below him, yet he could still hear the roc screaming.

He was at the very edge of the formations when he glanced back. The roc was finally out of sight, so Audun angled his head and body and took off back toward the nest, faster than most dragons and much faster than any bird as big as a roc could ever fly. Circling around, Audun sped back to the nest but was only part of the way there when he saw another roc far off in the distance, heading in the same direction. Audun didn't have much time. He focused on the nest ahead, and put all his strength into going even faster.

"Climb on!" Audun shouted, as he reached the boy. "Hurry, the other roc is coming!"

At the sight of a dragon, the baby birds squawked and fluttered to the other side while Owen scrambled onto Audun's back.

"Hold on tight!" ordered the dragon. He beat his wings and flew as fast as he could until they were well over the desert.

Audun had slowed to a more comfortable pace when Owen finally tried to talk to him. "Where are you taking me?" he asked.

"To the town where your aunt lives. It's where I dropped off your brothers and sister. They said it was where you were headed when the roc took you."

"I don't know how to thank you," said Owen. "I still can't believe a dragon is helping us. Why are you here, anyway? I've never seen a white dragon like you before."

"I'm from the Icy North. I've come looking for a desicca bird."

"A what? No, wait! I've heard of them, although I don't know very much. They're really rare, even more rare than rocs. The only place they've ever been seen is around oases. I guess that's where you should look. I wish I could tell you more."

"Actually, you've helped a lot. I'll head for an oasis as soon as I drop you off."

"It will be night by then. It gets awfully cold in the desert at night."

"I know," said Audun. "I'm looking forward to it."

Seven

When Audun woke the next morning the sun was already up and the sand was uncomfortably hot. As he flew over the desert, the light reflecting off the sand made his head hurt, but he'd already used up an entire day helping the children and didn't want to lose any more time.

Audun's head was pounding when he finally saw an oasis, small, yet with a glint of water, and an islet of stunted trees. He licked his dry, cracked lips, but despite the pain in his head and his ever-growing thirst, the young dragon was reluctant to land for fear that the oasis was either a mirage or a trap. The water looked so tempting, and the shade so inviting, however, that Audun circled the oasis, high enough that anything on the ground would have difficulty seeing him, but low enough that he could see if something moved.

When the oasis didn't disappear and he didn't spot anything dangerous, he flew down until he was close enough to see an ant waving its feelers from the tip of a nodding leaf. Audun settled to the ground and sniffed the water. It smelled as clean and pure as it looked, so he took a chance and sipped. The water was warm, but delicious. As it trickled down his throat, he gave up all caution and submerged his head, taking one enormous gulp after another. Fortunately for Audun, the pool of water was small and he had emptied it before he drank enough to make himself sick.

With water in his belly and the shade of the trees cooling his back, Audun would have been happy to stay and rest, but he knew that his blue and white scales would stand out against the gold and green of the oasis and were sure to frighten away the bird he had come to find. Spreading his wings again, Audun took off. Perhaps he'd find a desicca bird at the next oasis.

For the briefest moment Audun wondered if the desicca bird might not exist and if the king and his councillors were just trying to get rid of him. He might have given the thought serious consideration, if his grandmother hadn't promised to help him. Even if she wasn't happy with his choice, he knew that she would never betray him in such a way. And certainly Owen would have had no reason to lie. If the boy said the bird existed, Audun was sure that it did.

The sun was still high in the sky and Audun was beginning to feel thirsty again when he spotted something flying in the distance. Because it didn't move quite like a bird, Audun grew curious and swerved in its direction. As he drew closer he realized that it was a man riding on a magic carpet—the same bald-headed wizard he'd seen making the mosaic talk. Intent on following a pair of vultures, the wizard didn't seem to have seen Audun.

The young dragon watched as the man gestured at the sky. A small, dark cloud appeared overhead, scudding just above the vultures. Suddenly, a bolt of lightning shot from the cloud, forking to strike both vultures at once. Stunned, the birds tumbled to the ground. The wizard gestured again and sand rose into the air, shaping itself into a braided net which scooped up the birds and hauled them onto the magic carpet. Not caring to see what the wizard would do next, Audun turned and sped back the way he'd come.

The wind was beginning to pick up when Audun finally spotted an oasis even smaller than the first. As he spiraled down toward it, he saw a fat, yellow-brown bird with a bald head tottering awkwardly through the meager foliage surrounding the tiny pond. It looked just like the bird in the image that Frostweaver had shown him.

Not wanting to frighten the creature, Audun swerved away, but it was too late. His shadow had fallen on the desicca bird, which looked up in alarm. A moment later, the bird took off, flying away on broad, sturdy wings strong enough to support its chunky body. Audun followed the bird, hoping it would lead him to its nest, but instead it veered into the increasing wind. Soon the wind was so strong that Audun had to fight for every inch, yet the desicca bird was able to fly into it with no apparent difficulty.

When the stinging sand made his eyes tear despite their inner lids, Audun turned his head away and struggled to gain altitude, hoping to climb above the storm.

Afraid that the wind might tear his wings before he could escape, Audun strained to get above the blowing sand until he was so high that the air was thin and he had to fight to breathe. The golden cloud roiled and churned below him as he fought to stay above the storm. When the wind finally died away, Audun spread his wings to their fullest and let himself glide down to the hot sand.

Too tired to move, Audun lay on his side, dragging air into his aching lungs. He was still there when the sun went down, letting the night bring its welcome chill.

❧

As the sun came up, Audun raised his head and groaned. Another day of searching. Another day of little to drink and nothing to eat. At least now he had seen one of the birds. He even had a good idea of where he should start looking.

The storm had changed the face of the desert, erasing dunes here, creating new ones there. Once again Audun took to the sky, looking for the oasis where he had seen the desicca bird. He found it more quickly this time, for now he knew where to look. The precious patch of greenery and water had been ravaged by the storm, but not destroyed. Audun was certain that this was where the bird would appear. All he had to do was wait.

A new dune had formed close to the oasis. Landing halfway up, Audun inched backward so he was partly buried in the concealing sand, yet could still see everything that happened near the water. As the morning wore on, the sand became hotter, until Audun felt as if he were roasting alive. To his surprise, however, the spot between his back and his wing wasn't hot. In fact, it was the only spot that was comfortable.

It occurred to Audun that it might be the effect of the never-melting ice that he had stuck in his pouch, so he took it out and held it against his forehead, easing the ball of pain that had been forming between his eyes. Even without the ice, however, the area between his back and wing felt fine, so he reached in the pouch once more and removed the rest of its contents, including the square of woven frost. Although he'd assumed that he was meant to use it to keep the egg warm, he wondered if it would also work to keep him cold.

After returning the ice to his pouch, Audun spread the square over his back. Within a minute or two he began to feel cool all over. Comfortable now, Audun shifted back and forth, letting the sand cover him until only his head was free. He waited through the heat of the day, dozing now and then, and was rewarded for his patience when something flew past his face. The desicca bird had returned.

Audun kept perfectly still as the bird landed at the edge of the pond. It looked fatter than he remembered it and was even more ungainly as it waddled into the water. Stretching its neck, the bird's throat convulsed and, to Audun's surprise, a fountain of water gushed out, mixing with the water that was already there. As more and more water emerged from the bird, its sides shrank until it was as thin as the first image that Frostweaver had shown him. When it was finished, the desicca bird waddled out of the pond, which was now considerably larger.

Audun's stomach churned as he thought about what he'd just seen. He had drunk water from a pond just like that only the day before. It had tasted fine then, but the thought that it might have come out of a bird's stomach was revolting. He was trying not to gag when he noticed that the bird had gone to the base of a dune on the far side of the oasis and had begun to preen its feathers, leaving them with a glistening sheen that seemed to glue them together. When it finally seemed satisfied, the bird turned to the dune and began to dig, scrabbling at the sand and shooting it out behind in a constant stream. It continued to dig until its body was buried in the sand, yet it didn't show any sign of stopping. When it had completely disappeared into the dune, Audun realized that the bird was creating a round tunnel as wide as it was tall.

Although the bird was out of sight, sand continued to shoot out of the tunnel. When it stopped, Audun expected the bird to emerge, but at least five minutes passed before he saw movement and then it wasn't the bird at all, but a mottled brown and gold egg, rolling out of the tunnel as its mother pushed it from behind. The bird emerged only long enough to place the egg beside the water before returning to the tunnel. Twice more it brought out an egg, and each time Audun thought about rushing down to grab one, but curiosity made him stay where he was, waiting to see what would happen next.

When the last egg had rolled to a stop beside the water, the desicca bird tapped it with her beak once, twice, three times. Suddenly the egg began to rock wildly back and forth. A crack appeared in its side and a sharp yellow beak appeared. As the first baby emerged from its shell, the mother tapped the second egg, eliciting the same response. The third egg was a disappointment, however, for despite the mother's tapping, the egg remained motionless and no baby bird appeared.

Audun was mentally kicking himself for not taking one of the viable eggs before they hatched when he noticed that the babies were following their mother into the pond. Scrawny and yellow, the freshly hatched chicks staggered into the water and plopped down. While their mother stood beside them, chirruping softly, the babies sat patiently, gazing at each other and the new world around them. Audun wondered what was going on. Then he realized that even though they weren't visibly doing anything, the chicks were growing plumper. It wasn't until he saw the waterline receding that he understood what was happening.

The chicks had hatched from the eggs of a bird that carried water in her body and could deposit it at will, and now they were absorbing the water she had brought.

That's one way to give your babies water in a desert, thought Audun. *And that's why they're seen only near oases. They don't come to the oases. They make them!*

The two chicks were as round as snowballs when Audun's gaze returned to the last egg. He was going to have to visit another oasis in the hope that a second desicca bird might come along. And if none came . . . The remaining egg rocked slightly and Audun gasped. The baby inside was alive after all!

Moving carefully, Audun crept out of the dune, hoping the mother desicca bird wouldn't notice the sand trickling down the slope, or the continued rocking of her egg. She was still absorbed in examining her hatchlings so Audun dashed down to the water's edge, pulled the square off his back, and threw it over the egg. Picking it up in his talons, Audun leaped into the air, climbing high with powerful beats of his wings. The desicca bird squawked, but Audun was already far away, with the egg clutched to his chest.

Twice in two days he had stolen something from a mother bird. The first time he had felt triumphant. This time he couldn't help but feel guilty.

Eight

Word of Audun's return must have reached the council members the moment he set foot on King's Isle because he was taken directly to the audience chamber where they were already waiting. He had yet to relax his grip on the egg he carried; it was almost with reluctance that he unwrapped it from its covering and held it up for the king and his councillors to see. The older dragons leaned forward to get a better look. After a moment, Stormclaw turned to Frostweaver and raised a brow ridge.

The old dragoness gestured to Audun. "Bring the egg to me, young dragon. My eyes aren't as good as they were when I was your age."

Audun stood on his hind legs to show the egg to Frostweaver, and sand trickled from the spaces between his scales, dusting the floor. Although the sandstorm had polished the outside of each scale, it had also left him with sand in every crack and crevice. He'd already decided that the desert was a nice place for an ice dragon to visit, but he, at least, would never want to live there.

The sand crunched under his feet as Audun held the egg higher, being careful not to lose his grip. The dragoness leaned so close that the tip of her nose almost touched the egg. Turning her head to the side, she placed her ear against the egg and listened. When she finally sat back and turned to the king, a smile split her wrinkled face.

"It's a desicca bird's egg all right, and I can hear the chick moving inside," she told the king, as Audun covered the egg to keep it warm. "We can't waste any time. He has to take the egg to her now."

Stormclaw nodded. "And he will, soon enough. But first I want to hear what happened. Did you have any difficulty finding the bird?" he asked Audun.

The young dragon shook his head. "Not once I knew where to look, but if the human boy, Owen, hadn't told me, I'd still be combing the desert right now."

"When did you see a human?" asked Song of the Glacier.

"I saved his brothers and sister from a lion that was about to eat them. They were the ones who told me that a roc had carried off Owen. It was after they escaped from Desidaria right after the war."

The king's brow ridges came together in a frown. He glanced at the dragoness seated between him and Song, but all she could do was shrug. "There's been a war in

Aridia?" he said, turning back to Audun. "Who were they fighting?"

"The East Aridian army invaded the city. A lot of people were killed, including the king."

Frostweaver gasped; Stormclaw and his advisers exchanged glances. "That explains why there was neither a delivery nor a message," said the king.

"What else can you tell us about this war?" Song of the Glacier asked her grandson.

Audun told them everything he could remember, and when he was done he told them in greater detail about the lion and the roc and finding the desicca bird. The king had come down from his pillar to pace while the young dragon talked about the orphans in the city, but he didn't interrupt until Audun was finished. "You've done well, young dragon. Better than we expected. The news you brought has given us much to think about."

"Stormclaw," prompted Song of the Glacier.

"Ah, yes. Your second task," the king continued. "Because you have been so resourceful, and have shown real concern for the chick within the egg, we believe you are the ideal dragon to take care of this for us. Wave Skimmer will tell you what to do."

The dragoness seated between Frostweaver and the king waved at Audun to get his attention. She was plumper than Frostweaver and not quite as old, although her scaled face bore more wrinkles and creases. "I'm over here, young dragon," she said. "King Stormclaw seems to forget that you don't know who we are. My name is Wave Skimmer and my talent lets me see things far away, provided they're under or on top of water. And if the weather is good. And if I'm feeling up to it. Sometimes my back aches so much that—"

"Wave Skimmer!" interrupted the king.

"Oh, right. You're in luck today. I think we'll be able to see just fine. We need you to take the egg to the sea witch Nastia Nautica, and exchange it for a musical instrument called the Sea Serpents' Flute that she keeps in that rotting hulk she calls home. Here, I'll show you."

Picking up a wide bowl resting beside her, she spread her wings and stepped off the slab, landing on the floor with a thump. The bowl was filled with water that sloshed over the rim when she set it down. "Now watch," Wave Skimmer said, sticking her talon in the water and stirring it. A picture formed in the swirling water. It was hard to make out at first, but as Audun watched the image became clearer. An old mermaid with pale, nearly transparent hair and dark green scales on her lower half was holding a long, thin tube with holes running down two sides.

Wave Skimmer flicked her talon at the mermaid. "That is Nastia Nautica, and that," she said, circling her talon tip around the tube, "is the instrument you have to bring back."

The mermaid in the image looked up when Wave

Skimmer said her name, almost as if she had heard her. She began to look around, peering under tables and into chests. When she didn't see whatever she was looking for, she flipped open the curved lid of a sea chest and tossed the instrument inside. Bubbles escaped from the chest as she shut the lid and turned to sit on it.

"What's she doing?" Audun asked.

"Don't ask me," said Wave Skimmer. "She's as crazy as a sea serpent stuck in a waterspout."

Nastia Nautica spun around, her dark, empty eyes looking frantically from one side of the room to the other.

"Do you think she can hear us?" Audun asked.

The mermaid darted to the empty panes of the large window at the back of the room. Sticking her head out, she peered around, seeming disappointed when she pulled her head back in, her mouth working in a scream that Audun was thankful he couldn't hear.

"Huh," said Wave Skimmer. "I hadn't thought of that. Sure looks that way, doesn't it?" The old dragoness took her talon out of the water and the image vanished. When she stuck the tip back in, Audun could see rolling waves as if he were looking down at the water from above. "That isn't right," muttered the old dragoness. "Maybe if we go this way . . ." When Wave Skimmer angled her talon to the side, the image shifted as well. Now it looked like the waves were coming head on, as if the dragons were bobbing on top of the water. Audun noted that they were near an island with oddly shaped trees and what looked like a magic carpet on the sand. An old man was dancing around the carpet, waving something green in the air while sunlight glinted off his bald head.

"It's that wizard again," muttered Audun. "I wonder what he's up to now."

"Slush!" exclaimed the dragoness, and jammed her talon in the water until it scraped the bottom of the bowl. This time the image raced down to the bottom of the ocean until all they could see was brown muck.

"I went too far," murmured Wave Skimmer, pulling her talon back just a bit. "There, that's better." The image of an old, round-bellied shipwreck appeared, the timbers broken and half-covered with seaweed. Brightly colored fish darted in and out of the openings while a long, thin creature like a flat snake undulated past. "It's not much to look at, but the old witch has lived there for years," said the dragoness.

Suddenly, Nastia Nautica shot out of one of the larger openings, frightening a school of small, bright yellow fish that darted out of her way. The sea witch looked wildly around, but didn't seem to see anything. Shaking her fist at the ocean outside her door, she retreated into her wreck.

"Where is this?" asked Audun.

"That's easy," said Wave Skimmer, taking her finger out of the water. "Go due south for three days. When you see a cone-shaped island puffing smoke, head west until you see three islands in a straight line. Look for the sea witch's wreck near the island shaped like a seagull's head."

"Why don't you show him a map like I did?" asked Frostweaver.

Wave Skimmer glared at the older dragoness. "You do things your way and I'll do them mine. Now, if you don't have any other questions . . . ," she said, turning to Audun. When he shook his head, she flew back to her perch atop the slab, her wings creaking with each beat.

"You forgot the amulet," King Stormclaw reminded her.

"Oh, right! Silly of me. He's going to need that." Peering down at Audun she told him, "Now, I'm sure that like most ice dragons, you can hold your breath underwater for a good long while. However, you won't be able to hold it while you talk to the sea witch, so you'll need this amulet I'm going to give you, if I can just find it." The old dragoness patted her slab. "Let me see . . . No, it's not . . . I know! I must have put it in my pouch." Her voice became muffled as she buried her face under her wing. "No, it's not . . . Ooh! What's this? Tsk, tsk. I'd better have a doctor look at that before it gets any bigger. Now let me . . . Here it is! I was sitting on it. This is your amulet."

Snagging the chain with his talon, Audun held up the embossed amulet so he could examine it. Waves surrounding a round bubble rolled across the amulet. For a moment, Audun thought the waves were moving.

"That amulet is yours now, so put it on and don't take

it off. It will let you breathe underwater for as long as you're wearing it. Take it off and you'll drown. If you're underwater, I mean. Any questions?"

"Just one," said Audun. "I'm supposed to take the egg to the sea witch and trade it for that flute. Does she know I'm coming?"

"Nope. She has no idea," said Wave Skimmer.

"Is there anything I should know about her?"

"You shouldn't trust her. Nastia Nautica's a slippery one. Any *other* questions?"

Audun shook his head and the old dragoness sat back with a soft grunt. "Well then, as I said before, you need to hurry. The chick won't stay alive in that egg forever. I don't know why the old sea witch wants it, but she won't trade for the egg unless the chick is still alive."

"I'll leave right away," said Audun, but King Storm-claw was talking to his councillors again. Audun heard a few words: ". . . send someone to find out . . . ," and ". . . no one who can . . . ," before his grandmother called him over. She gestured for him to follow her behind her slab so they could have a moment of privacy.

"I wanted to tell you that you did very well with your first task," Song told him. "Just be careful around the sea witch. Nastia Nautica has no scruples. She'll do anything to get what she wants."

Audun had a lot on his mind as he climbed the ramp to the top floor and the exit of the island stronghold. He was grateful to his grandmother for taking his side and worried that the king might never see why he had to be with Millie. And what about Millie? Her mother had taken her away because of him. He didn't know anything about her mother, except that she was a princess, a witch, and a Dragon Friend. Was she good to Millie? Had she taken her away to punish her? What was she doing right now? Was he wasting his time hunting for an egg and negotiating with a sea witch when he should be rescuing his beloved?

Audun wasn't looking where he was going as he left the ramp and almost ran into two dragons that were blocking his way. One was Hildie, looking bored. The other was an older male dragon he had never met before. "Audun!" cried Hildie, her face lighting up. "I heard you were back. Are you staying long?"

"No, I'm on my way out now, actually," he said, trying to edge past.

Hildie frowned ever so slightly, then quickly sidled up to the older dragon and stood so that their sides were touching. "Wait, you have to meet my suitor, Ice Rider. He got his adult name last year, isn't that right, dear?" The adoring look she gave him was so unlike the bored expression she'd been wearing just a moment before that Audun was surprised. Apparently Ice Rider was as well, but he seemed to like it; he lifted his tail and wrapped it around hers in a possessive way.

"That's right, sweetness," he said, smiling at her.

Turning to Audun, Hildie said, "He's the champion ice floe rider. He can ride a floating piece of ice for miles."

"How nice," Audun told the dragon. "I'm sure that comes in handy at times." As he squeezed past them, trying to keep the egg he cradled against his chest from getting squashed, he noticed the look of disappointment in Hildie's eyes.

"Audun!" squealed Loolee, as she barreled off the ramp. "I heard you were back. Do you want to ride down the chute with me? I had so much fun last time."

"I'm sorry, Loolee, but I can't today. I have to go somewhere now. Maybe I'll be able to slide with you when I come back."

"All right," the little dragoness said, her crest drooping.

"And we'll talk, too, then, won't we, Audun?" called Hildie as he neared the door to the outside.

"Of course," he said, but instead of thinking about talking to Hildie, he was already wondering what he could possibly say to a sea witch.

Nine

A udun may not have had a map this time, but he did know how to follow directions. He flew due south for three days, stopping to catch fish and to drink from rivers, and later to catch even bigger fish from the ocean. He took time out to sleep twice, once amid the ruins of a castle, after getting permission from the banshee who lived there, and once on a tropical island whose only occupants were crabs and seabirds. Both nights he had difficulty falling asleep because he was thinking about Millie. Audun took good care of the egg, carrying it gently and making sure it was wrapped in the square so that the temperature was just right.

If it hadn't been for the smoke, he would have missed the cone-shaped island that Wave Skimmer had mentioned. He'd been looking for the smoke for the last half day, but he smelled it before he saw it. Turning west, he began to look for the three islands all in a row, but didn't spot them until late in the day.

Not wanting to face the sea witch in the dark, Audun spent the night on the island shaped roughly like a seagull's head, although he thought it looked more like a crow. He was worried about the baby bird because it had been in the egg for much longer than its nest mates, so every once in a while he pressed his ear against the egg and listened. If he waited long enough, he was rewarded with the smallest of sounds, and so knew that the baby was still alive.

He woke early the next morning when the sunlight turned rosy outside his eyelids. After breakfasting on a plump fish, he flew out over the water, the amulet's chain around his neck. Unlike the murky water in the Icy North, this water was clear and he could see far into its depths as he skimmed the tops of the waves.

Audun circled the island. When he reached the spot where he had started and still hadn't found anything, he widened the circle and searched again. He did this three or four times, until he finally saw the wreck just beyond an enormous bed of seaweed. The ship had sunk in one piece. It had been a large ship, and sturdily built, although time and the sea had left gaping holes big enough for entire schools of fish to swim through. One fish was so huge that Audun was sure that it, at least, couldn't fit through the openings. Nearly twenty feet long, the fish's gaping mouth took up most of its pointed face and was filled with dragon-sized teeth. It swam with the confidence of being the biggest predator around. Audun watched as it passed over the wreck and back again. Finally, it seemed to grow bored and swam away, but the young dragon waited until it was out of sight before heading down to the wreck.

He didn't want to startle the witch, so he swam around the wreck quietly, wondering how to find her. At the squared-off back of the ship he found the window that he'd seen in Wave Skimmer's bowl of water. He peered through the window, trying to see the dim interior, and suddenly there she was, staring back at him with eyes like dark, bottomless pits. The witch's pale, green skin looked taut and ageless, but it was her cloud of nearly colorless hair and her horrifying eyes that made her look so old.

"What do you want?" Nastia Nautica demanded.

A jellyfish undulated past Audun, trailing ribbonlike tendrils behind it. Squinting her eyes in annoyance, the sea witch pointed a finger at the creature. The tendrils flailed and began to tie themselves in knots while the jellyfish wobbled in agitation.

Unable to bear the creature's agony, Audun hoped that distracting the sea witch would make her leave the jellyfish alone. "I've come to trade something for a musical instrument that you have in your possession. I have something I believe you would like."

"What musical instrument?" asked Nastia Nautica, turning back to Audun and letting the jellyfish get away. "I have lots of them. I'm a very musical person."

"It's called the Sea Serpents' Flute."

"Really? Now why would a dragon want to torment a sea serpent until it flees? Is it anyone I know?"

"I doubt it," said Audun. "Are you interested in making a trade?"

"What do you have? That flute is one of my most prized possessions. I won't let it go for just..." When Audun held up the covered egg, Nastia Nautica leaned out the window saying, "What's that? Unwrap it and let me see."

Audun was reluctant to unwrap the egg. After seeing what the witch had done to the poor jellyfish, he knew that she liked hurting living creatures. But he had been sent to get the flute and he wasn't going to go back without it. Gritting his teeth, Audun slowly unwrapped the egg, revealing the distinctive mottled shell.

Nastia Nautica gasped. "Is that what I think it is?" she said, crawling halfway out the window. "Give it to me! I have to see if it's alive."

"The instrument...," said Audun.

"I'll get it! Just let me see that egg!"

Audun would have held on to the egg, but he was taken by surprise—the sea witch snatched it from him, and shook it hard. Placing her ear against the egg as she retreated into her wreck, she listened for a moment, then chortled with glee. "I've finally got it! Now that little witch will learn a lesson she'll never forget."

"About the trade...," said Audun.

The sea witch sneered at him. "You're a fool, dragon. You should never have given up the egg so easily. Here's your trade!" Holding the egg with one hand, she made circling motions with the other and a dark, solid-looking bubble formed on her palm. Audun was backing away when she hurled it at him. The bubble exploded, its force flipping the dragon head over tail all the way to the bed of seaweed.

As a black fog dragged at his mind, he thought about Millie. She'd never let magic stop her and neither would he. Shaking with the effort, Audun fought against the darkness, willing it away until he was able to raise his head from the silt of the ocean floor. Looking around, he spotted Nastia Nautica swimming in the opposite direction with the egg clutched in her hands. He would have to follow her, but first there was something else that he needed to do.

Audun was angry. The sea witch had taken something he wasn't even sure he wanted to give up. Knowing it was a living creature that she would probably mistreat made it that much worse. And for all he knew, she might have swum away thinking that she had killed him.

Audun didn't have time to find his way through the witch's ship to the room where she kept the flute, so he decided to use the window. It wasn't big enough for a dragon Audun's size, but he drew away from the wreck, tucked his wings tight against his body, and used powerful strokes of his legs and tail to propel him through the water and smash through the window frame, splintering the wall around it.

In an instant Audun flipped open the lid of the trunk he had seen in Wave Skimmer's image. What he hadn't seen in the image, however, was the nest of sea snakes writhing in the bottom of the trunk.

The snakes hissed and stared up at the dragon with their cold eyes.

"I don't have time for this," Audun growled, as he reached toward the trunk. The sea snakes might be venomous, but they would break their fangs before they'd ever pierce his scales.

"Ordinarily, we wouldn't say anything," said one of the snakes, raising its head above the rest, "but you're one of the great ones and worthy of our respect."

"The sea witch has cast a spell on us," added another. "We must stay in this chest and guard the flute. Please don't blame us if we can't let you have it."

"What if I set you free?" asked Audun, his talons poised over the chest.

The snakes shivered in ecstasy at the thought. "Can you really do that, Great One? Do you really have the power? We would be forever grateful if only you could help us!"

"Just watch me," Audun said, as he turned around. Dragging his tail in front of him, he swung it around with a *whump*, pulverizing the chest and sending the sea snakes flying around the room.

"We're free!" cried a snake. The other snakes cheered.

Audun plucked the flute from the shards of splintered wood while the sea snakes gathered around him. The flute was bigger than he had expected, but he was still able to fit it in the pouch under his wing. Squeezing back through the hole where the window had been, he turned to follow the sea witch's scent through the water.

"What about us?" asked the snakes. "What should we do now?"

"It seems to me that you have two choices," said Audun, glancing at the little faces clustered at the splintered window. "You can stay here and let the sea witch know how you feel about being locked in a chest, or you can go back to wherever it was you came from and get on with your lives." Audun could hear them hissing among themselves as he swam away.

Following a scent through water wasn't much harder than it was to follow one through air. It helped that the amulet made breathing underwater so easy. Sea creatures gawked at the blue and white dragon as Audun coursed back and forth, tracking the sea witch. Her smell was slightly sour and distinctive enough that he didn't confuse it with other odors.

Moving as silently as possible, Audun followed the sea witch into a cave. After only a few yards, the cave narrowed into a tunnel that headed downward before abruptly changing direction and angling up. He moved more cautiously as the tunnel became so narrow that he feared he might get stuck, but it soon widened into a high-roofed chamber. The tunnel had been dark, but the chamber was filled with a pale green light that seemed to come from green stones embedded in the walls. Strange plants and animals grew in the cave, but any creature that could move fled when it saw Audun.

The dragon had gone only a few feet into the cave when he saw the sea witch. She was crouched beside the egg, which had already begun to crack. *I'm too late,* he thought, certain that the baby bird would drown if it hatched here, at the bottom of the sea.

A hole appeared in the shell and the baby's yellow beak poked through. More cracks appeared and the baby emerged, its beak opening and closing as if it were gasping.

Audun rushed farther into the cave to try to save the baby bird but slowed as he realized that the hatchling was growing rounder and fatter. By the time Audun had taken three steps, the baby that had started out smaller than a human boy's fist was as big as Audun's head. Three more steps and the bird was twice that size. It was soaking up water just as its siblings had at the oasis, but with water all around, this baby was doing it much faster.

"You're going to kill it!" Audun shouted.

Nastia Nautica whipped her head around, making her

hair swirl behind her. "So you followed me. And I thought my sharks would be fighting over your carcass by now." The baby bird continued to grow as Nastia Nautica swam back and forth in front of Audun, blocking his way. "It might die, it might not. It will soak up some of the water; the rest it will turn into air. What difference does it make as long as it does its job before it dies?"

The little bird burped and a bubble floated out of its mouth. Suddenly, the sea witch darted forward and ripped the amulet from around the dragon's neck. With a flick of her fingers, she encased the amulet in a bubble and sent it shooting out the entrance of the cave. Sneering at the dragon, the sea witch said, "You'd better hope that the bird doesn't die until it empties this cave or you'll die with it. What a dilemma—save the bird and you die, or let it finish soaking up the water and filling the cave with air and you live, for a little while at least."

Audun knew just how long he could live on the air in his lungs. It was enough to let him get to the surface, if he left right away. "You can't do this," he said, and watched the precious air bubbles trickle past his lips.

Nastia Nautica laughed. "I can do whatever I want, and you won't be able to stop me. You're going to be too busy sucking up air," she said, pointing at the ceiling where the water level had already dropped.

Audun growled at the witch as she swam to the side and let him pass. He was picking up the baby bird when Nastia

Nautica backed into the cave entrance, saying, "You really aren't very bright, are you? I wanted this cave empty of water so I could use it as a cell for a little thief who thinks she can get away with stealing my pearl. Do you see those green stones in the walls? They give off light, but that isn't all they do. They wipe out any magic used around them, so neither my prisoner's spells nor your magic will work down here. I bet you didn't know that your amulet stopped working the moment you entered this cave. You've already used up most of your air! Once again, you've helped me out through your stupidity. You'll be my test case. If the cave will hold you, it should hold my little prisoner as well. Oh, and by the way, you won't be able to get out even if you can breathe underwater. Not after I do this!"

With a flick of her tail, the sea witch turned and darted down the tunnel. A moment later, Audun heard the rumble of stones falling as she blocked off the entrance to the cave.

They were trapped! Now Audun would never see Millie again and . . . He took a deep breath of the air at the top of the cave and tried to calm himself. The baby bird made a chirruping sound and waddled a few steps closer. The little creature didn't seem to mind being underwater. His body was so big now that his head looked like a tomato resting atop an enormous pumpkin and his legs were two little twigs that probably couldn't have held him up if he had been on dry ground.

Bending his neck until his eyes were level with the

bird's, the young dragon said, "How are you doing, little fella?"

"Mama!" said the bird, gazing at Audun with a look of adoration.

Audun jerked his head back. "I'm not your mother. My name is Audun and I'm going to rescue you."

The little bird bobbed its head up and down as if in agreement. "Mama!" it said again.

Audun was about to protest, but he felt a growing tightness in his chest. The air in his lungs was almost gone. If he didn't do something soon, he might actually die down here. Glancing up, he saw that the water level had dropped by a third. While the baby bird continued to swell, Audun swam above the water and took a deep breath. The air smelled like fish and seaweed, both of which Audun liked. At least he could breathe while he tried to think, but he still didn't have long. If they didn't go soon, the baby bird would be too big to fit through the tunnel even if it wasn't blocked. And the sea witch was bound to discover that he'd taken the instrument and freed the snakes. He was sure she'd come back then, but if Audun had his way, he and the bird would both be long gone.

Ten

Leaving the baby desicca bird on the floor of the cave, Audun slipped down the tunnel to see if it was truly blocked. He was able to get past the point where the angle of the tunnel changed direction, but only a few feet farther he ran into a plug made of boulders. Knowing that the sea witch's word was worthless, he tried to use his magic to move the boulders aside. Try as he might, he couldn't budge even the smallest pebble. He was still trying to make the boulders move themselves when the sea snakes arrived.

"What are you doing?" asked the first snake to wriggle through a crack between the boulders.

"Trying to get out," said Audun.

Another snake appeared, and another and another until a mass of squirming bodies filled the water around Audun and he couldn't see his talons in front of his face. "Why don't you go between the rocks like we do?" asked one of the snakes.

There were too many snakes to tell them apart, and the way they kept sliding over and around one another would have made it impossible, so Audun didn't even try. "I'm too big. Now get out of my way so I can see what I'm doing."

"We want to help you," said a snake.

"How can you . . ." Audun stopped when he began to feel the tightness in his chest. Knowing that he didn't have any air to waste, he shuffled backward until he reached the cave behind him. By now the baby bird was nearly as big as he was and the water level was so low that the dragon had only to stretch his neck to breathe. When he dropped his head again, the water around him was once more filled with sea snakes.

"Why are you here?" he asked them.

"To help you," said one.

"We have to," said another. "We tried to go home, but the witch's magic won't let us."

"We have to protect the flute, no matter where it is."

"You have the flute, so we have to stay with you."

"What can we do to help?"

Audun sighed. He knew that a magic compulsion could be very strong. Even if his magic was working, he wasn't sure he'd be able to break it. If he didn't want the snakes getting in his way, he'd have to give them something to do, although he doubted they could really help him. "Why don't you go see how many boulders the sea witch put in front of the opening?"

"We can do that!" said a snake, and they all turned and swam into the tunnel in one apparently solid mass.

"Are you all right, little one?" Audun asked the baby bird. He couldn't see its legs at all now under its grossly engorged body.

"Mama!" cried the baby bird, rocking toward Audun.

The dragon looked up as the first sea snake returned. "How many boulders did you see?"

"A whole lot!" said the snake.

"Can you give me a number?" Audun asked. "You can count, can't you?"

"What does that mean?" asked another snake.

"Never mind," Audun said. "You just stay here and keep your eyes on the bird. Don't let anything happen to it."

"But we need to stay with you!"

"Not this time," said Audun. Rising up on his toes, Audun filled his lungs with air until he couldn't hold any more. After giving the baby bird a gentle pat, he backed down the tunnel so his tail would be toward the boulders. When he reached the plug, Audun moved his tail to the side, rested his weight on his front legs and kicked hard with the back ones. One kick shifted the boulders, making debris swirl around him. It took two more kicks before the boulders shot out of the tunnel, startling a school of orange and white striped fish.

Some of the sea snakes had followed him despite what

he'd said. They cheered, writhing in joy. "Now you can get out!" said a snake, twining around his ear.

"Not yet," Audun said, and he hurried down the tunnel. There was very little water left in the cave when he arrived and Audun wasn't sure he'd be able to get the bird out, but when he touched it, the water in its belly sloshed around, changing the bird's shape enough that he thought he might have a chance.

The bird was so big now that Audun could no longer get a grip on it. Instead, he rolled it toward the tunnel, letting the little bit of water left in the cave support some of its weight. When he reached the entrance to the tunnel, he had to push and squeeze, pinch and shove the bird through the narrow opening. He thought the bird was stuck at the point where the tunnel changed direction, but a little more pressure on one side and its round, spongy body squished through.

Audun was relieved when the baby bird popped out of the tunnel like a cork out of a bottle. Although he was no longer afraid that the bird might drown, he was worried about what would happen to it out in the ocean where the volume of water was so huge. He didn't have much air left himself, after working so hard to get the bird out of the cave.

There hadn't been enough space in the tunnel for the sea snakes to help him much, but once in the open ocean they gathered around, waiting to be told what to do. "You can help me push it to the surface," he said.

With the snakes pushing alongside him, Audun was

making good headway when the fish with the pointed face appeared from the direction of the sea witch's wreck. Audun wasn't afraid of the fish, but he could already feel the tightness in his chest from lack of air.

"Shark!" hissed the snakes, moving away from the bird to place themselves between the dragon and the fish.

"I know you want to protect me," said Audun, "but I need some of you to push the bird to the surface while the rest go find my amulet. It's a piece of gold on a chain that the sea witch took from me."

"We can find it," the snakes replied, and a moment later half of them were swimming back toward the bottom of the sea. Audun watched to make sure that the remaining snakes were indeed pushing the bird, albeit more slowly, before he turned to face the shark.

"Why are you here?" Audun asked, trying to ignore the tight feeling in his chest.

"I'm hungry," said the shark. "I want to taste that thing you were pushing. Get out of my way or I'll eat you instead."

"Just try it!" Audun snarled, baring his fangs.

Suddenly, Audun felt the overwhelming urge to inhale. His air was gone. He'd have to surface or drown. Either way, he wasn't going to be able to help the baby desicca bird any longer. If only . . .

And then the shark was there, jaws snapping and teeth grazing the scales on Audun's neck. The dragon fought back in a desperate frenzy. His fangs pierced the rough skin of the shark even while white lights exploded in the darkness.

The shark writhed, its tail whipping the water as Audun released his grip and bit again, deeper and harder, only to feel his jaws grow slack as he began to lose consciousness.

"We got it!" a snake's voice whispered in Audun's ear as the shark broke free and turned to rip at the dragon's side. Something cool settled around Audun's neck while the shark snapped at him, trying to penetrate the rock-hard scales. Within a few seconds, the dragon was able to breathe. He could feel the scrape of the shark's teeth even as he started to come around, and then the dark fog was gone and he was back. With one swipe of his tail, Audun knocked the shark spinning through the water.

The shark shook itself and turned to charge at the dragon again. When it was only a few yards away, Audun threw back his head and roared. Ripples of sound hit the shark like mallet blows to its snout, forcing it to turn aside. Audun was preparing to fend off another attack when the shark shook its head and sped away.

The sea snakes cheered, their tails slicing through the water, but Audun wasn't ready to celebrate yet. All the while he had been fighting the shark, the baby bird had been soaking up more water, becoming wider and harder to move. It took all of the young dragon's strength and that of the sea snakes as well to shove their charge to the surface of the water, and even then the bird grew heavier and heavier as they propelled it toward the nearest island. When they finally rolled the baby bird onto the sandy beach, Audun was so tired that he was close to collapsing.

"Get rid of that water!" he told the bird, and gave it one last shove. Then, while the sea snakes watched from just beyond the surf, Audun lay his head on the sand and let the darkness overwhelm him.

Eleven

*I*t was morning when Audun came fully awake, although he seemed to remember more than one sunset since he first lay down. The baby bird was nestled against his side, muttering about being hungry. It was back to its normal size. Audun raised his head and saw that he was only a few yards from a pool of water that hadn't been there before. A deep channel had been etched into the beach where the excess water had drained into the sea. Apparently the baby bird had rid itself of the water right where it landed.

Audun was stiff and sore when he stood, but he had one more trip to make before he could return to King's Isle to present the flute to the council. Picking up the baby bird, he carried it past the island's tree line to the underbrush, where insects would be easy to find. While the hatchling ate, Audun returned to the ocean for a quick breakfast of fish, then retrieved the bird and rose into the sky. The oasis where he'd found the egg was at least two days' flight away, but he had to return the little creature to its mother.

Audun had been gone for over a week by the time he returned to King's Isle with desert sand still grating between his scales. Finding the mother bird hadn't been easy, but it had been well worth the effort to see her joy when she finally saw her hatchling for the first time. Fortunately for Audun and the baby bird, the mother had accepted it back, although the baby still seemed to think that the dragon was its mother, too.

The first dragon Audun ran into when he set foot in the king's stronghold was Frostybreath. The big ice dragon seemed happy to see him, patting him on the back so hard that Audun nearly lost his footing. "Welcome back, young dragon. You were gone so long that we thought we'd never see you again. The king and his councillors are going to be happy to see you. And so is Loolee. Make sure you ride the chute with her. It's all she's been able to talk about since you left the last time."

"I will," said Audun. He didn't want to disappoint the little dragoness again.

"I'll go on ahead and let the king know that you're here, but you might as well go down to the antechamber. I'm sure he'll want to see you right away."

Audun was on his way down the ramp when he passed

a gaggle of dragonesses going the other way. They all seemed happy to see him, but it was Hildie who stopped to talk while her friends continued on. "What have you been doing?" she asked. "You look different."

"I've been in the desert," he replied, thinking that she must be referring to the sand he was still shedding as he walked.

"Hmmm," Hildie said, looking him up and down. "I didn't know a desert could do that to you."

Audun excused himself and continued down the ramp, but somehow he knew that she was still watching him.

Audun had never thought much about his appearance. He'd always been the average length for whatever his age happened to be and he'd always kept his scales fairly presentable, but he'd never preened the way some dragons did, or paid someone to burnish his scales to a semi-sheen. It came as a surprise, therefore, when he paused long enough to see his reflection in the ice and it wasn't at all what he'd expected. True, his scales were the same blue and white they'd always been, but now they gleamed in the torchlight like well-polished metal. He also looked older; he'd lost the rounded cheeks of a teenage dragon and acquired a more angular, adult look. Although he hadn't grown any longer, he seemed bigger, with well-defined muscles and broader shoulders. When he turned this way and that to see himself better, it was obvious that he had been working hard and eating little. Perhaps that was what Hildie had meant.

Frostybreath was waiting for him on the ramp. They nodded once at each other, then the older dragon ushered him into the audience chamber and left, shutting the door behind him.

Audun felt uncomfortable as he stood before the king and his councillors, waiting for his turn to speak. He wasn't happy with them for sending him on a mission that had endangered an innocent life. It was hard to think of a diplomatic way to tell them this, though, while they talked among themselves. Their voices were too quiet for him to hear except for a few phrases like "... not at all what I expected," "... couldn't have been nicer ... ," "... someone will have to go ... ," and "... know that you have fish eggs on your chin?"

Finally King Stormclaw turned to the young dragon and said, "I've been reminded that I haven't properly introduced my councillors to you. You've met Frostweaver and Wave Skimmer, and of course you know Song. This," he said, indicating the gray-and-white-scaled dragon seated beside Audun's grandmother, "is Vision Seeker, a truly gifted dragoness who is sometimes able to see into the future."

Audun dipped his head in respect, but the old dragoness just snorted and said, "Did you get the flute?"

"I have it here," he said, holding it up so everyone could see it.

"Did you have any problem with the sea witch?" asked Wave Skimmer.

"Nothing I couldn't handle," said Audun. "She wanted the egg so she could make it hatch and use the baby bird to suck the water out of a cave. Did you know why she wanted it before I went? Did you know that she wouldn't care if the hatchling lived or died?"

Wave Skimmer shook her head. "We didn't know what she wanted the egg for, although we had a good idea, considering the nature of the bird. What happened to the hatchling?"

King Stormclaw leaned over the edge of his slab to glare at Audun. "Did you leave it with the sea witch?"

"I couldn't," Audun said, straightening his back and returning the king's glare. "I took it back to its mother in the desert."

King Stormclaw looked satisfied. He glanced at Song and nodded. "You were right about him."

Audun glanced from the king to his grandmother, confused.

"I told King Stormclaw that you would not only get the flute from the witch, but also keep the baby bird safe," said Song of the Glacier.

"We needed the flute," said the king, "but we had no intention of hurting the baby."

"You could have told me," Audun muttered.

"Yes, and we should have," said his grandmother. "You must excuse us. We've had other things to worry about of late."

"Tell him!" said Wave Skimmer. "If you don't, I will!"

King Stormclaw nodded. "There's something else you should know. We've had a most unexpected visitor in your absence. Princess Emeralda, the Green Witch, came to see us. It seems that her daughter is pining away. She refuses to eat and doesn't sleep, so her mother came looking for you. I didn't know how powerful the witch's magic was until she said that she used it to trace you here."

"She says that her daughter swears she loves you so much that she will never love another," interrupted Wave Skimmer. "I must admit, the girl sounds like a true dragoness. When I was young, I had a number of friends who swore they would rather die than give up the one they loved. I think it's so romantic!"

King Stormclaw cleared his throat. "The Green Witch is a much better human than I expected. And a much better dragon," he added, at a small sound from Song. "Word of the war between East Aridia and Aridia has spread. The Green Witch has heard of our ties to Aridia and understands our concern. She explained that she doesn't care about jewels, and that Greater Greensward has had difficulties of its own with the East Aridians. She came to the stronghold to offer us a pact of alliance should we need it."

"I thought it was so nice that she asked," said Wave Skimmer.

"We told her that we would discuss it and send her word of our decision when it had been made," said the king.

119

"What about Millie?" Audun asked anxiously. "Is she all right?"

"I'm sure she is now," said his grandmother. "Her mother said that she's going to withdraw her objections to her marrying you."

"Imagine a human objecting to her daughter marrying an ice dragon!" snapped Vision Seeker. "She should be grateful an ice dragon wants to marry her!"

"Can I go see Millie?" Audun asked, suddenly so excited that he found it hard to stand still.

"Actually, we have another task for you," said the king. "The girl's mother understands that we're in the midst of a difficult time and will tell her daughter as much."

Audun held the flute out to the king. "What should I do with this?"

"Take it with you," said King Stormclaw. "We need you to deliver it to a family of giants traveling on the Eastern Sea. They have been friends to ice dragons for many years and we are happy to help them when they find themselves in need. Frostybreath will give you the directions."

❧

Frostybreath was waiting for Audun outside the chamber, but he wasn't alone. Loolee was there, wriggling with anticipation and talking nonstop about sliding down the chute. Hildie was there as well, along with another dragon that

120

Audun had never met before. Unlike Ice Rider, the dragon Hildie had introduced him to during his last visit, this one was much older and not nearly as athletic. He looked closer to Audun's father's age than to Audun's, and his ponderous belly was encrusted with jewels, a typical dragon way of showing off wealth and protecting his more tender regions.

"Audun," said Hildie, pushing herself in front of the others, "this is—"

Loolee grabbed hold of Audun's leg and clung to it. "I'm ready to go down the chute," she cried, her eyes wide with excitement as she gazed up at him. "Can we go now?"

"Loolee!" Audun had never had a younger sibling and neither had any of his friends, so a playful little dragoness was new to him.

"Audun, I wanted you to meet—," Hildie tried again.

Loolee began bouncing up and down, crying, "You promised, Audun, remember?"

Audun sighed. "I can go with you one time today."

Shrieking with delight, the little dragoness took off up the ramp. Audun was about to follow her when he remembered something. "You have some directions for me, Frostybreath?" he asked, turning to the big dragon.

"You go ride the chute," the big dragon replied. "I'll meet you at the door and tell you how to get to the islands."

"But, Audun," wailed Hildie. "I need to talk to you!"

"Sorry, but I'm already short on time. It will have to wait until I come back." Audun may not have had a lot of experience with young dragonesses, but he did know that he didn't want his name added to Hildie's list of suitors.

Twelve

Frostybreath was good at giving clear directions. For the first half of the trip, Audun found himself flying over familiar territory. He saw the distant mountains where the witch's servants had imprisoned his family, and flew over the plains and forests that he had crossed while looking for Millie. Later that same day he looked down to see a marshy area where a dragonlike beast called a knucker was chasing an unfortunate deer. He circled for a minute, wondering if he should look for fish in the marsh, but continued on, his stomach growling from hunger. Just beyond the marsh lay a forest of scruffy pine which continued to the rocky shore of the sea. It wasn't as blue or as clear as the sea where he'd found Nastia Nautica and he couldn't see as far into its depths, but he did see schools of fish from time to time. He had a full belly by the time he reached the island where the giants' boat was beached.

The giants' ship was much bigger than the wreck that was the sea witch's home, with a mast at least fifty feet tall.

It rested on a beach of silvery sand with shallow ditches on either side. Two enormous boys were standing where the wavelets washed onto the beach, tossing rocks as large as Audun's head into the water. A woman was seated on the sand, with her head bent so that her long, brown hair hung over her face. She was sobbing and her shoulders shook with every breath she took. It was obvious that something was terribly wrong. Suddenly, Audun regretted taking the time to slide down the chute with Loolee.

The young dragon was trying to decide where to land when he noticed ripples of water arrowing toward the beach, aimed directly at the woman. "Watch out!" Audun shouted. Thinking that a sea monster was about to attack her, he tucked his wings to his sides and plummeted to the sand, pulling up short in front of the giant woman. Audun turned his back to her and faced the water, preparing to fight.

He had already tensed his muscles and spread his wings to make himself look bigger when the ripples faded away and another giant stood up, shedding a torrent of water. At least twenty-five feet tall, he was bigger than the woman and the boys. "Who's this?" boomed the giant, brushing his dripping hair out of his eyes and looking warily at Audun. Thick sheets of water sprayed across the beach, drenching Audun and making him stagger.

Audun bowed his head and said, "King Stormclaw and his council sent me. I brought you this." Reaching into his flap, he took out the flute and laid it on the ground at the giant's feet.

"Ah," said the giant, giving Audun a halfhearted smile. "I was afraid he hadn't gotten my message. I'm not sure it will do any good now. It's been so long . . . I didn't see anything," he told the woman seated behind Audun.

The woman's crying became so loud that each sob hurt Audun's ears. He moved away when the giant gestured for one of the boys to pick up the flute. Although the boys looked just like the giant, they weren't nearly as tall. Audun decided they must be his sons.

Audun had to brace himself as the earth shook from the giants' footsteps and it wasn't until they were all sitting down that he was able to say, "May I ask what happened?"

"Our daughter is gone," said the woman, dabbing at her tears. "The sea monster took her."

"Let me explain," said the man. "My name is Hugo and this is my wife, Mona, and our boys, Clifton and Tomas. We'd been visiting the islands, seeing if we'd like to settle here, when we stopped to take on more fresh water and supplies. Mona and I were collecting seaweed with the boys just over there," he said, pointing down the beach, "when our little girl, Penelope, disappeared."

"She's only three," wailed her mother.

"We think a sea monster took her. Shortly before she disappeared we saw a hideous beast with a long, whiplike tail jump out of the water as if it was trying to get a good

125

look at us. We've been searching for her for days, but all we've found are some prints in the sand."

"Don't forget the picture," said Clifton, the taller of the two boys.

Hugo sighed. "The boys found a picture made of seashells. They thought it looked like their sister."

"It did look just like her, Papa!" said Tomas. "It was so good an artist must have done it."

Hugo shrugged. "I didn't see it myself. The waves had washed most of it away by the time I got there. If it was as good as the boys say, whoever made it must have seen Penelope. We thought they might want a ransom, but they never sent us a message of any sort. However, it wasn't the picture that interested me as much as the marks in the sand. They were just above the waterline; the waves hadn't reached them yet. It almost looked as if someone had pressed a cup over and over into the ground. The only thing we could think of was that a sea monster must have left the marks."

"Which means that some horrible fiend had the sea monster carry her off," said Tomas. "Those monsters aren't smart enough to do a picture that good."

"We don't know anything for sure," said Hugo. "Just that we think a sea monster was involved somehow. That's why I asked an eagle to carry a message to King Stormclaw. I'd heard of the Sea Serpents' Flute and knew Stormclaw could get it if anyone could. I thought we could find out what happened to her if we could talk to the sea monster."

Clifton held up the flute, which looked like a child's tiny toy in his hands and would have been lost in his father's. "What happens if I blow into this?"

"The sea witch who I got it from said that it would torment sea monsters and make them leave," said Audun.

Hugo looked puzzled. "I'd heard that it will calm sea monsters so you can talk to them."

"That may be true," Audun replied. "I wouldn't trust anything that sea witch says; she's a notorious liar."

"Do you still think you should use it, Hugo?" his wife asked. "We wouldn't want to torment them and drive them off if they have Penelope with them. They might hurt her . . ."

"If they haven't already," murmured Clifton.

His mother's chin wobbled, but she managed to say, "Or abandon her, and then we'd never find her."

"That's a good point," said Hugo.

Audun cleared his throat. "Maybe I can help. I'm pretty good at tracking things, even underwater. If sea monsters took her, I should be able to find her. Can I see something of hers, as well as the place where you found the prints?"

"I'll get something that belongs to Penelope," said Mona, her eyes glistening with hope.

"And we'll show you where we found the picture and the prints!" exclaimed Tomas.

The ground shook so much as all the giants got to their feet that Audun couldn't stand. He was stumbling around when he finally spread his wings and rose into the air, although he didn't go very high.

It looked like it was going to take Mona a few minutes to get something of Penelope's, so Audun followed the boys. When they crouched beside something on the sand, Audun landed and bent down to look. Clifton said that he had placed spindly pieces of driftwood around the marks on the beach, but there were only a few indentations and the blowing sand had made them indistinct. Audun examined them for a moment, noting the acrid scent of whatever had made them, then the boys showed him where the picture had been. Most of the shells had washed away; Tomas had stacked the rest in a pile just beyond the water's reach. Audun picked up one of the shells and sniffed it. The shell carried the same scent as the marks in the sand. He set it down when Mona arrived with Penelope's shoes, which the girl had taken off while playing on the beach. They, too, had a very distinct smell.

"I think I'm ready now," said Audun. "But first, tell me, can your daughter swim?"

"Like a fish," said Hugo, who had come with his wife. "We made sure all three children could swim before we set sail."

"Where did you spot the sea monster?"

Hugo pointed out to sea. "Just past those rocks. There, where the waves are breaking."

"Then that's where I'll begin," said Audun. After

assuring himself that the amulet was still around his neck, he told the family of giants that he would do his best to find Penelope, and dove into the middle of a curling wave before it could crash over his head.

Although he had hoped to find Penelope's scent, it was the smell from the beach that Audun detected first. It was stronger than any other scent he found, as if whatever had made it had just passed by. Audun followed the trail like a hound would a rabbit, with his nose quivering and all his attention focused on that one telling odor.

The water was colder here than where Nastia Nautica lived, but Audun liked it better this way. The water farther south had been so warm that it had made him drowsy, but the cold water rushing against his scales as he sped beneath the waves now was invigorating. The fish weren't as brightly colored here, but there were more of them, and he would have been easily distracted if he hadn't been on such an important mission . . . or hadn't just eaten.

The scent grew stronger as Audun swam and he was convinced that he must be getting close. Suddenly, he glimpsed something nearly as big as himself swimming just above the edge of a rocky outcropping. Drawn by the scent, Audun followed the creature, noting the long whip-like tail that propelled it through the water. The beast was easy to see against the browns and grays of its surroundings because its long, thin body was colored a contrasting orange and yellow. As Audun drew closer, he saw that rows of thin legs ending in suckers were tucked under the monster's body, and its eyes, when it turned to look at him, were enormous.

The creature blinked, as if in surprise at seeing a dragon, and began to swim more rapidly. When it looked back a short time later and saw that Audun was still following, its tail became a blur and it sped away faster than Audun would have thought possible. Sure that he had found the sea monster that had taken Penelope, Audun raced after it.

The creature twisted and turned, swimming around obstacles as it tried to lose the young dragon. When it sped through a school of fish so quickly they didn't have time to get out of the way, so did Audun. When he raced through a gap in the side of a shipwreck, so did Audun. They passed islands and a peninsula that jutted out into the sea without Audun losing sight of the monster.

The water became deeper and colder. They circled the peak of a mostly submerged mountain, startling huge fish that flashed blue and silver as they changed direction. Every so often the sea monster would turn to see if Audun was still behind him, and each time the dragon was a little bit closer. Audun wasn't aware of how far they had traveled until they entered a trench that split the floor of the sea in two. He had heard about the Mary Alice Trench, named after two mermaids who had entered it on a bet and never returned, but he didn't know anyone who had actually gone there. Loathsome creatures supposedly inhabited its depths, which ran deeper than Audun had ever gone, but he followed the monster, not wanting to lose it.

The water around them grew even darker as they traveled downward, and Audun began to feel pains in his chest and limbs. When the sea monster's swimming became more labored, the dragon was sure that the creature was feeling similar discomfort, but they continued to go deeper until Audun could scarcely see. Strange creatures swam past, illuminating their way with lights they carried on their bodies. Some had little lanterns dangling from their heads while others had rows of glowing spots on their sides. A few darted away at Audun's approach, while one with ferocious teeth set in huge, gaping jaws swam a little bit closer, but none were brave enough to come after a dragon.

It was so dark now that Audun was following the sea monster by its scent alone; and then he encountered a strong mineral smell that nearly overwhelmed all the other odors. A few minutes later, he spotted the glow of a fire in the water ahead. Thinking he'd seen the sea monster pass in front of it, he swam toward the light, but it was so bright that it made him blind to everything beyond it.

Enormous plumes of fire and gas were erupting from a hole in the seafloor, heating the water. Clusters of tall tubes sprouted from the ground around the hole and Audun wondered what they might be. A slim, wormlike creature poked its head out of one of the tubes and eyed him. When he did nothing more threatening than look back at it, the worm said, "Hello!" in a cheery voice.

Instantly, a hundred other worms popped out of a hundred other tubes.

"Who are you talking to?" some said.

"Are you talking to me?" asked a dozen others.

"Look, we have company!" said the worms who had noticed Audun.

"Are you a fish?" asked three or four, while twenty wondered aloud what he could possibly be.

"I'm Audun," replied the young dragon, who had been taught to always be polite. "I'm a dragon."

"Ooh!" exclaimed nearly every worm. "A dragon!"

"What's a dragon?" only one was bold enough to ask.

"I'm sorry. I'd like to stay and chat, but I'm looking for someone. Have any of you seen a sea monster with a whiplike tail who passed by here just a moment ago? We were together, but I seem to have lost him."

"What's a sea monster?" asked some.

"What's a whip?" asked others.

"What's a tail?" asked the smallest worm in the shortest tube. When the rest turned to look at him, snickering, he disappeared into his tube and refused to come back out.

"We saw something big go that way," said the first worm. It jerked its head in a direction Audun never would have guessed. "It wasn't nice like you. It didn't stop to say hello."

"They rarely do," said another worm.

"How true," said at least a dozen, sounding mournful.

"Thank you very much," said Audun. "You've been very helpful."

"You're welcome," said all the worms at once.

"Good-bye," Audun called, as he turned to follow the sea monster.

"Good-bye!" they all called back.

"Such a nice dragon," said one of the worms, as Audun swam away.

"What's a dragon?" asked a chorus of wormy voices.

Audun swam into the darkness, hoping the worm had been right, but he didn't have to go far before he picked up the sea monster's scent again. Soon light began to relieve the gloom enough that he could see the walls of the trench on either side. A few minutes later he spotted the sea monster in the distance.

Audun had just left the trench when he saw bubbles from a channel of water rushing by faster than the sea around it. He watched as the sea monster hesitated, then plunged into the current and was swept away. Determined not to be left behind, Audun darted forward and dove in after the already disappearing beast.

Although the current carried him forward at an amazing pace, it was carrying the sea monster just as quickly. Audun was exhausted, but he'd have to swim even faster if he wanted to catch up to the monster. It wasn't long, however, before the monster glanced behind him and saw the advancing dragon. With a swish of its tail, the beast slipped from the current. If Audun hadn't been watching closely, he would have been carried far past the monster, but he reacted quickly enough that he dropped out of the current only yards behind the monster.

The sea monster looked tired now, too, and didn't go far before turning to face Audun. Gathering his strength, the young dragon closed on the beast who met him with a slash of his tail. Audun bit the tail and the monster turned to grapple with him, fastening its suckers onto the dragon's scales. The beast pulled and would have ripped some of the scales from Audun's body if the dragon hadn't bitten one of the monster's legs, hard.

"Wait!" shouted the sea monster. "I have to know— why are you chasing me? What have I ever done to you? I don't even know you."

"You took a little girl," growled Audun. He was surprised to hear the sea monster laugh.

"Is that what this is about?" the beast said, relieving the pressure on Audun's scales. "Why didn't you say so in the first place?"

Audun shook the monster until its teeth clacked. "This isn't a joke," he hissed.

"Of course it isn't," the monster hurried to say. "If you mean that giant hulking girl, we didn't take her. She followed my friend Blooger. We've been trying to send her home ever since."

"What do you mean by 'followed'?" asked Audun.

"We were over by the island where the tastiest seaweed grows, resting after we'd eaten," said the monster. "Blooger was asleep in the shallow water when something grabbed one of the growths on his back and tried to pull it off. He swam away, of course, and it wasn't until he was almost home that he realized something was following him. He heard splashing and an awful wailing, and when he looked back he saw an enormous child floundering in the water. Blooger couldn't just leave the child there to drown! Anyway, he called to me and together we took the girl to our home, which was much closer than hers. That child weighs too much for either one of us to carry by ourselves and it was a struggle for the two of us."

"And so you just kept her? You didn't even try to take her back? Do you know how worried her parents are about her?"

"We tried to tell them! I went back to the seaweed island and left a picture of her on the sand. I drew arrows, too, pointing the way to our home, but they never came. Blooger and I were beginning to think they didn't want her. I've been back there every day hoping to lead them to her, but those people are always throwing stones and I can't get close enough to talk to them. I was on my way home after stopping by there when you started chasing me."

"Take me to the child," said Audun, releasing his hold on the monster. "Perhaps I can carry her."

"You're welcome to try," said the sea monster. "My name is Squidge, by the way. And you are . . . ?"

"Audun," he replied. "I'm from the Icy North."

"Well, Audun from the Icy North, let's hope you're a lot stronger than Blooger and I. The sooner we get that girl back with her parents, the happier we'll be!"

Audun wasn't sure how far he could trust Squidge, so he stayed close to the sea monster all the way to the entrance of a tree-shaded lagoon. The young dragon saw the giants' child right away. She was seated in the shallow water, playing with something that she held in her hands. Not wanting to frighten the girl, he climbed out of the water and walked toward her along the beach so that she'd have plenty of time to see him coming.

"Penelope," he said, as he got closer, "my name is Audun. I've come to take you to your parents."

The girl glanced up at him and smiled. It was obvious from the clean tracks on her cheeks where tears had washed away the dirt that she'd been crying, but she didn't look upset now. "We go see Mama and Papa?" she asked.

"That's right," said Audun, relieved that she seemed to be unharmed. He walked closer, wondering where the other sea monster was, and aghast that they would leave a young child alone in the water. Then he saw that she wasn't alone at all. What he'd thought was the sandy bottom of the lagoon was really an enormous oval of sand-colored flesh that rippled at the edges. Penelope was sitting on it, playing with a flower, although when he got closer he realized that it wasn't a flower, but a fleshy growth sprouting from the monster's back. A veritable garden of the growths dotted the monster, but most of them were too short to reach above the water.

"This is my friend Blooger, who I was telling you about," Squidge said, swimming to the shore where the dragon stood. Sticking his head under the water, the sea monster spoke to his friend. Although Audun couldn't see its eyes, he was sure that the beast was looking at him.

When he'd told Squidge that he would take the girl back to her parents, he hadn't even thought about her size—she was almost as big as Audun.

"So you'll tell her parents that it was all a mistake?" asked Squidge. "We didn't take her, she just sort of came to us."

Audun nodded. "I'll tell them as soon as I get her there. But that might be a problem. I thought I could fly her back, but I'm not sure I'll be able to lift her. She looks awfully . . . solid."

Squidge sighed. "I was afraid of that. I suppose Blooger and I could help you. We might be able to get her all the way there if three of us carry her. Although I don't know how . . ."

"I have an idea," said Audun. "Are there any vines on this island?"

"I don't know," Squidge said. "I haven't gone past the beach and Blooger never leaves the water."

"I'll go look," Audun said, already on his way to the trees.

He was back a few minutes later, laden with long, thick vines. Squidge helped him make a sturdy net big enough to hold Penelope. They were able to convince her to sit in the net only after Squidge told her that she could keep one of Blooger's flowers, much to his friend's dismay.

When everyone was ready, Blooger swam out of the lagoon with Penelope on his back, while Audun supported much of her weight from above and Squidge pushed from behind. Progress was slow as they crossed the sea between the islands, and they had to wait once for a whale to pass, but they eventually had the island in sight and could even see the mast of the giants' ship.

Audun was already thinking about taking a quick leave of the giants when the first stone hit the water, narrowly missing Squidge. "Penelope!" screamed the girl's mother from the shore.

"I'm coming, Audun!" bellowed Hugo, as he waded into the water. "Leave them alone, you miserable beast!"

It occurred to Audun that their little procession might not look quite right from the island. He doubted that the giants could see Blooger, so it probably appeared as if Audun was carrying Penelope in a net while another sea monster chased them.

"It's all right!" he shouted, ducking as another stone flew over his head. "The sea monsters are helping me!"

The barrage of rocks stopped as suddenly as it had started. While the giant family stood on the shore anxiously awaiting Penelope's arrival, Audun and the monsters labored to push, drag, and carry the now-laughing child through the waves to the beach.

"Mama!" she shouted. Pausing long enough to rip a flower from the monster's back, she hopped to her feet and scrambled onto the shore, where her family waited with open arms.

The sea monsters had no intention of sticking around, but Audun convinced them to wait long enough to tell the giants what had happened. Hugo and Mona listened, skeptical at first, but with growing belief when they saw their little girl's fascination with the flowers.

"And remember how she wandered off when we were cutting logs to build the boat? We found her in that meadow filled with wildflowers," Mona reminded her husband.

Hugo nodded and bent down to speak to the sea monsters. Keeping his voice soft out of consideration for the smaller creatures, he said, "I don't know how to thank you. My family is everything to me."

"We're so sorry for ever thinking that you had carried her off," Mona told them. "Is there anything we can do to make it up to you?"

"Just don't throw stones the next time you see us," said Squidge.

Although the giants promised never to throw anything at the sea monsters again, Squidge kept eyeing them warily and he and Blooger left soon after. It wasn't until the monsters had gone that Hugo turned to Audun and said, "Thank you for everything. You came so far, and helped us so much. How can we ever thank you?"

"There's no need," said Audun. "I'm happy I could help. I came on behalf of King Stormclaw and his council, so you can thank them if you'd like."

"But all they wanted you to do was bring the flute and you've done so much more. Tell me, where are you going next? Can we at least give you a ride in our ship?"

"Thank you, but it will be quicker if I fly," said Audun. "I'm returning to King's Isle. I'm helping the king so he'll agree to teach me how to become a human."

"Really? How very odd. Why would you want to do something like that?"

"Well, there's this human girl . . . ," Audun began.

"You're doing it for love! That's wonderful! Perhaps we can help!" Mona exclaimed. "Wait right here!"

Audun had no idea what the giant woman had in mind, and he was even more confused when she returned with a barrel in her arms.

"Here," she said, setting it in front of Audun. "Take this with you. It's a lotion I make myself. Giants have a very strong odor, but we don't like it any more than anyone else does. Slather some of this lotion all over yourself and you'll no longer smell like a dragon. We've known a few dragons who can turn into humans. Even when they have a human body, they still smell like dragons unless they use this. You won't have to use it often; once every few years should suffice."

"Thank you!" said Audun. "I never would have thought of this. Are you sure you can spare the whole barrel?"

Hugo laughed, making the ground shake along with his stomach. "That's one thing we'll never have in short supply!"

"I can always make more if we run out, which shouldn't be for years," Mona said. "Thank you again, Audun. We'll be forever in your debt."

Placing the barrel in the net he'd used to carry Penelope, Audun said farewell and rose into the air. Although he'd been working hard to do whatever the king and his council had asked of him, this was the first thing anyone had done to help him be like a real human. He wanted to stop running errands for everyone else and start on his own task. As soon as he got back to the island, he'd tell the king and his council that it was time he learned how to be a human.

Thirteen

Audun wasn't surprised when Frostybreath met him at the entrance, but he didn't expect the dragon to lead him down an extra level to Song of the Glacier's rooms. His grandmother was waiting for him and she greeted him with delight. "I knew you could do it! We saw part of your actions in Wave Skimmer's bowl of water. I'm so proud of you, Audun. All you went through to help that little girl!"

"She wasn't so little," Audun murmured, stretching to relieve the stiffness in his back. "I've worked hard to do what the king asked of me. Would someone either teach me how to be a human or tell me that I'm free to go see Millie?"

"That's one of the things I wanted to talk to you about," said his grandmother. "It has come to my attention that a young dragoness is interested in having you as her mate. You need no longer worry about learning to be a human just to win a mate for yourself. There have never been as many female dragons born as there were males, which is why many male dragons live their entire lives as bachelors. That need not be the case for you, however. If you are willing to forgo this scheme of yours to woo a human, you could have a marvelous and long life with a true dragoness."

"It's Hildie, isn't it?" asked Audun. "But that's just it. I already know that Millie is the one I want as my mate. She is a true dragoness *and* a true human. She is the one I love. I don't love Hildie. She doesn't stir my heart the way Millie does. I don't lie awake at night thinking about Hildie; the last dragoness I think about before I fall asleep and the first one I think about when I wake is Millie. I thought you, of all dragonesses, would understand."

His grandmother sighed. "Ah, but I do. I just thought you should know that you have a choice. If the girl is your true love, you are already on a path that you cannot change. Now, do you really still want to learn how to become a human?"

"Yes, of course!" said Audun. "I mean, I'm glad I got Millie's mother's approval, but there's still the rest of her family. And there's so much more of Millie's life that I can share if I can be a human with her."

"I'm glad to hear that," said his grandmother. "There's something I want to tell you that we should have told you long before this. We had you find the baby desicca bird because we wanted to make sure that you would be the best kind of human before we showed you how to be one at all. Turning into a human is easy, once you know what to do. The ability is inside every dragon, but not every dragon is capable of being a good one. However, you excelled at the task, and you did something else that we hadn't expected. You learned things while you were in Aridia that our regular contacts should have relayed to us. It wasn't until you told us about the fighting in Desidaria that we knew our contacts were in trouble. We have strong ties to Aridia; it's where the gem mine I told you about is located. Any upheaval in the kingdom affects us as well.

"When you came back with the egg containing the baby desicca bird, King Stormclaw saw how useful you could be to us. After that, he stopped testing you and has been giving you jobs that we've needed someone to do, only we're so shorthanded that we don't have anyone we can send."

Audun was incredulous. "You mean the king tricked me?"

"I mean we've needed your help and, at this point, *we* need *you* to learn how to become a human. You are the only one capable of going on a very delicate and important mission. Are you ready to learn how to make the transformation?"

Audun's heart began to beat faster as he realized what she was asking. "I sure am!"

His grandmother cleared her throat. "I was fortunate enough to be selected to help you." Opening her talons,

144

she revealed a ring bearing a large, green stone surrounded by smaller, red ones. "This will help you become a human the first few times you change. After that, your body will remember the way and you will no longer need the ring. At that point, all you'll have to do is will it to happen. For now, however, put this on."

Audun trembled as he took the ring from Song and slid it over a talon. He was examining the ring when his grandmother stepped so close that their foreheads were touching. "Now, I want you to close your eyes and think about what it is that you want to become. Think about being a human—with only two legs, no wings, no scales, no ridge . . ."

Audun laughed self-consciously. "You make it sound as if I will be losing so much and gaining nothing."

"You understand at last," his grandmother said, but her voice was only a whisper because Audun was already beginning to change.

What began as a hum inside his head grew louder and louder until he could hear nothing else. His heart had already been beating rapidly, but now it beat so hard that he feared it was about to pound itself right out of his chest. After the air in his lungs left his body in a *whoosh*, he found that he was unable to take a truly deep breath. When his muscles began to change and the skin beneath his scales to burn, he staggered and would have fallen if his grandmother hadn't been there to hold him up.

"Open your eyes," she said finally, only this time her voice was loud and clear.

When he did, everything had changed. His grandmother, who had always seemed small and delicate, now appeared huge and powerful beside him. His own body was small and helpless now, with his head reaching only as high as her chest and the span of both his arms together shorter than the length of her neck. He stood upright on only two legs, with a spine that held his head high. Raising the hand that bore the ring, he found that he had hair on the top of his head and ears on the sides. He had a nose instead of a snout, which struck him as funny. When he tried to speak, his voice came out sounding rough and raw. Although his ears were different, he could still hear well, although not as well as when he had been a dragon. His eyesight was different, too; things weren't nearly as distinct and colors didn't look the same.

"Try walking," said Song, her voice sounding loud in his ears even though she had moved to the far side of the room.

He moved a foot forward, but his joints didn't behave the way he expected them to and he had to grab hold of a table to keep from falling. The smooth wood felt odd and he realized that skin without scales was much more sensitive to texture. He took another step and, with his grandmother's encouragement, began to walk around the room, to stop and touch things, to look at them from a whole new angle. The furniture seemed bigger now, the room itself enormous, but as he stepped from one place to another he began to feel more in control.

"What do I look like?" he asked, running his fingers through his hair.

"See for yourself," said his grandmother. "There is a mirror in the drawer of that table."

Audun struggled to pull the mirror out of the drawer. Although it would have been small for a dragon, it was big and awkward for a human. He needed to use both arms to carry it to a chair where he propped it up so he could get a good look at himself. Taking a step back, he studied his reflection. Audun's shoulder-length hair was silvery white. He had a strong chin and prominent cheekbones, just as he did as a dragon. His eyes were the same vivid blue they had been in his dragon form, although he laughed to see eyebrows on his face. "I know all humans have these," he said, tracing one eyebrow with a fingertip, "but what are they for?"

Song of the Glacier shrugged. "I don't know. Perhaps to keep the rain from running into their eyes? They don't have two sets of eyelids like we do."

"That makes sense." Audun glanced down at his naked body, marveling at how vulnerable humans were, with nothing covering them but soft flesh. He prodded his well-muscled arm and pinched the skin on his bicep. "It's a wonder humans can survive at all. They have nothing to protect them."

"Except their wits," said his grandmother. "And for most of them, that's more than enough. Do you think you can handle walking as a human?"

"I think so," Audun said, nodding.

"Then I want you to turn back into a dragon. You need to be able to turn both ways as quickly as possible."

"All right," said Audun, and he closed his eyes again.

The transformation into a dragon was easier, and when Song had him turn into a human again only a few minutes later, he found that easier still. They spent the next few hours in the room while he changed from dragon to human and back again, and the more time he spent as a human the better he became at moving as one. After a time he was able to change in either direction in the blink of an eye. When his grandmother saw that, she took the ring away.

"You need to be able to do it on your own," she said, as she slipped the ring into a drawer in one of the tables. "A ring like that would give you away to anyone who knows what it means. And wearing an expensive-looking ring might not always be a good idea around certain humans, who are always aware of such things. Don't forget that even though you might look like a human, you are still a dragon at heart. Humans find it easy to lie, while honor is so ingrained in dragons that only those who are sick in their heart or mind may lie easily. Be careful if you find yourself in the position where you cannot tell the truth. Only bad will come of it if you do."

"I'll remember," Audun replied.

"So, are you comfortable enough as a human to go out in public as one?"

"I think so," Audun said, wondering what Frostybreath and the others would say when they saw him.

"Then put these on."

Audun had seen Millie change from a dragon back into a human, and each time she'd had clothes on when she became a human. As a dragon he had never worn clothes, so he'd been without them as a human as well. He supposed that he couldn't go out in public that way. Audun's grandmother helped him open the barrel that Mona had given to him. Dipping his hands into the barrel, he covered his body with the thick lotion that immediately soaked into his skin. Although he fumbled with the clothes at first, Song made some suggestions and he guessed the rests; he soon stood before her, dressed and ready to go.

"I had bumps on my skin before I put on the clothes," he said, rubbing his arms through the sleeves. "I guess that happens when humans are cold."

Song of the Glacier smiled. "You still have a lot to discover. Just don't let it overwhelm you." Crossing to the table, she opened another drawer and took out a small pouch. "Put this in your pocket," she said. "You'll need coins in order to buy anything."

Reaching into the drawer once more, she took out a rolled-up tapestry and spread it open across the top of the table. "This is a map to the Magic Marketplace. No one knows where the marketplace is located and one may go there only through a map such as this. You're to go to the market as a human and buy a gift for a self-indulgent person. It's for a human male, so don't get anything for a dragon."

"Who is this man?" asked Audun. "Buying something for him would be easier if I knew something about him."

"We've learned that our contacts were killed in the war. Because we have no other way of learning what's going on in Desidaria, we were forced to piece together bits of information we've received from them in times past to learn what needs to be done now. All I know about the man for whom you're buying the gift is that he's the castle steward and indulges himself whenever possible.

"We're sending you to the Magic Marketplace because you can get just about anything there and everyone likes magical gifts. In your case, you can look around while you practice walking and talking as a human. Now, remember, you'll have to be careful not to draw undue attention to yourself or let anyone know what you really are if you want to survive. There are humans out there who hate dragons and would love to kill you while you're weak and vulnerable.

"To get to the marketplace, all you have to do is touch the fountain pictured in the tapestry. To return, you must touch the actual fountain. There are witches at the Magic

Marketplace, as well as other creatures, some who are in disguise, some who are not. Nearly everyone there has magic of some sort. Talk only when necessary, make your purchase, and return as soon as possible."

"I'm not sure I'm ready for this," Audun said, glancing down at his legs, which no longer seemed to want to move. "What if I forget how to be a human while I'm there?"

"You won't," said Song of the Glacier. "You are a dragon, no matter what you look like on the outside, and dragons can handle anything."

Fourteen

The Magic Marketplace wasn't at all what Audun had expected. It looked a lot like it did in the tapestry, but even a magic picture couldn't convey the noise, the smells, or the hustle and bustle of the real thing.

There were more humans there than he had ever seen in one place, but humans weren't the only ones who frequented the market. He saw a banshee buying ointment for red eyes and a centaur examining hoof polish at the same stand. A leprechaun was haggling with a stall owner over the price of a gold pot while only a few stalls away a nymph bought fruit from a goblin. There seemed to be more witches and wizards than anything else, but as Song had warned, not everyone was what they appeared to be.

"Move it, buddy," a goblin said, having arrived at the market right behind him.

Audun stepped out of the way, saying, "Pardon me," and bumped into a dog.

"Careful!" growled the dog, before stepping off the

raised platform surrounding the fountain and scurrying away.

Audun climbed down the steps carefully; he hadn't practiced with stairs and wasn't quite sure how to do them. When he reached the cobblestones that paved the streets of the marketplace, he stopped to get his bearings. He'd seen a few stalls that interested him from the height of the fountain, but now he wasn't sure which way to go.

He was looking around when a sultry voice called to him. "Might I interest you in some spices?" It was a witch with eyelashes and hair of real gold and a face too perfect to be real. "I have spice to make the nostrils burn and to cool a steamy temper. This one smells of a summer's day; sniff it and you'll hear bees buzzing and feel the heat of the sun. In this basket I have moregano and lessregano. Use one to fill a glutton's appetite and the other to make anyone hungry. Of course, I have the ordinary spices like frankincense and myrrh," she said, pointing from one basket to the next. "Can I interest you in cinnathinamin? One teaspoon a day and you'll lose weight in a trice. But then, I guess you wouldn't need that, handsome." The witch smiled and looked at him through her eyelashes in a way that might have made a normal man weak, but dragons are immune to such ploys. He shook his head and moved on.

"Maybe later," she called after him.

"Fabric for your sweetheart?" asked the fairy at the next stall. "Think of what she'd look like in a gown made of this!" Bolts of corn silk and spiderweb lace were piled atop woven goose down and a swath of cloth made of highly colored fish scales. Cloth of gold vied for space on the table with cloths of copper and lead. The fairy shooed a mouse away from the cheesecloth, but it had already nibbled a hole in one corner.

A man who looked as if he might be part ogre called from the stand across the way, "Get your bottomless tankard here! Fill it full of ale once and it will never be empty again!" Seeing a young mother carrying an infant in one arm, while holding the hand of a small child, he crossed to the other side of his table and held up what looked like a wad of cloth. "I have bottomless diapers as well! These diapers never need changing. They'll soak up anything . . ."

"Except the smell!" said a gnome at the stall beside his. "What you should be selling are bottomless trash cans to hold all the garbage you're spewing."

"Why, you little runt," the big man growled, showing fangs half as long as his fingers. "I ought to . . . Wait a minute. A bottomless trash can . . . That's a good idea. I can see everyone wanting one of those!"

Audun moved on, attracted by a sweet voice singing just a few stalls away. A marmoset was seated on the table, singing a song about blue skies and green leaves while a cat played a fiddle beside it. An old woman sat unmoving on a stack of crates behind the table, her eyes glazed over as if her mind was somewhere else. Audun peeked into a box on the table and was surprised to see three fully grown dogs no larger than chipmunks trying to jump out. Not one of them was making a sound, although their mouths were working as if they were barking. "Get your exotic pets!" shouted the cat with the fiddle when he saw Audun.

"Not today," Audun said, wondering if the cat was for sale, too.

Although Audun had seen many interesting things, he had yet to find something he liked. True, the object was supposed to be for a man, not a dragon, but Audun was waiting to find something special. He was passing a stand where a wizened, little old woman was selling shoes when he overheard a loud man's voice saying, "I don't care if you have phoenix feathers and unicorn horns. I need dragon parts. You wouldn't have any dragon scales, would you? Or perhaps a talon or two?"

A rack displaying necklaces made from various kinds of fangs and teeth stood between him and the customer, so Audun couldn't see him at first. "And why would you want a dragon scale?" asked the woman. "Don't you know that dragons never shed their scales? The only way you can get one is if they give it to you or they die and you pry it off them. You want some idiot to risk life and limb so you can pretend you killed a dragon?"

"Humph!" the man declared. "I don't have to explain myself to you, you knucklehead! But I can't believe you don't have the scales, at least. Dragons have an impeccable sense of direction. You carry one of their scales and with the right spell you can find anything, including people. Anyone with half a brain in his head knows the real value of a dragon scale! A simple yes or no would have sufficed. Now you've wasted my time!"

Audun's stomach churned at the thought of the man's shopping list. He half-expected to see some sort of horrible monster when the man stepped away from the stand and Audun saw his face for the first time. His skin was weathered as if from long exposure to the sun. A drooping mustache blended into a short beard, nearly concealing his mouth. Both mustache and beard were white, as was the fringe of hair rimming his shiny, bald scalp. *It's the wizard who made the mosaic speak in East Aridia!* Audun thought, and gasped.

Turning away, the wizard glanced at Audun and saw his horrified expression. "What's wrong with you?" the old man asked. "You look as if I'd asked her to skin your mother."

"I don't . . . I can't . . . ," Audun began. Too appalled and upset to think of what to say, he fled, unaware that the old man was still watching him.

Suddenly, the market no longer seemed quite so much fun. Audun wanted to leave. He would buy something . . . anything . . . for the self-indulgent man, and go back to the dragon stronghold as soon as he could. To think that there were monsters walking around loose who would kill a dragon for its scales . . .

Thinking back on everything he'd seen, Audun decided to return to the stall where the man was selling bottom-less tankards. Any self-indulgent man would surely love a tankard that never went dry. He was on his way there and was passing a stand displaying magic swords when he saw the old man's reflection in one of the shiny blades; the wizard was following him.

A large group of people were coming down the aisle, laughing and talking as they headed for the food stalls. Audun waited until they had almost reached him before stepping into their group, leaving the wizard stuck behind them. When he thought the man couldn't see him any-more, Audun slipped between two stalls and into the next row, where he had to wait for a procession of goats pulling heavy carts.

A stand selling seeds displayed its wares only a few feet from Audun. GIANT SEEDS! read one sign. BUYER BEWARE! read another. Smaller signs on each box described the con-tents within. There were beans for giant beanstalks for vis-iting friendly giants, peas for giant pea pods that could be turned into boats, pumpkin seeds for those wanting a new coach or small cottage, as well as onion seeds for recluses who wanted to keep everyone away from their cottages.

Audun stared blankly at the seeds as he tried to decide what to do. He had to get the tankard—it was the reason he had come and he wasn't about to go back empty-handed—but he didn't like the way the bald-headed man was following him.

"So what will it be?" asked a voice. Audun turned around. The bald-headed man had come up behind him and was studying the young dragon-turned-man the way a physician might a patient. "They don't sell seeds for gunga beans or hot flami-peppers here," the man said, smirking.

"I've never heard of either of them," said Audun, edging away.

The wizard followed him, sniffing. Audun was glad he'd used the giant's lotion and didn't smell anything like a dragon. When the man frowned and looked down at Audun's hands, the young dragon was grateful that Song had made him take off the ring, for this man acted as if he might actually know what it meant.

"I say we shouldn't take them, Ratinki," a woman at a nearby stall declared. Audun turned at the sound of the familiar voice. The two women who had flown their brooms out to meet him at the castle in Upper Montevista were standing in front of the magic-arrow seller and they both looked angry. "The last arrows we bought from him kept coming back," continued Klorine. "Who's to say these will be any better?"

"But those arrows were supposed to come back!" said the stall owner, a tall, thin man with a long, crooked nose.

"That's what made them so special. They were reusable arrows that you didn't have to look for. They returned to their owners when a magic word was spoken."

"And spitted them like trout on a stick!" exclaimed Ratinki.

The man glanced around, his eyes becoming frantic when he saw how many people had stopped to listen. "That's why I included a free shield with each purchase of ten arrows or more! Your soldiers were supposed to use the shields to catch them!"

"Well, they didn't! They used their bodies instead. Come on, Klorine, let's go find some arrows that work," Ratinki said, and the two witches turned away. "We have a big order to place, but we're not getting them here."

"I told you I'd give you three bundles of my new arrows to replace the ones you didn't like," the stall owner called after them. "Three bundles! That's a good deal. These new arrows glow when the archer says a magic word. It makes them easy to find after a battle."

"Glow schmo," grumbled Ratinki, as the two women neared Audun. "We need arrows that hit their target, not look pretty lying on the ground."

It occurred to Audun that the two witches might help him get away. Although he found it difficult to lie, that didn't mean he couldn't find a way to use the truth to his advantage. He waited until Klorine and Ratinki were close before stepping in front of them, saying, "Ladies, I wonder if I might ask you a question? Do either of you know why dragon scales are considered to be so special?"

"Because they're tough!" snapped Ratinki.

"Because they're pretty?" asked Klorine.

Audun shook his head. "I can't believe he's right about you two ladies."

"What are you talking about?" demanded Ratinki.

Audun stepped aside so the women could see the balding man behind him. "This man says that anyone with half a brain knows the real value of a dragon scale lies in its ability to help you find things!" he said, quoting the old wizard.

"He does, does he?" Ratinki said. "Why, if it isn't Olebald Wizard. Half a brain, huh?" The old witch advanced on Olebald and began stabbing him in the chest with one of her knobby, crooked fingers. "I'll tell you who the idiot is, you old sack of hot air! Why, I remember the time when you . . ."

As Audun joined a family group walking past, he couldn't help but smile at the look of frustration on Olebald's face. The old man was trying to speak, but neither of the witches would let him.

With Olebald no longer dogging his heels, Audun hurried to the stand where the tankards were being sold. Hoping to be gone before the wizard found him again, he plunked down his money, snatched one of the tankards, and dashed to the fountain.

"Stop," shouted the owner of the stall. Then he glanced down at the money and didn't say another word.

"That was awful," Audun muttered, as he reached for the lip of the fountain. "I hope I never have to go shopping again!"

Fifteen

A heartbeat later, Audun opened his eyes and found himself standing beside the tapestry in his grandmother's rooms with his finger still touching the picture of the fountain. He jerked his hand away as if the tapestry could burn him, and bumped into a slender statue of a dragon. The statue clattered to the floor, but luckily didn't break. A moment later his grandmother poked her head through the doorway.

"You're back!" she said, her eyes alight. "How did it go? Did you get the gift?"

Audun held up the tankard, saying, "I got a bottomless tankard. I hope it's good enough."

"It should do very well," said Song. "How was your visit to the marketplace? Did you have any problems passing yourself off as a human?"

Audun paused long enough to turn back into the more comfortable form of a dragon, then nodded and said, "There was an old man. I knew he was a wizard because

I'd seen him doing magic. He acted suspicious, and I'm pretty sure he thought I wasn't a human. I caught him looking at my hands and sniffing me. He followed me around until I got two witches to distract him."

Song of the Glacier sighed. "I was afraid something like this might happen. Humans never can mind their own business, especially the ones with magic. I want you to tell me exactly what happened. This may be nothing, or it may mean we're in real trouble."

The young dragon told his grandmother how he'd overheard the wizard asking about dragon scales and how he'd followed Audun. She looked interested when he told her about the two witches, but it wasn't until he told her that they'd called the man Olebald Wizard that she really looked worried and began to pace the width of the room.

"What did he do when you left the stall?" she asked, turning around. "Did he follow you again?"

"Not that I saw," said Audun. "But then, I didn't stay around to make sure. I bought the tankard and came straight back here."

"I don't know many wizards," Song said, pacing again, "but even I've heard of Olebald. He's a tricky old man without many scruples who'd do just about anything to get what he wants. If he really suspects that you might be a dragon, he might try to follow you. Humans are always looking for dragon lairs. Sometimes it's to steal our treasures. Other times it's to steal pieces of our bodies in the hope of tapping into our magic. Even the skull of a dead dragon has a powerful magic that few wizards can match.

"I'm not sure Olebald has the necessary magic to follow you here, but it wouldn't hurt to take a few precautions. Roll up the tapestry and bring it with you. We need to put it somewhere safe."

"Like in a treasure chest?" asked Audun, as he rolled the tapestry into a long tube.

"That might work," said Song, "but I was thinking more of tossing it into a deep pit or setting it adrift on an ice floe. Hurry. We might not have much time."

Audun gathered up the tapestry and followed his grandmother out the door in time to hear her call to the guards. The two guards on duty came lumbering around the corner with Frostybreath close behind. "We may have a problem," Song told them. "A wizard may be coming here through my tapestry."

"Can we destroy the tapestry before he gets here?" asked one of the guards.

Song shook her head. "Magic tapestries are not easily destroyed."

"Audun!" called a feminine voice. He looked away from his grandmother, who was still explaining the problem to the guards, and saw Hildie hurrying down the corridor. "I heard you might be here," the young dragoness said, brushing past the big dragons. "We need to talk."

"This isn't a good time, Hildie," Audun replied, noting

that the guards' expressions were turning fierce as Song told them about the wizard.

"That's what you always say!" Hildie yelled. "The last time you were here you said we would talk the next time you came and you're here now! You're not getting out of talking to me this time!"

"Audun," said his grandmother, "we need to go now. The guards think the ice floe is our best option."

"I'll talk to you later, Hildie," Audun said, shouldering the tapestry as he tried to walk around her.

Hildie stepped in front of him, blocking his way. "You're not going anywhere until we talk about this! I have to know—are you going to declare yourself, or am I going to have to choose one of my other suitors?"

Audun was so surprised that he fumbled the tapestry and almost dropped it. "I'm sorry, but there must have been some sort of misunderstanding. I never was one of your suitors and I'm sorry if I gave you the impression that I might be. I think you're a wonderful dragoness, but I'm in love with someone else."

"I thought that might be it! Is it one of the dragonesses here? It isn't Patula, is it? Why, I'll . . ."

"No, Hildie, it's not. She's not anyone you know. It's—"

A heavy weight hit Audun's shoulder, almost knocking him down. "Audun, watch out!" his grandmother screamed.

The weight was still there, so the young dragon rose onto his back legs and heaved the thing off. Olebald went flying and hit the wall with a *thunk*. Audun was backing away when the old wizard staggered to his feet, shaking his head and swearing. The two dragon guards converged on the wizard, who raised a gnarled magic wand and waved it in their direction. A gray haze filled the air and the guards began floundering around as if they couldn't see.

Olebald had turned toward Audun when Frostybreath sprang in front of him and exhaled at the wizard. The air crackled around him as his beard turned stiff and cold and frost sparkled on his bald head. Olebald's movements were slowed, but he was still able to raise his wand. Frostybreath exhaled again. A thicker layer of ice formed on the old man, and he grew still, his eyes glazed over.

"I don't know how long this is going to last," said Frostybreath. "I thought one breath would be enough to hold him."

"Watch him," said Song. "If he so much as twitches, breathe on him again. We're going to have to find somewhere we can lock him away where he can't get out. As for you, Audun," she said, turning to her grandson, "give me the tapestry. You have to leave before the old fool can cause any more trouble."

Gesturing for the young dragon to follow her, she led the way back into her suite of rooms and closed the door. "Take this," she said, handing him the tankard and a sack to put it in, "and go to the capital of Aridia. Look for the human girl who doesn't belong. She's an orphan and we believe she's living in the castle."

"Song of the Glacier!" shouted Frostybreath. "He's moving!"

"Then breathe on him until he's an ice cube!" she called back. Turning to Audun one last time, she pointed at a door he hadn't noticed before. "That will take you to another corridor. I don't have time to tell you anything else. Go now—and hurry!"

Sixteen

The royal castle of Aridia had been built with thick walls and blocky towers to withstand the desert storms. Tall dunes had settled against the walls of Desidaria, making it almost indistinguishable from the desert itself. As Audun circled the city from a distance, he wondered if the presence of the dunes had helped or hindered the invading army.

In early evening Audun landed behind a dune not far from the main road into Desidaria. Burying himself in the sand so that only his face was exposed, he waited until the gates were closed and the caravans that arrived too late to gain entrance had begun to set up camp for the night. He was about to crawl out of the dune when he realized that anyone riding a magic carpet would be able to see him from above, so he waited until dark, when the traffic in flying carpets had died down, before he shook off the sand and turned into a human.

Careful to avoid the more heavily guarded camps, Audun slipped among the tents looking for groups that seemed to feel safe enough to relax and enjoy themselves. While the men sat by the fire drinking and telling stories in increasingly loud voices, Audun rifled through their saddle-bags until he found the clothes and coins he was seeking. He was sneaking out of the camp when he overheard a man telling the others about what life had been like under the old king.

"King Cadmus was fair, I'll give him that much," the man said in a gruff voice. "My brother worked in his kitchens for twenty years. He said Cadmus cared about his people and always made sure no one went hungry."

"He had to," said a man with a whiny voice. "He was stingy with his wages, despite his hoard of precious gems. Cadmus's, brother, Dolon, pays better. I'm glad he's king now. I've heard he's hiring, which is why I've come looking for work."

"Cadmus wasn't stingy. He was careful with the royal treasury. Mark my words—Dolon'll spend it inside a year."

"You can bet Dolon won't be spending his money on paying work crews to push the dunes back," said the man with the gruff voice. "He'll get King Beltran's wizard to do it. He's nearly as old as the last wizard we had and I've heard that he's almost as powerful."

"I have no stomach for wizards," whined the second man, "but wizard or no, I'm going to get a job in the castle. It's the best pay around and no one else is hiring. I heard Smugsby, the steward, is the man to see."

"That's right," said a different man. "Just make sure you take him something good. The better the gift, the better the job."

Some of the men left the campfire after that and Audun had to hurry to get out of their way. As he hid behind one of the tents with the clothes and coins he'd stolen, two men went past, talking in voices so low that no one, other than a dragon, could have heard them. "I don't know much about King Dolon," murmured one of the men, "but I doubt he'll run out of money soon. His men contacted me last week to say that my nephew had been orphaned and I needed to come get him. It took me a few days to gather the money. They called it a gift for King Dolon, but for all their demanding ways and the amount of money they want, it's ransom if you ask me."

"Hush!" said the man's companion. "You never know who's listening these days."

A few minutes later Audun was back behind the dune changing from the clothes he'd been wearing into ones that matched those of the other travelers. After tucking away the small sack of coins he'd stolen, he turned back into a dragon and buried himself in the dune once again. The temperature dropped and Audun drifted off to sleep, smiling as he dreamt of Millie.

Audun woke the next morning before the sun was up, but not before the caravans had already begun to break camp. He turned back into a human and slipped into line behind other travelers even as the gates were opening. The crowd surged forward, shoving Audun to the edge, near where a group of soldiers on horseback waited to enter. He was nervous at first, remembering how the horse had reacted when he arrived in the castle courtyard in Greater Greensward, but when nothing happened and the horses ignored him, he stopped worrying that the animals might give him away.

Intent on their own business, none of the people around him showed any interest in a boy dressed in a plain, brown tunic, dusty leggings, and the typical head covering of desert dwellers, which suited Audun just fine. He moved forward, shuffling one step at a time as the people in the front of the line were admitted. As he waited, he listened to the chatter going on around him. Most of it seemed unimportant, but he began to listen in earnest when he heard soldiers lolling by the side of the road mention missing children.

"You see these blisters?" one soldier asked of another. "The day after I got here they sent me with a patrol to look for Cadmus's brats. I nearly died out there, it was that hot. My brain was cookin', my skin was sizzlin', and I got blisters poppin' up like mushrooms on manure. The captain wouldn't let us turn around until we found those kids, but they'd disappeared like magic had carried 'em off. We were out there a whole week."

"Stop your bellyachin', Narwool," said the soldier

behind him. "We've all been out in the desert. We know what it's like. I was in the patrol that had charge of the wizard's enchanted vultures that he sent out to look for the children. He had little crystals tied around their necks. I heard the old man could see through those crystals as if he was there himself, no matter how far or high the birds flew. Of course, those birds splattered gook on the crystals every time they ate. It was our job to keep the crystals clean. Do you know how revolting it is to clean up after a vulture? It was the worst job I've ever had."

"They never did find those kids," said the soldier beside Narwool. "I was there when King Dolon heard they were missing. I've never seen him that angry before. He hates those kids with a vengeance. Do you think he would have killed them if they hadn't disappeared?"

"Those brats got out just in time, if you ask me."

Audun would have liked to have heard more, but the crowd had moved forward and it was finally his turn to pass through the gate. Three soldiers guarded the entranceway, yet only the oldest turned to look at Audun. The other two were more interested in talking to a pair of young women who didn't seem interested in leaving.

"So what do we have here?" demanded the soldier. Audun's breath hitched in his throat and he gazed at the man blankly, wondering how he could possibly have known that the young dragon masquerading as a human wasn't what he seemed. But then the soldier added, "Why are you here, boy—business or pleasure?" and Audun exhaled in relief.

"I'm looking for a job," he said, glad he had heard the men talking the night before. Obtaining a job in the castle would be the best way to get inside and would give him a legitimate reason for being there while he looked for the girl.

"Do you have a trade? What is it you do? Nobody is going to employ a boy your age who doesn't have any skills."

"I'm going to see the steward, Smugsby, at the castle. I understand they're hiring."

The soldier nodded, suddenly looking bored. He held out his hand and grunted, then seemed annoyed when Audun didn't respond.

The woman in line behind Audun bumped him with her basket and whispered, "Don't you know anything, boy? Give him a coin. There's some of us what's in a hurry."

Audun fumbled for the small purse in the folds of his tunic. He had no idea how much the coins were worth, so he hoped the one he took out would be enough. The old soldier grunted when he saw it, and glanced at his companions, who were still talking to the young women. When they didn't look his way, he tucked the coin into his own pocket. Giving Audun a slightly more respectful look, he nodded and let him pass as the woman behind him shuffled to the front of the line.

Although Audun could see the castle towering above the much shorter buildings of the city, the streets were laid out in such a confusing way that he kept finding himself in dead ends and roads that looped around to take him back to where he'd started. As a dragon he would have spread his wings and flown straight to the castle, but now he had to walk wherever he wanted to go and he wasn't used to it. Soon his feet hurt and his legs ached, neither of which had ever happened to him before.

The area around the gate had been crowded, but the farther he went into the city, the fewer people he saw. Many of the buildings had been damaged or destroyed by fire. Abandoned possessions, broken and trampled into the mud around some of the larger, more prosperous-looking homes, gave evidence of looting. The few people that he passed hurried away once they saw him returning their gaze.

After a time Audun heard voices; he followed them to a square, empty except for women who were hauling buckets of water from a well. The castle was so close now that it blocked half of the sky. He could make out the damaged battlements, but they weren't in as bad shape as he'd expected.

If the group of women hadn't been there, he might have gotten a drink from the well, but he was still too self-conscious about posing as a human to want to start a conversation. He was about to continue on to the castle when he thought he saw Owen, the boy he had rescued from the roc, crossing the far end of the courtyard.

"Owen!" he yelled, drawing all eyes in their direction.

The boy stopped and stared, appearing stricken at hearing his name. Audun started toward him, but the boy took off, running into one of the alleyways that led from the courtyard. Audun had become adept at walking with human legs and feet, but running was another matter. After taking only a few running steps, his feet went out from under him and he sprawled on the smooth cobblestones. The women laughed at his clumsiness, making him feel even more self-conscious.

"Walk much or just practice a lot?" shouted a girl nearly his own age.

Peals of laughter rang out and Audun's face reddened. He was never going to be able to pass as a human long enough to find the girl. Scrambling to his feet, he fled the courtyard, forgetting about following Owen as he made his way to the castle once more.

❧

A crowd had already gathered by the time Audun reached the entrance to the castle, and once again he had to stand in line. Fortunately, only a short time later a guard led the job seekers into the castle, where he left them in a room too small for their numbers. While some of the men began to argue over the few available benches, Audun took a seat on the floor. Even in human form, he was taller than most, and stronger than all of them. He could have won any fight with ease, but dragons rarely fought unless it was over something of great importance.

Audun hadn't been there long before he recognized the voices of some of the men from the night before. They were talking about the jobs they hoped to secure even as they were led one by one to meet with the castle steward. Only a handful of hopeful faces remained in the room when it was Audun's turn.

A pinch-faced little man led him down the corridor to another room, where two men sat behind a wooden table looking tired and bored. His escort said, "Master Smugsby, sir, here is the next applicant," then waited while the larger of the two men set a scrap of meat on a platter, licked his greasy fingers, and nodded. The nervous-looking assistant seated beside him took a sheet of parchment from a pile and glanced up at Audun, his quill pen in his ink-stained hand.

Smugsby, the steward, looked as if he'd never denied himself anything. A golden chain gleamed from the folds of a tunic made of deep red fabric embroidered in threads of blue and yellow. Each finger of the hand resting on his bulging stomach bore a glittering ring and when he burped he patted his mouth with a delicate lace handkerchief. Behind him rested a treasure trove of bags and boxes, evidence of the applicants who had visited the room before Audun.

"What's your name, boy?" Smugsby asked Audun, as the other man dipped his pen into a pot of ink.

"It's Audun, sir," he replied, glancing at the man who had begun to scratch on the parchment with the pen. "I'm from the north."

Smugsby snorted and said, "I don't care where you're from, boy, just what you can do for me. What jobs have you had in the past?"

"None, really," said Audun. Performing tasks for the dragon king and his council didn't seem to count as a job.

"A son of the privileged class? There are a lot of you looking for work just now. We'll try not to hold it against you." Smugsby chuckled with his mouth open, showing Audun the gaps between his teeth. Turning to the other man he said, "Write that down—no prior work experience. What about skills?" he asked, turning back to Audun.

The dragon-turned-human thought hard. As a dragon he had plenty of valuable skills. He could fly, swim, hold his breath for a long time, find things by their scent, and slide down the ice on his belly. As a human he couldn't do any of those things, except maybe the belly sliding. He could grip small items easily now and his skin was more sensitive without his scales, but he didn't think the steward would find either of those things impressive.

"I assume from your silence that you don't have any skills," said Smugsby, as the other man's pen scribbled away. "So tell me, lad, why should I hire you?"

Audun's expression brightened. Here was a question he could answer. Swinging the sack onto the table, he took out the tankard and handed it to Smugsby. "Because I brought you this."

Smugsby glanced at the tankard and scowled. "I should give you a job because you brought me an ordinary tankard? The thing isn't even made of silver! Do you honestly think I'd demean myself by accepting anything less?" He glanced at the man beside him, who was writing down every word. "Scratch that out, Pringle. I told you there have been rumors that the king might start looking at the books."

The man beside him looked pained. "I'll have to redo the entire page. Scratch-outs aren't allowed in the official records."

"So do it," snapped Smugsby. "But first you can escort this young scallywag out of the castle."

Pringle sighed, crumpled the piece of parchment, and stood up. "Come with me, young man. You shouldn't have wasted Master Smugsby's time like—"

"But you haven't even tried the tankard!" Audun told the steward. "Fill it with your favorite ale. Or wine if you prefer," he said, talking faster as Pringle came around the table. "It's a magic tankard. Fill it once and it will never be empty again."

Smugsby quirked one eyebrow. "Magic you say? Now, where would a boy like you get a magic tankard?"

Audun was about to tell him that he'd bought it at the Magic Marketplace, but Smugsby waited only a heartbeat or two before saying, "I like a man who can be discreet. Pringle," said the steward, as the other man reached for Audun, "do as he says. Fill it with ale—no, make that an expensive wine just in case, then bring it to me. If this boy is telling the truth, he'll be rewarded with a job, but if he's lying to the king's steward, I'm sure they can find room for him in the dungeon."

While Pringle went to do the steward's bidding, Smugsby sat back in his chair and smiled at Audun. "You've provided me with entertainment, boy, something I rarely get these days. If you are telling the truth, I'll have a magic tankard and a boy working for me who has enough skill to beg, buy, or steal one, any of which would be useful to me. If you are lying, I'll see you thrashed and thrown into the dungeon for the rest of your days, which would be diverting in itself. Ah, there you are, Pringle. I hope you got me something tasty. I've worked up a thirst talking to the young scamp."

Smugsby took the filled tankard, being careful not to spill a drop. Tilting his head back, the portly man began to drink. Both Audun and Pringle watched his Adam's apple bob up and down as he took one gulp after another. Audun glanced at Pringle as the steward continued to drink. The man had looked skeptical at first, but his eyes grew wider and his jaw began to sag as Smugsby showed no sign of stopping. When the steward finally lowered his hand, smacked his lips, and sighed, Pringle ran around the table to look in the tankard. Even from where he stood, Audun could see that wine filled the tankard to the brim.

"Excellent!" Smugsby said, wiping his face, which had grown pinker with each gulp. "It looks like I've got a bottomless tankard, and you, my boy, have got yourself a job."

"What should I write down?" asked Pringle, picking up a new sheet of parchment.

"Write that the boy is intelligent and will do admirably as my new assistant," said Smugsby. "Then take him to get a new suit of clothes and his sleeping assignment." He smiled as he turned to Audun. "You'll start work in the morning. Come see me then."

"But what do I do about the other applicants?" asked Pringle. "Don't you want to see them?"

"Not today," said Smugsby, smiling into the depths of the tankard. "Tell them to come back tomorrow. I'm going to be busy for the rest of the afternoon."

Seventeen

$\mathcal{P}$ringle took Audun down another corridor and into a small room where he dug through a trunk and found a plain blue tunic and brown leggings, much like the ones he was wearing himself. He handed over a pin identifying Audun as one of the steward's men and said, "You'll sleep in the room at the end of the corridor. Take one of those pallets," he added, indicating a pile by the door, "and find a space on the floor. You'll be eating with the rest of the servants. At first light, be in the room where you spoke with Master Smugsby to get your instructions for the day. Now, be off with you. I'm a busy man and you've already taken up too much of my time."

Audun nodded, too excited by his success at getting a position in the castle to think of all the questions he should be asking. While Pringle retreated down the corridor, Audun picked up the cleanest-looking pallet and hefted it onto his shoulder. A trio of maids so alike that they had to be sisters watched him walk to the end of the corridor with obvious interest, but Audun simply said hello and continued to the room, mindful that these girls looked as if they belonged together. Although he really didn't know what a girl who didn't belong would look like, he was certain that she wouldn't have family around.

The room was larger than the one he'd been given when he first arrived at the dragon stronghold, but the walls were lined with rolled-up pallets so Audun knew that come nightfall he'd be sharing the room with quite a few others. In the meantime, the remaining hours until supper were his own and he decided that it was the perfect opportunity to go exploring and begin his search for the girl. Hoping to blend in, he changed his clothes and tucked his old ones inside the bedding on the pallet before setting it against the wall. He would find the girl right away, if he was lucky, and never have to come back to this room again.

Audun headed toward the Great Hall first, having passed the entrance in the corridor when he was walking with Pringle. Song of the Glacier had told him to look for an orphan girl who didn't belong. Galen, one of the boys he'd found in the desert, had told him that all the children who'd been left without parents had been brought to the castle. Didn't that mean that none of them really belonged? He'd have to find the orphans and see if one of the girls stood out from all the rest.

Once he stepped inside the Great Hall, he realized that it was bigger than the dragon king's audience room. He stood gaping at the high ceiling and weapon-decorated walls until he heard a group of pages and younger squires making rude comments about the peasant from the country.

"Don't pay them any mind," a dirty-faced boy with scruffy brown hair said, stopping by Audun's elbow. There was a smudge of ash on his upturned nose and one of his front teeth was chipped. He looked as if he couldn't be more than nine or ten years old and the top of his head scarcely reached Audun's chest. Obviously a servant, he was carrying rags and a bucket and was dressed in a soiled tunic and patched leggings with shoes so ragged that most of his toes were showing. Although humans rarely washed and usually smelled of body odor or perfume, this boy smelled like he'd rolled in a pigpen *and* hugged an old billy goat. Audun didn't care. He thought most humans smelled bad, anyway. "They want everyone to think they're sophisticated," the boy continued, "but half of them are from the country themselves."

"I'm surprised there are so many people here," said Audun. "Did they all come with King Dolon?"

"Just the ones who are acting all puffed up like they're something special," said the boy, glancing at a young woman walking heedlessly through a cluster of people who stepped aside as she'd obviously expected them to do. "That's Dolon's daughter, Gabriella. She used to be called Gabby, back when her uncle was king. The nobles who are

183

here were either Dolon's friends or the ones who changed allegiances as soon as they saw which way the wind was blowing."

"What about you?" asked Audun. "It sounds like you've been here awhile."

"I have, one way or another," said the boy. "My name is Jim."

"I'm Audun," he replied. "I'm pleased to meet you, Jim. But should you really be telling all these things to a stranger?"

Jim shrugged. "Why not? No one cares what someone like me thinks. To most of the people here, I'm practically invisible unless they need me for something. You will be, too, once you stop gawking and making yourself obvious. Just act like you've been here for years and know exactly what you're doing."

"Good point," said Audun. "I'll have to try harder."

"You do that," Jim said, backing away. "See you around," he added.

Audun watched as Jim slipped through the crowd without anyone looking his way. People in the Great Hall made him feel uncomfortable, so he followed Jim's suggestion and tried to act like he knew what he was doing as he started to leave the room. He had almost reached the door when it occurred to him that the Great Hall might be just the place to find the girl, since it seemed that nearly everyone passed through it. Instead of leaving, he walked to the wall as if to inspect a tapestry that he'd seen from a distance, intending to watch the comings and goings from the side of the room.

The sound of a scuffle in the middle of the Hall drew his attention. Jim was on his knees, cleaning up spilled ale. The same pages who had mocked Audun were now gathered around Jim, calling him names and trying to push him over with their feet.

"The filthy pig reeks! He'd do well to dump that water on himself, not the floor."

"Maybe we should help him. Hand me the bucket, Ronald, and we'll give him a bath!"

"I wouldn't do that if I were you," said Audun, putting his hand on the page's shoulder. "No one deserves to be treated like that."

"Who are you to talk to me that way?" asked the page. "You're new, but I can tell from your clothes that you're just a servant. You shouldn't even be talking to me. I'll report you and see that you get punished for this."

"Really?" said Audun. "And while you're reporting me, you should add that you were trying to keep another servant from doing his job, and because you both live off the king's treasury, you've been wasting the king's money. Just how kindly do you think he'd feel about that?"

"Why I . . . We were just . . ."

"I thought so," said Audun. "If you don't like the way someone smells, then stay away from him." Nodding to each of the boys, Audun walked away, leaving the pages staring.

"We'd better get out of here," Jim said, tagging along at Audun's side. "They could easily change their minds and report you."

Audun shrugged. "I'm not afraid of them."

"Maybe not," said Jim. "But I am. I appreciate what you did. No one has stood up for me for a long time, but I'm afraid this will only make things worse. Take my advice and steer clear of them. That's what I do." The boy gave Audun a pat on the arm, leaving a dirty handprint, then ran off through the door leading from the Great Hall.

Audun was disappointed in himself. He shouldn't have butted into a conversation that didn't involve him if he didn't want to be noticed. But then, he couldn't just let those older boys pick on Jim. It was getting harder and harder for him to blend in. Someone was sure to ask questions about him if he kept drawing attention this way. Taking Jim's advice, Audun left the Great Hall.

He drifted through the corridors, learning his way around the castle while keeping an eye out for the girl, but when the light outside the narrow windows began to fade, he followed the scent of cooking food to the kitchen. Audun was a door away when he once again heard familiar voices and peeked into a room just off the kitchen. Nearly a dozen people were seated at a long table and among them were some of the men who had sat with him in the waiting room that very morning. Seeing Audun in the doorway, one of them called out, "So you got a job, too! Congratulations! Come in and join us."

When the man slid over to make room for him, Audun took a seat, not knowing how to refuse.

"I'm John, and the ugly cuss on your other side is Gib," said the man who'd moved over. "What job did you get?"

"I'm working for the steward," said Audun, as he accepted a platter from a pretty girl with freckles and a friendly smile. Although supper wouldn't be served for over an hour in the Great Hall, the servants who would be doing the serving there were already sharing their meal with a few friends and acquaintances.

"Lucky you!" laughed John. "I'm a server, until I find something better. I didn't know it until I got here, but my brother Patrik got his old job back. He's head baker and the best one this castle has ever seen. Here, try some of his bread. Then tell him how good it is. That's him in the doorway."

Dragons don't eat much besides meat and fish, but Audun took a small hunk of bread and bit into it, just to be polite. The outside was crusty while the inside was soft and chewy, much like an oyster. He thought it was probably very good, if you liked bread, so he had no problem calling, "It's delicious!" to the man in the kitchen doorway.

Patrik grinned and nodded, making Audun feel as if he'd finally done something right. No one seemed to notice that he didn't finish the bread, although they made comments about how much sausage he was able to eat.

Seated with the new people were servants who had been there during King Cadmus's reign. Audun learned that although the king, his family, and many of his nobles had run away or been killed, many of the servants who had stayed behind had continued working in the same jobs they'd held before.

As Audun listened to the conversations around him, it was the older servants who proved to be the most informative. While some gossiped about the love lives of their fellow servants and others talked about members of the nobility who had recently moved in, it was the woman seated at the end of the table who really sparked his interest. "I don't care what you say about Princess Gabriella. She doesn't hold a candle to my little Shanna! I was nursemaid to all four of Queen Floradine's babies and was there when the good queen died at Shanna's birth. That little one stole my heart. It was nearly the death of me when I heard that the poor darlings were lost in the desert."

"She doesn't seem very upset now," Audun whispered to John.

Gib must have heard him, because he leaned closer and whispered, "There are rumors that the children still live. They say that those rumors are all that keep her going. Meg couldn't stop crying the day they disappeared. We all thought their uncle Dolon had had them executed, but no one does that and then spends so much time looking for them."

A man on the other side of Gib nudged the woman beside him and whispered something in her ear. She glanced toward the doorway and her mouthed crinkled in distaste. Audun let his gaze follow hers and was surprised to see Jim. When Audun smiled, the boy waved a greeting, but didn't cross the threshold until Meg called, "Come in, boy. Look at you! You're all skin and bones. I've seen boiled chicken bones with more meat on them than you have. Patrik, serve up a plate for our Jim, won't you, please, darlin'?"

"He'll do it, too, seeing that Meg asked," Gib whispered to Audun. "Patrik has been sweet on Meg for years. He told me all about her long before I ever came to the castle."

"Wouldn't he give the boy a plate, anyway?" asked Audun.

Gib shook his head. "No one goes near the boy if they can help it, except Meg, that is. The rest of us stay away from him and he stays away from us. Get a good whiff of him and you'll know why."

Audun watched as one of the scullery maids handed a plate to Jim. The boy ducked his head and whispered his thanks, but the maid had already hurried away, holding her nose. Jim sighed and took the plate to the corner, where he sat on the floor with his back to the wall and tore the meat with his teeth. Audun decided that the boy must be ravenous.

"What about Davie?" asked someone farther down the table. "Any word on how he's doing?"

"Dolon beat him the night before last when the poor man was slow to refill the tankards at the head table," Gib told Audun. "No one's seen him since."

Smithson shook his head. "It wasn't Davie's fault that he was late. It was his turn to take the food to the south tower. You know he has a soft spot for those orphans, locked away waiting for their families to come for them. He always dawdles when he goes there. We've been short-handed," he said, glancing at the new servants. "It'll be better now that you're here."

"What's this about orphans?" asked another man who had also been hired that day.

"After he took over the city," said Gib, "Dolon had his soldiers go through the streets, looking for orphans from wealthy families. The children were brought here to the castle. He said it was so he could take care of them, but he locked them in the south tower and sent word to their relatives that they should come fetch them. He told the head cook that we weren't to give them but the smallest portions of food. 'Let their relatives bear the brunt of their expenses,' he said. We do what he orders us to, officially, but we can't stand to see the wee mites go hungry, so we take a little extra when we can."

"He's stingy with the orphans because of all the prisoners he's got locked away in the dungeon," said another voice. "Not that he gives *them* much to eat."

"Anyone know how many are down there now?" asked Gib.

Someone Audun couldn't see said, "I used to know, but they haven't let me down the steps since Dolon took charge."

Audun noticed a look pass between Smithson and the head cook, who had come to the door. "That's it, everyone," the cook said abruptly. "Time to take the supper to the Great Hall. You've had your share of food and gossip. Now, let the mighty lords and ladies enjoy theirs!"

Eighteen

udun woke early the next morning hoping that he could locate the girl and be headed back to the dragon stronghold before the end of the day. He had found his way to the south tower the night before, although it had been heavily guarded and he hadn't been able to get in.

He reached Smugsby's office before anyone else, then had to wait for nearly an hour before Pringle showed up to tell him that the steward was feeling ill and wouldn't be in until later. "He has a bad headache," he said, giving Audun an accusing look. "I daresay it's because of that tankard you gave him yesterday. He should be back by this afternoon. Come here after the midday meal so he can tell you what to do. In the meantime, familiarize yourself with the castle if you haven't already. Master Smugsby will expect you to know your way around, given you've had so much free time."

"Yes, sir," said Audun. Of course, he had something else in mind.

The kitchen was bustling with activity when Audun reached it just a short time later. It was still early, so he didn't think anyone had carried the orphans' meal to the tower yet. He found the baker, Patrik, in the heart of the large, chaotic kitchen. When Audun asked if he could help out in any way, perhaps by taking the orphans their food, the baker seemed happy to accept the offer.

After collecting the pot of porridge and some bowls, Patrik handed him several loaves of hot, crusty bread. "Take these for the guards. They'll be more likely to let you take the food to the children if they have their own breakfast to eat. You'll want to go up the tower to make sure the orphans are being treated well, and that the food is really going to them. Oh, yes, and these are for the cat." Audun couldn't understand why the man handed him three pieces of meat wrapped in an oiled cloth, but he wasn't about to object. Surely a cat wouldn't need all three pieces, in which case, he could have a taste himself.

It wasn't until after he had given the bread to the guards positioned outside the door and had started up the steps that he understood about the cat. He had climbed only half a dozen steps up the narrow spiral staircase when something landed in front of him, yowling like a banshee. It was an orange tomcat as big as a large dog and it had three very different heads. The one in the center was big and blocky with a ragged ear and a scar down one side of its face. It was spitting and snarling at Audun. The one on the right was more refined, although it was growling deep in its throat. The third head was rounder and had short, little ears. Its sweet face had a more pronounced nose that it kept in the air, sniffing the meat.

Audun reached into the pocket where he'd stuffed the cat's breakfast. He'd seen the length of its nearly dragon-like claws and the sharpness of its daggerlike teeth, and he felt sorry for any unprepared intruder coming up these stairs to take a child home without paying the ransom. Whoever the wizard was that was helping King Dolon, he seemed to know what he was doing.

At the top of the tower, Audun found the children playing with a few broken toys while an old woman with a sour face watched over them. Her eyes lit up when Audun gave her the last of the bread, and she retired to a chair in the corner to eat.

The children gathered around Audun as he served their porridge, smiling shyly whenever he looked their way. None of the five little boys or three little girls appeared to be more than seven years old. If they'd been wearing anything of value when they were found, it had been taken away; they were dressed in clothes much like those of the servants. Even so, everything they wore was clean and they looked healthy.

While the children ate, Audun squatted down beside them, and spoke to them in a kind and encouraging way. Although they had been shy at first, they soon told him their names and what toys were their favorites. Then a little boy named Ortzi told him that his uncle was coming for him that very day. When the other children told Audun in excited voices about the impending arrival of their relatives, he began to wonder how any of them could be the one he had been sent to find. The little girls were the most animated, and although they didn't belong in the castle, they did have someone with whom they belonged. Nothing seemed particularly out of place. Surely none of them needed to be rescued.

There was no sign of the cat when Audun returned down the stairs carrying the empty bowls, which was just as well because he was trying to remember exactly what his grandmother had said in those few hectic moments before he left the dragon stronghold. He was sure she had said that the girl was an orphan, but he couldn't recall her saying anything else about her. If only that wizard hadn't shown up and they'd had more time to talk.

Audun returned the bowls to the kitchen and swiped a chunk of raw meat for himself while the cook had his back turned. Next, Audun decided to look around outside. He took the closest door leading into the courtyard and found himself near the stables. As Audun passed an open door, he glanced inside and saw a boy entering an empty stall a little farther in. The boy was the same size as Owen and had the same color hair. Audun was wondering if he should say anything when the boy raised his head. It *was*

Owen and he didn't seem happy to see Audun. He took off, running into the dimly lit depths of the stable.

Audun was peering into the darkened stalls when Owen stepped out of a doorway and they both stumbled. While Audun was trying to get them both back on their feet, he felt Owen's arm wrap around his neck and the cold blade of a knife press against his throat.

"Why are you following me?" Owen demanded.

Audun inched his hand between them, ready to break the other boy's grip. "I want to help you," he said. "I don't mean you any harm."

Owen pressed the knife a little harder. "Who are you? I've never seen you before."

"Yes, you have," said Audun, as he shoved the hand that held the knife aside, and jumped out of Owen's reach, keeping his eyes on the boy. "It's just that I didn't look like this then. I helped you once before. I want to help you now. What are you doing here? You are the prince they're all talking about, aren't you? It's too dangerous for you to be anywhere near this castle."

"I'm not telling you anything!" Owen said, waving the knife in Audun's face.

Realizing that he wasn't going to get anywhere without revealing who he was, Audun said, "I helped you escape from the roc's nest. My name is Audun."

Owen looked confused. "How is that possible?"

At least, thought Audun, *there's no one around to hear this.*

Shrugging, he said, "Humans have their magic, we dragons have ours. So why are you here?"

Owen lowered the knife and used the back of his other hand to wipe sweat from his forehead. "I heard that my father isn't dead after all. He's still alive and locked in his own dungeon. I've come to free him. Did you mean it when you said you want to help me?"

"Any way I can," said Audun.

"Then come back here tonight at midnight. You can go with me to get him out of the dungeon. I could use the help of someone like you."

"I'll be here," Audun said, even as Owen slipped into the shadows and disappeared. He was scarcely out of sight before Audun realized he should have asked if Owen had noticed a girl who didn't belong. He hurried after him.

Audun walked behind the stable and had almost reached the top of the manure pit when he heard someone shout. A slight figure was standing on the edge of the pit waving its arms in the air. Audun realized it was the boy, Jim. "What are you doing?" he shouted, just as Jim jumped into the pit below. Audun ran as fast as he could to the edge. To his amazement, Jim was rolling around in the smelly mixture, coating his clothes and body and making small grunting noises.

Seeing Audun, Jim stopped rolling long enough to sit up and shout, "Hello!"

"Are you hurt?" Audun asked, although he could tell

that the boy was fine even before he began to pick his way down the slope.

Jim was laughing when Audun finally reached him, looking happier than Audun had ever seen him. His laughter transformed his face, making him look less like a lost waif than a mischievous prankster.

"I'm right as rain," Jim said, climbing out of the pile.

"Physically, maybe," muttered Audun, running his eyes over the boy's thin frame. "But you must be crazy to jump in that."

"No, I'm not. Meg made me take a bath today," he said, as if that explained everything. When Audun's expression remained blank, Jim added, "Most people don't bother me when I smell. I mean, honestly, would you?" Raising one of his arms to his face, Jim took a deep sniff. Rolling his eyes, he stuck his tongue out of the side of his mouth and pretended to faint.

"I thought you were on fire or someone was chasing you," said Audun. "If I'd known you were just being an idiot, I never would have gotten so worried."

Jim blinked and looked up at Audun. "You were worried about me?" he said, as if he were pleased. "No one ever worries about me."

"Meg does," said Audun, giving Jim a hand out of the manure.

"Meg worries about everyone," Jim said. "I think it's part of her job."

"And what's *your* job exactly?"

Jim shrugged. "I clean up messes that no one else wants to touch. I run errands that no one else wants to do."

"In other words," said Audun, "you make yourself invaluable."

Jim gave him a sideways glance as if surprised that someone had figured it out. "I guess you could say that."

"And what else do you do?" Audun asked. "You have complete run of the place. I bet you know everything that goes on here."

"I guess you could say that, too," Jim said with a smirk. "I know that Smugsby has a killer headache and that he blames a certain person who gave him a certain tankard. I'd tiptoe around him if I were that person."

"Thanks for telling me. Now, tell me one more thing: have you seen a girl who doesn't belong here? One who might be in danger?" Audun asked, trying to sound casual, as if the question weren't uppermost in his mind.

Jim glanced away, but not before Audun could see that his eyes looked troubled. "No. I don't know anyone like that."

Audun nodded. He didn't want to scare the boy off. "Well, then, what about places? I bet you know your way around this castle pretty well."

Jim snorted. "Better than anyone. I know more secrets about this place than the men who built it. There are secret passages everywhere. I know three ways to get into the king's own chamber, and only one of them is through the door."

"What about the dungeon? How many ways do you know to get in there?"

"You aren't asking about the front door, where you have to go past two sets of guards and a trapdoor that would send you straight to the netherworld if you took one wrong step, are you? You want to know about the back way, where no one can see you and you have to watch out for rats and things that give you nightmares even during the day."

"That's right," said Audun.

"Did you want to see these places yourself?"

Audun nodded. "Now, if you have the time."

Jim took his mission very seriously. He warned Audun to be quiet and, once they had passed the stables, looked high and low to see if anyone was watching them as they approached the far side of the castle. They had rounded the corner of the keep when Jim stopped suddenly and said, "That's odd. Those weren't there when I was here last." He pointed along the back of the keep to a group of figures that were standing in their way.

"What are they?" Audun asked, squinting into the sunlight. They looked like tall, thin people with upraised arms, but they were too tall and too thin to be real.

"They're some kind of plants," Jim said, approaching them cautiously. "Look, they're covered with prickers."

"How long ago were you here last?"

"Right after I came to live at the castle. Before the wizard came. Do you think he had something to do with this?"

"I wouldn't be surprised," said Audun.

As they got closer, Audun saw that they really were plants. Gray green in color, they each had two armlike branches that reached toward the sky and sharp, spike-like growths that covered them from top to bottom. Jim and Audun were almost among them when the plants began to move.

"Watch out!" Jim shouted, as the plant closest to Audun swung a branch at him.

Audun jumped back, and the branch barely missed him. Drops of liquid quivered on the tips of some of the spines. "We're not going any farther now," said Audun, taking another step back. "Where exactly is the opening to the dungeon?"

"There," Jim said, pointing at a patch of tall, normal-looking weeds by the base of the wall. "There's a hole with a grate in front of it. The hole is small, but it gets bigger inside. We'll never get there, though, not with these plants guarding the opening."

"I'm sure you're right," said Audun, but he was already thinking of ways he could do just that.

The sun was high overhead by the time they returned to the stables. "Thanks," said Audun. "You were a big help. Just don't tell anyone what you showed me."

"Who—me? You're the only person I've talked to since Dolon took over. No one else is worth the bother. Say, aren't you supposed to go see Smugsby soon? I've heard he has a whole lot of things for you to do." Grinning at Audun once more, Jim darted off around the manure pile and up the hill to the castle keep.

Jim was right; it was time to go see Smugsby. Only a few minutes later, Audun was passing the Great Hall. He heard the commotion of an excited crowd. Lords and ladies dressed in fine clothes pushed past him to stand shoulder to shoulder with scullery maids and undergrooms while the words "marvelous" and "wonderful" rang out around them. Audun worked his way into the crowd and finally, after crawling under a table and stepping on a few toes to get people to move, he was able to see Princess Gabriella and the man he assumed was her father, King Dolon, greeting someone he had yet to see. It wasn't until the crowd parted so that the new person could come forward that Audun saw his face. To the delight of everyone except Audun, Olebald Wizard was back.

As the old man's head turned his way, Audun ducked and melted into the crowd.

Nineteen

Jim had been right about something else, too: Smugsby was in a very bad mood.

"Someone who hates me sent you with that blasted tankard, I know it!" he growled, when Audun walked in the door. "Either I didn't give him a job, or he didn't get what he thinks he deserved. You brought me that . . . that *thing* so I'd drink myself to death!"

Audun shook his head. "That isn't true. I brought it because I thought you'd like it."

"I do, and that's the problem," Smugsby said, rubbing his temples. "I wouldn't be too pleased with myself, though, if I were you. Every time my head pounds, I'm going to think of more work for you, and right now it feels like it's the midsummer celebration and everyone is dancing on my skull! Go see Pringle. He's got a list of things I want done today. And don't dawdle if you want to keep your job."

True to Smugsby's word, Pringle kept Audun running

all afternoon. He took a message to the captain of the guard, then brought back his reply. He rushed to the city with a note for a man who sold wine, and as soon as he returned he was sent back to the city with a note for a wool merchant.

Audun was relieved when Pringle finally told him that the rest of his errands would be inside the castle. He was walking through the Great Hall when the floor beneath him trembled and a loud rumble filled the air. A passing guard smiled in a knowing kind of way and said, "Must be that wizard. I expect we'll have a lot of that kind of thing going on with him in the castle."

Audun frowned. It had been easy enough to forget about Olebald Wizard while he was in the city, but he'd have to remember to stay on guard if he didn't want the wizard to see him.

Late that afternoon Audun was returning with a message from the king's chancellor when he saw an enormous man come out of Smugsby's office. His shoulders were broad and his arms and legs muscled as if he lifted heavy objects daily. Although Audun was sure he'd never seen the man before, there was something familiar about the way he held his head. He nodded at Audun and winked, as if about to say something, and might have if Pringle hadn't stuck his head out the door and told Audun to come in.

"Who was that?" Audun asked, shutting the door behind him.

"A new guard," said Pringle. "He's big enough to intimidate anyone, don't you think?"

"Indeed," said Audun.

He wouldn't have thought any more about the new guard if the man hadn't kept popping up. Audun saw him while passing through the Great Hall on two different trips, then once outside the kitchen, and again in the corridor by the room where he'd left his pallet. Although the man never spoke, Audun could sense his eyes following him every time they met. At first he thought the man might be working for Olebald Wizard, but he discarded that idea when the man didn't approach him and neither did anyone else. Surely if Olebald knew he was there, Audun would no longer be walking around freely. But, the man made him nervous.

The sun had already set when Audun finally finished his work for the day. After making sure that no one, including the new guard, was following him, he slipped through a door and hurried around the side of the castle. He was about to do something he had told himself he wouldn't do while on the castle grounds, but it was the only thing he could think of that would take care of the spiky plants. For just a few minutes, Audun was going to have to turn back into a dragon.

He waited until he was in the deepest shadows close to the wall of the keep before closing his eyes and thinking about being a dragon. When he next looked up, his eyesight was back to normal; washed in a pale light, the plants were no longer the dull grayish green they'd appeared through human eyes, but now showed patches of ultraviolet and a white so bright that Audun had to look away. The plants seemed to be watching him. He took a step closer and they swayed in his direction ever so slightly—as if a gentle breeze had blown them. When he was a few yards away, they began reaching for him.

If Audun had been a fire dragon, he would have blasted them with a heat so intense they would have blackened and withered like daisies in a forest fire. But because he was an ice dragon, he coughed. It wasn't a loud cough, just the kind that ice dragons do when they are mixing the noxious gas stored in a sac near their lungs with the air they are about to exhale. When he did exhale, the gas formed a small cloud that was colorless and nearly invisible. As the cloud drifted through the cluster of plants, they jerked back and then began to shrivel and die. Not a single desiccated plant stirred as Audun walked between them to the grate in the wall.

About two feet across and built into the wall for drainage, the grate covered a round opening at the bottom of one of the walls. Time and rust had loosened it so much that Audun was able to lift it free with no effort at all. The opening was too small for a dragon as big as Audun, and since he had to change back, anyway, he crouched down and, a moment later, tried to see if his human form could fit. Although it was tight, he was able to wriggle inside. He thought about going to look for the king himself, but he had no idea what the man looked like or what he would do with him once he got him out, so he wriggled back through the opening and set the grate where it belonged. Midnight was only a few hours away and Audun guessed Owen would be furious if he rescued the king without him.

❧

The full moon was peeking over the castle wall when Audun returned to the stable yard. Owen had yet to arrive, so Audun sat on the ground to gaze up at the sky while he waited for the prince. It wasn't long before he heard someone approach, but the boy who sat down beside him was Jim.

"I wish I could fly away from here," Jim said, sounding wistful.

"Where would you go if you could?" asked Audun.

"Somewhere I wouldn't have to hide and could just be myself. The problem is, I wouldn't know how to get there."

Audun felt sorry for the boy. He pretended not to notice Jim scrub his eyes with the back of his hand as he climbed to his feet.

Jim straightened his back and glanced at Audun. "Where's your friend?"

"What friend?" asked Audun.

"The one who's meeting you at midnight. I told you I know everything that goes on around here."

"He should be here soon," said Audun.

"Who is that?" said a voice out of the near-darkness. "I told *you* to come. I never said you could bring someone else."

Audun waited while Owen came close enough that they could see each other clearly. "I didn't invite him, but it might not be a bad idea to have him along," said Audun. "Jim knows his way around the castle better than anyone."

"He doesn't know it better than I do," Owen snapped. "Look at him—he's a kid. He'll just get in the way."

"I can help!" Jim rushed to say. "And I bet I know ways into the dungeon that you've never seen."

Owen narrowed his eyes. "He told you we were going to the dungeon?"

"No, I just know a lot of things," Jim said. "And I'm small. I can fit places you can't."

"All right," Owen said. "Since you already know all about it, you can come, but stay out of my way. And it's up to you to keep an eye on him," he added, glancing at Audun.

"No problem," said Audun, giving Jim a pointed look.

Owen acted as if he knew where he was going, but when they reached the base of the first tower, he stopped and kicked at a pile of gravel. "I know it was here," he said. "I found the tunnel years ago when I was playing with my friends. It was behind a couple of big boulders."

"I think Dolon had it filled in after he took over the castle," said Jim. "If it were daylight out, you'd see the new stones and mortar."

"There was another, smaller entrance," said Owen, "but it had a grate over it. I don't recall exactly . . ."

"It's this way," said Jim. "Follow me!"

He took them around the castle wall to the side he had visited with Audun earlier that day. It was darker there because the tower itself was blocking the moonlight, but with his sharp dragon eyes, Audun could see the ground where the spiky plants had been standing. It looked ghostly in the gloom, as if a patrol of guards had been mown down and deflated at the same time.

"What happened to them?" Jim asked.

"Looks like something killed them," said Audun.

Jim glanced at him in exasperation. "I know that! I just wonder how."

Owen nudged the limp remains of a plant with the toe of his shoe. "Could have been a lot of things."

The prince seemed to be having difficulty determining where to step, so when he stumbled and nearly fell, Audun set his hand on his arm to guide him. Owen tried to shake him off, saying, "I don't need your help."

"What harm is there in accepting what little help I can give you? Or would you rather trip over a rock and break your neck so that your father rots in the dungeon for the rest of his life?"

"Well, if you put it that way . . . ," said Owen.

"It's over here," Jim called from the middle of the dead weeds.

Audun helped the prince down the slight incline, the weeds crunching beneath their feet. Releasing his grip on the prince's arm, he lifted the heavy grate as easily as if it were made of paper, then bent down to peer into the opening.

"It's a tunnel," said Jim, squatting beside him. "It opens into another tunnel that goes all the way under the dungeons. It smells in there and there're a lot of rats, but there's water running through the bottom."

"An underground river runs beneath the city," said Owen. "It's why Desidaria was built here and why we rarely run out of water. I've seen it on my father's old maps." Reaching into his tunic, he pulled out a candle and flint. "We can light this in the tunnel. Stay here. I'll go first."

"I think I should go first," said Audun. "You never know what you're going to find in a place like this."

"I'm not going to argue about it," Owen said. "Just stay here until—"

"Come on in," Jim called from inside the tunnel. "There's plenty of room in here."

"People are supposed to listen to princes," Owen grumbled, as he crawled through the opening. Audun followed, reaching back to grab the grate and pull it roughly into place. When he turned around again, Owen had lit the candle and was holding it up to examine their surroundings. The tunnel was wider than the opening to the outside, but still not big enough to allow them to stand. It went back only a dozen yards or so before ending in a mound of stone and gravel. The sound of rushing water was audible even near the opening and grew louder the farther in Audun went.

"The other tunnel is this way," Jim said, as he scurried off, still doubled over, into a side passage. "We'll have to go down because it's under this one and . . . Hey! It's filled with water! It wasn't the last time I came here, I swear it!"

"I believe you," Audun said, squeezing in beside Owen and Jim. The tunnel was short, ending in a hole in the ground as wide as the tunnel itself. Water rushed only a foot or so below them. "I bet the wizard brought the water level up just so people couldn't get into the dungeon through these tunnels."

Owen nodded, the flickering light of his candle making his shadow on the wall nod with him. "The whole castle shook this afternoon. I even felt it outside."

"What are we going to do?" asked Jim. "I know of two other ways in, but if this tunnel is flooded, they will be, too."

"I'll go," said Audun.

"Don't be ridiculous," Owen said, scowling. "You won't be able to breathe in there and there's no telling how far you'll have to go before you reach air again."

Jim shook his head. "You can't go in! I've been down there and I can tell you that it's a really long way. I suppose we can check the other openings. Maybe one of them . . ."

"You said yourself that if one is flooded, the others will be as well. I'm a strong swimmer and can hold my breath for a very long time, much longer than either of you. I'll have the best chance of getting in there and back out again." Although Owen knew that Audun was really a dragon, Jim had no idea. The last thing Audun wanted to do was let someone else in on a secret that no one was supposed to know.

Owen held up his hand in protest. "It's my father and—"

"Exactly," said Audun. "I don't want to be the one to tell your father that you died trying to rescue him. Don't worry, I know what I'm doing."

"You won't have any light," said Owen. "How will you see where you're going? I have another candle, but it won't do you a bit of good underwater."

"I can see in the dark better than you can," said Audun. "There is one thing, though. I've never met your father or seen what he looks like. How will I know who to bring back? From what I've heard, Dolon has been collecting prisoners in the dungeon since the day he took over the castle."

"Here," said Jim, reaching into the neck of his tunic. "I have this." A jeweled locket lay on his palm and when

212

he pressed a tiny knob on the top it split in half, revealing a miniature picture on each side. "That's my father," Jim said, pointing to the picture on the right. The man was dressed in heavy robes with a jeweled chain around his neck. Jim tapped his finger against the other picture. "And that's King Cadmus. He and my father were friends." The king was a distinguished man with hair as blond as Owen's.

The prince glanced up and gave Jim a searching look. "Your father was the gem merchant, wasn't he? My father counted him as a good friend."

"This should help," said Audun, examining the miniature portrait of the king closely. "There is one other thing that might be useful. Would you happen to have something of your father's, Owen? Perhaps a piece of clothing that you took with you when you left?"

Owen looked thoughtful but shook his head. "The only thing I have of my father's is this ring," he said, holding up his hand. "He gave it to me for safekeeping just before Dolon's men took him away."

"That might work," said Audun. He pulled Owen's hand closer as if to get a better look, and quickly sniffed the ring. When he had a good sense of its owner, Audun turned and lowered his legs into the water before anyone could stop him. It was warm, with a strong current that Audun hadn't anticipated.

"Are you sure you want to do this?" asked Jim. "I

mean, you're the first friend I've made since I got here and I really don't want to lose you."

Audun grinned. "I don't want to lose me, either. Don't worry, I'll be back before you know it." The last thing he saw before the current carried him away were the worried faces of his two new friends.

As the water swept Audun under the castle, he considered changing into a dragon, but the space was narrow, and he didn't know how wide it would be up ahead. He'd never taken off the amulet that allowed him to breathe underwater, so he wasn't worried about air. However, his human body was far more fragile than his true dragon self, a fact he'd forgotten when he had said that he would go. The current was fast, and if it hadn't been for his dragon strength he would have been hurled into the wall. As it was, it took all of his efforts to stay in the center of the channel while avoiding the debris that churned in the water around him.

After what seemed like hours, Audun finally saw a glimmer of light ahead. He was swimming toward it, hoping that it was an opening into the dungeon, when he sensed a change in the current. Something big was coming.

Even with the eyesight of a dragon, Audun couldn't see more than a few feet away in the darkened water. He was turning in a circle, trying to see what was coming up behind him when a tentacle wrapped itself around his neck and jerked. Audun flailed his arms as the tentacle dragged him backward. There was a loud sucking sound and he slid down the gullet of a river monster.

The tentacle let go with a slurp and Audun slid on his back down a bumpy surface. He was stunned. He'd never been swallowed before and it wasn't at all what he would have expected: he hadn't been chewed into bits, nor was he dissolving in a vat of stomach acid. Instead, he floated in water that smelled faintly of rotting fish and was warmer than the water he'd just come from. The light he'd been trying to reach was still visible, although it was wavery, as if he were looking through a thick layer of ice. The roar of the underground river was muted.

Audun twisted his body around until he felt footing below him. Using his hands and feet, he tried to climb up the bumpy surface, but it gave too easily under pressure; he felt like he was climbing in old fish pudding. He could always turn into a dragon if he had to, but the thought of doing it inside another living creature made his stomach turn. There had to be another way out.

Water sloshed around him every time the creature moved. With his hand touching the inside of the beast, Audun could feel its body slosh, too, which made him realize just how much of the monster was made of water. It seemed more like a water-filled bladder armed with a tentacle than like the sea monsters Audun had met near the islands. And if it really was mostly water . . .

Audun reached into the satchel where he'd hidden the

objects he usually carried in the pouch under his wing. The piece of ice felt colder in his human hand than it had in his dragon talons and he dropped it sooner than he'd intended. It fell into the water which instantly turned slushy with the cold. The monster shivered and Audun's human body shivered with it.

A groaning sound filled Audun's ears and he looked up as a wave of warm water washed over him. It took only moments before this water had turned slushy as well. Hoping that the monster would groan again, Audun doubled his efforts as he fought his way to its mouth. He was ready when the creature's jaws gaped open. Grabbing hold of the creature's lip, he somersaulted out of the beast and into the underground river which was already turning colder. Although he kept his head down, he grazed his back on the ceiling of the tunnel, cutting through his clothes and scraping away skin.

With powerful thrusts of his legs and arms, Audun swam away from the monster toward the light in the ceiling. It was another wide hole covered with a metal grate. Audun struggled against the current, trying to stay under the opening long enough to grab hold of the grate. It took all his strength, but Audun was able to push it aside and pull himself out of the river with a *whoosh!*

He stood for a moment, trying to get his bearings as water sluiced off his clothes. Squelching with every step, he began to search for Owen's father.

The only light in the otherwise dark dungeon came from smoking torches that sputtered at the slightest puff of air. At first, Audun caught only a faint whiff of the king's presence, and thought it might have been left from visits in times past. That changed, however, when Audun reached the intersection of two corridors and the scent became much stronger.

Although he tried to be as quiet as possible, even the small sounds he made drew the prisoners to the doors of their cells. A few of them watched him walk by in silence while others cried out, asking for his help, yet each time he tried to talk to one of them, they were too frightened and distrustful to listen to what he had to say.

Finally, he noticed a man who pressed his face against the bars in the square window of his door and didn't hide when Audun approached. "Be quiet, you idiots!" the man shouted, making his long, scruffy beard bob up and down. "Can't you tell—that's a dead man walking there. You don't want the kind of help he can give you!"

"Pardon me," said Audun, "but I was wondering if you know where the king is being kept."

"Why?" asked the man. "Do you want to drag him off to drown him so you'll have company in your watery grave?"

"Not at all," Audun replied. "I'm not dead and I don't want to hurt anyone. I'm here to help the king escape."

"Really? In that case, I'm the king. Which one are you looking for?"

"King Cadmus," said Audun.

"Well, then, I'm King Cadmus! Let me out."

Audun sighed. "I can't take everyone in the dungeon, and if I let you out they'll all want to go. I'm here to rescue the king. Once I get him out, I'm sure he'll do his best to come back and free the rest of his subjects."

"Why would he want to do that? There are murderers and cutthroats down here. Most of these men deserve to be right where they are. I'm different, though, so let me out."

"Why are *you* in here?"

"Because I'm King Cadmus, remember? You have a very short memory, don't you, boy?"

Audun peered at the man. He was old and wrinkled and his beard must have taken years to grow. The man in front of him didn't look anything like the clean-shaven man in the picture and he smelled so awful that Audun's eyes teared. "Never mind," Audun said, as he turned away. "I'll just have to keep looking."

"Don't be a dunderhead!" yelled the man. "I'm Cadmus and you have to get me out."

"No!" shouted a prisoner on the other side of the corridor. "I'm Cadmus. Take me with you!" Audun glanced at him, but he was much too young to be the king.

While voices up and down the corridor clamored that they, too, were Cadmus, Audun went from window to window, trying to find the prisoner who looked like the man in the picture. None of them were right, however. Some were too young, some too old, some had eyes too far apart or noses too small, yet now that they knew that Audun was there to free the king, every one of them claimed to be King Cadmus. Unfortunately, they all smelled horrible.

Reaching the end of the row, Audun closed his eyes. Taking a deep breath, he tried to sort out the awful smells. There, that was it. It was true, Cadmus was here, but he was behind him. Audun retraced his steps all the way back to . . . Audun groaned. The crazy old man he'd been talking to was Cadmus after all.

"I told you so," said the king.

"Why don't you look anything like the picture you gave the gem merchant?" asked Audun.

"Is that the picture you saw? I must have given that to him six or seven years ago. I pass out so many of those things that it's hard to keep track. I've had a beard for the last five years at least. Now, how about letting me out?"

"I'm doing this on your son's behalf," Audun said, wrapping his fingers around the window bars. With one powerful jerk, he yanked the bars from the window, but left the door still in place.

"Is that the best you can do?" asked the king. "I can't fit through that little hole. I may have lost weight, but I'm not a skeleton like that guy." Audun peered behind the king at the skeleton sitting in the corner. Someone had rearranged his bones so that he was in a sitting position, with one knee resting on the other and his hands palm up beside him. An old metal cup had been placed on one of his hands so that he looked as if he'd been drinking.

"I'm not finished," said Audun. Bracing his feet against the wall on either side of the doorway, he gripped the door through the window hole and pulled. The top of the door broke free, leaving the bottom intact.

"You're not very good at this, are you?" said Cadmus. "Why, if it were up to me—"

"Pardon me, Your Majesty," Audun said, as he reached through the opening and picked up the king. "We don't have time for criticism."

Slinging the king over his shoulder, he turned and started down the corridor while prisoners shouted and pleaded for him to take them, too. He really would have taken them with him if he could have, but he knew that the return trip wasn't going to be easy. In view of what had happened on his way in, he was already considering how he was going to carry the king back with him. It had been difficult enough to fight the current when he was by himself, but carrying this old man would make it that much harder . . . unless, of course, Audun was a dragon.

Putting aside the concerns that had made him refrain from changing into a dragon earlier, Audun resolved that he would have to return to his normal shape if he were to have any chance of reaching the outside world. He had even thought of a way to keep the king from seeing his true form. He hoped the old man wouldn't be able to feel the difference between human and dragon once they were in the water.

After setting the king beside the opening to the tunnel, Audun took Frostweaver's fabric from his satchel and held it up so King Cadmus could see it. "We're about to go into some very cold water. This magic fabric will keep you warm, but you have to keep it over your head, so you won't be able to see anything. Don't struggle while I carry you, or I might lose my grip and drop you. Do you understand?"

"Of course I understand," grumped the king. "What kind of idiot do you think I am? You're going to carry me to who knows where and I won't be able to see where we're going until we get there. And if I try to get away, you're going to drop me." King Cadmus peered over the edge into the ink-black water where chunks of ice floated by. "I see what you mean by cold. I thought you were making up excuses for wrapping me in a blanket so I couldn't see where we were going. Who would have thought there'd be ice in the desert? So how am I going to breathe down there?"

Audun didn't think he had any choice; he had to tell the king about his amulet. "I'm wearing something that lets me breathe underwater. I believe you'll be able to breathe, too, as long as I'm carrying you. It's an—"

"You *believe*? You mean you don't know? Now, isn't that a fine kettle of fish! I'm supposed to trust you with my life and you don't even know what you're doing! And this is all on my son's behalf? Which son is it? I have three, you know. Do they know what you're up to? Maybe they're out to kill me, too. Never mind. They're all good boys. We'd better get out of here before those fool guards wander down this way in one of their drunken stupors and trip over us. Hand me that fabric. I'll do it myself. I don't trust you not to . . . There, that's it," King Cadmus said through the fabric. "I'm trussed up like a goose and ready to go. I don't care how you get me out of here. Just do it! Hey, are you going somewhere? You're not going to leave me here!"

Audun had slipped into the river feet first and was treading water. While the king flopped around like a blindfolded fish, Audun changed back into a dragon. It was a relief to be himself again, and the current that had felt so strong and cold before now seemed gentle and refreshing. Because the hole was too small for him to fit through as a dragon, he reached up with both forelegs and plucked the king off the floor. Careful not to poke the man through the fabric with his talons, Audun dove into the river and swam upstream, easily maneuvering around the debris.

The king had begun to struggle as soon as he entered the water. Audun worried at first, but the old man continued to

222

shout and thrash around long after he would have drowned if the magic hadn't been working. Satisfied that the king was all right, the dragon sped through the water, reaching the hole in the ceiling near the outer wall in minutes.

With a powerful heave, Audun tossed the king through the opening onto the floor of the tunnel. He heard Jim and Owen shout, but by then he was so busy focusing on turning back into a human that he missed whatever they were saying. A moment later he pulled himself out of the water, landing on his stomach beside the partly unwrapped king with an *oof!*

"You got him!" Owen shouted, pounding Audun on the back.

"You shouldn't have doubted me," Audun said, although he'd had moments when he'd doubted he could do it himself.

"Your friend swims like a fish," said the king, as he kicked the cloth off his feet. "I wouldn't have thought he was human if I hadn't seen it with my own two eyes. Didn't feel like a human, though." He rubbed his chest where Audun's talons had pressed against him. "Strongest grip I ever felt."

Owen put his arm around his father's shoulders. "Thank goodness for that. But now we have to get you out of here, Father. I have a horse waiting in the city. You two should come with us," he added, glancing from Jim to Audun. "This is no life for you here, Jim. And I can use your help, Audun. My father and I are going to get his throne back."

"Jim should go," Audun said. "But I have to stay here. I came to Desidaria to find someone and I'm not leaving until I do."

Twenty

The sun was coming up as Audun helped Owen hide King Cadmus in a wagon that would take him off the castle grounds. After wishing his friends well, Audun sneaked through the back door of the kitchen behind a yawning scullery maid and trudged down the corridor to the Great Hall. His clothes still damp, he sat on a bench to wait until it was time to see Smugsby.

Exhausted from the sleepless night, Audun dreaded all the tasks the steward was bound to have waiting for him. He thought about abandoning the job altogether so he could focus on looking for the girl, but then he would probably be kicked out of the castle. Perhaps he could hunt for the girl while he was working, provided he wasn't too obvious about it. He'd already decided that he would talk to every girl in the castle if he had to, in order to find the one he was meant to rescue. After that, he would go straight to Greater Greensward and tell Millie how much she meant to him, and this time nothing was going to get in his way.

Audun was about to get off the bench and go see Smugsby when four guards approached him. The big man who'd been made a guard just the day before was among them. Audun thought they were headed for the next table, and was surprised when they stopped beside his.

"You're coming with us," said one of the men. Audun recognized him as a guard from the orphans' tower.

"What's this about?" Audun asked, getting to his feet.

"Treason," the guard answered. He refused to say anything more, even as they hustled Audun through the Great Hall, along the corridor, and down the steep stairs to the dungeon.

Audun wasn't worried when they marched him into an empty cell and manacled him to the wall. He knew he could get out at any time: he was sure that the chains couldn't withstand a dragon's strength, but he was curious enough to want to know why he was being named a traitor. They couldn't know of his actions during the night, unless . . .

Audun sniffed the air. Could they have captured Owen and Jim while they were helping King Cadmus off the castle grounds? If so, they would be in the dungeon as well, but he couldn't sense either of the boys, and with such a distinctive odor, Jim would have been easy to smell.

Audun watched the guards as they prepared to leave the cell, taking the torches they'd brought with them. Although three of the guards hurried out of the cell without a backward glance, the new guard paused at the door, letting the light of the torch he carried play over his features. And he winked.

Audun's jaw dropped. He wanted to ask the guard who he was and why he had winked, but the man was gone before he could get the words out. As the door slammed shut, Audun closed his eyes and shook his head. He'd really messed things up this time. Not only had he not found the girl, but he'd gotten himself locked away, and now he'd have to free himself without revealing his true nature. He was wondering how things could have gone so wrong when he heard footsteps. Light filled the small square window again.

His answer came when two visitors unlocked the door and one of them, a man dressed in a billowing robe decorated with spinning silver stars, jerked his cupped hands into the air, sending a ball of pale, blue light through the cell to bob just above Audun's head. Ever since he'd seen Olebald in the Great Hall, Audun had suspected that it wouldn't be long before the wizard knew of his presence in the castle. He had hoped, however, that it would take a little longer than this, and that he might actually be able to leave before the wizard could find him.

As the two men drew closer, he recognized the other man as the one who had greeted Olebald on his arrival, the one he'd assumed was King Dolon. Shorter than his brother, Cadmus, Dolon's hair had yet to turn from silvery gray to white and his beard was just a fringe on his chin.

"So this is the one who's come to kill me," said Dolon, peering nearsightedly at Audun. "He doesn't look like an assassin."

Audun's head shot up. "What? I never tried to kill anyone."

Olebald snorted and stomped across the filthy floor to glare down his nose at Audun, even though the boy was a good eight inches taller and the wizard had to tilt his head back to do it. "Don't lie to us, boy. Why else would you be here? You got a job under false pretenses—bribing a court official with a forbidden magical gift."

"Oh, dear," said King Dolon. "Is it really forbidden? I was so hoping to get one for myself. I've heard those bottomless tankards are wonderful, especially when you plan to entertain, and you know my wife intends to have all her relatives visit now that she's queen. Those people can drink more in one hour than a ship's crew the first day in port."

"Well, of course *you* can have one, Your Majesty," said Olebald. "I'll get you one myself if you'd like."

King Dolon looked pleased. "Very thoughtful of you, old fellow. I'd like mine filled with mead. I'm partial to it myself, and I don't see why the wife's brother can't drink mead instead of the imported wine he's always demanding."

Olebald sighed. "As you wish, Your Majesty. Now, about the boy . . ."

"What boy? Oh, yes. Him. He looks like a nice enough boy. Handsome, too. Just the sort my daughter would be interested in meeting. Do you suppose you can arrange that as well?"

Olebald ground his teeth and, in an obvious effort to remain patient, said, "He's here to kill you, Your Majesty. That's why he's in the dungeon."

"I told you, I'm not here to kill anyone!" said Audun.

"Then why are you here, if not to overthrow King Dolon and put his brother back on the throne?"

King Dolon nodded. "Someone set Cadmus free last night. Was it you? Because if it was, I'd like to know how you did it. Quite an amazing feat actually, what with the river and the monster and all. I was astounded when Olebald thought of so many marvelous traps. I never would have come up with any of them in a million years."

"That's why I'm here, Your Majesty," said Olebald. "To protect you from nefarious scoundrels like him."

"I'm not here to hurt King Dolon!" Audun said again.

"He certainly is vehement. Are you sure he isn't innocent?" asked the king.

"Don't listen to him, Your Majesty. He has to lie about it. It's part of the assassins' code. They never admit that they've come to kill someone, even under torture."

"Oh, dear, we're not going to torture him, are we? You know I don't like that kind of thing."

"We could torture him," said Olebald, "to try to learn

if he has any accomplices, but I don't believe it would work. No, we'll just execute him quietly, if that's all right with Your Majesty."

"Yes, indeed, that's much better," King Dolon said, looking relieved. "You'll handle all the details, won't you, Olebald?" The wizard nodded, and the king added, "That's a good fellow. I knew I could depend on you. Now, if we're finished here, I suppose I'll be off."

Olebald ran to the doorway and stood just inside, watching the old king go. "I thought he'd never leave," he said, once the king's footsteps stopped ringing in the hall. The old wizard waved his hand, creating a blue cloud that drifted to the door, closed it with a *whump!* and remained to swirl in front of the window, preventing anyone from seeing inside the cell. Turning back to Audun, Olebald rubbed his hands together, saying, "Tell me what it would take to get you to turn back into a dragon."

Audun shook his head, not sure he had heard him correctly. "Pardon me?"

"You can either show me your own true self right now, which would save us both so much trouble, or I could show you a way I've devised that will change you, whether you want it to or not."

"What are you talking about?"

Olebald smiled, but in a not-very-friendly way. "Some time ago I came across a spell that would give me exactly what I'd been dreaming about for years. A nasty little witch exiled me to a tropical island where the memories of a group of witches had been kept. Although most of them had been freed, I found one bottle still intact, buried in the sand. I freed the memories in exchange for the witch's strongest spell, one which will turn me into the most fearsome dragon alive. All I need are a few key ingredients and I'll never again have to follow the orders of a sniveling king who has no idea how to rule a kingdom. I'll be the one with all the power and everyone will have to listen to me!"

"Do you honestly think a simple spell is going to turn you into a dragon? There's a lot more to it than that."

"Really? Like what?" Olebald said, his eyes lighting up.

"I'm . . . not sure," said Audun.

"Why don't you turn into a dragon and show me? I'm sure you're a most handsome beast."

"Why do you want *me* to turn into a dragon so badly?"

"Would you believe—I'm curious?"

"Not in the least. And I doubt it's because you want to see what I look like while I change. Unless . . . What precisely did the spell say you needed to turn into a dragon?"

"Just a dragon scale, a dragon talon, a dragon eyeball, and a dragon jaw. Nothing you'll miss too much."

"Sorry, but even if I wanted to give you the scale and the talon, I believe I'd really miss the eye and the jaw."

"I wasn't asking for them," said Olebald. "I was just telling you what I'm going to take once you change back into a dragon."

"You're crazy. Why would I turn back knowing that you want to tear off bits of me? I'm not going to do anything to help you."

"I can see you aren't going to cooperate," Olebald said with a sigh. "Fortunately, my plans don't depend on your goodwill." Reaching into his robe, Olebald took out a silk pouch and opened it, revealing a green stone the size of a large man's fist. Bathed in a pale light, the stone illuminated the cell like an eerie, flameless fire. The moment the stone left the pouch, the ball of blue light that had been bobbing above Audun's head flickered and went out and the silver stars on Olebald's robe stopped spinning.

Audun recognized the stone, having seen many just like it studding the wall of Nastia Nautica's underwater cave. What he didn't understand was what the wizard thought he could do with a stone that wiped out magic.

"This stone has many properties," said Olebald. "Even the sea witch I acquired it from didn't know them all, but I've been experimenting with it. I believe that while no one can do magic in its presence, if you were to swallow it, it would force you to turn back into a dragon. In essence, it can change your form only from the inside—and then only by returning you to your real shape."

Audun was incredulous. "You want me to swallow that rock? That thing is huge! I couldn't get it down, and if I did it would kill me."

Olebald shrugged and took a step toward Audun.

"Great discoveries often involve great sacrifices. I don't need you to be alive to get the parts I require. It will make it easier for me if you aren't. Now, open wide and we'll see if this fits."

"Mmph!" said Audun, pressing his lips shut and turning his head to the side. He struggled as Olebald grabbed his head and tried to pry his jaws far enough apart to shove the stone between his lips. Unable to use his magic in the presence of the stone, the old man had to rely on his not-so-great strength and was losing the battle when the cell door burst open, admitting a slender, young, blue and white dragoness with lovely green stripes.

"He hasn't hurt you, has he, Audun?" asked the dragoness. Audun wondered how this stranger knew his name. Only four feet long, she was probably about the same age as Loolee. Audun was certain that he had never seen her before.

"Mmph!" said Audun, still trying to keep his mouth shut.

"Get away from him, you horrible monster!" the dragoness roared. With one beat of her wings, she landed on Olebald and knocked him to the floor. She was so small, however, that once he was down, he was able to fend her off with one arm while the other clutched the stone to his chest.

"If I can't get ... what I want ... from one dragon," Olebald said, grunting with exertion, "then I'll get ... it from . . . another!" The old wizard shoved the little drag-oness to the ground, pinning her beneath his knees. She flailed at him with her wings, batting the stone to the floor where it rolled well out of reach. With both hands free, the old wizard tried to rip one of her scales loose. The drag-oness screamed and snapped at him with her sharp baby teeth.

Audun groaned. If only the stone had rolled in his direction, he might have been able to toss it out the door and turn back into a dragon. Now that the little dragoness was in danger, he *had* to become a dragon to save her. Whoever she was, she couldn't possibly know the danger she now faced.

Audun dragged at the chains that bound him to the wall and for the first time noticed that they were new and not like the chains he'd seen in the cells while looking for King Cadmus. These were made of bright, shiny metal with no sign of rust; it was all he could do to bend them, let alone break them.

While Audun thrashed around, jerking at the chains, he called out to the dragoness, "Hold on! I'm coming!" When the dragoness let out a pitiful mew, he threw himself against the chains. With no scales to protect him, the metal cut into his skin, making the manacles slippery with blood.

Audun turned his head as the floor shuddered under the pounding of heavy feet. Suddenly, an enormous dragon head filled the doorway, its mouth open in a roar that shook the walls of the cell and made dust sift through the stone ceiling. Olebald looked up from the dragoness, his eyes as big as platters and his face turning pale. Snarling, the dragon thrashed its head from side to side as it fought to work its way into the room. With a sickening grating sound, the mortar that held the stones of the doorway crumbled and the dragon staggered into the cell.

The dragon was more than twice Audun's normal size, with burly muscles and a ridge as sharp as blades. When he roared again stones fell from the ceiling and screams of terror echoed from the neighboring cells. Audun had never been so happy to see anyone as he was to see Frostybreath at that moment.

Olebald cowered against the floor with his arms crossed in front of his face as if they could protect him. The little dragoness looked just as frightened as she crawled toward the wall, away from both the wizard and the dragon.

"So you thought you'd get away," Frostybreath growled, thrashing his tail behind him as he strode toward the wizard. His tail hit an ancient skeleton, knocking it across the cell where it shattered against the far wall. "Did you really think I wouldn't find you again?"

The old man stammered, powerless against the dragon without his magic. He scuttled backward until he reached the wall and couldn't go any farther.

Frostybreath turned to Audun and shook his head, saying, "You certainly know how to get yourself into a mess."

The little dragoness's ridge was raised in anger when she flew at him shouting, "Don't you hurt my friend!"

"Who is this?" Frostybreath asked, as he caught the little dragon with his talons. She fought, scratching and biting.

Audun shrugged. "I don't know, although she seems to know me. Would you mind," he asked, pulling his arms as far from the wall as he could get them.

Frostybreath grunted. Stretching out his neck, he breathed on the chains, making them so cold that they became brittle. He was reaching out to break them when Olebald got to his feet. While the big dragon turned back to the wizard, Audun lunged against the chains, snapping them. He didn't hesitate, but dashed to where the green stone still lay and snatched it up from the floor. Running to the door, he pitched it down the corridor where it skidded through the dust and debris and finally disappeared through a hole in a grate to the water below.

Still in the doorway, Audun closed his eyes and turned back into a dragon. Hearing a gasp behind him, he turned around and saw the little dragoness looking from him to the blue cloud that had formed between the wizard and Frostybreath. The big dragon looked stunned. Audun didn't know why until he saw tendrils reaching from the blue cloud to wrap themselves around the dragon's throat.

The wizard had his back to Audun, who knew that he had only seconds before Olebald used the blue cloud against him as well. Without making a sound, Audun launched himself at the old man, knocking him to the floor. The impact stunned Olebald for a moment, which was just long enough for the cloud to falter and fall back in on itself. Released from the cloud, Frostybreath snarled and stalked toward Olebald. The old man was shaking his head when the big ice dragon breathed on him. A look of horror stiffened on his face as Frostybreath froze him as solid as an ice cube. The blue cloud imploded with a small *pop!* leaving the room too dark for a human to see. Fortunately, it wasn't too dark for dragons.

"I should have done that the last time," the big dragon said, sitting back on his haunches.

"You're a dragon!" breathed the little dragoness, staring at Audun.

He noticed that one of her front fangs was chipped. She reminded him of someone, but he just couldn't remember who. "Yes, I am," he said, still studying her face. "Thank you for coming to my rescue, but do I know you?"

The dragoness nodded and a moment later Jim stood in front of him, looking up at him with the same worshipful look that the dragoness had been giving him. Audun gasped and said, "Jim?"

"It's Gem, actually," she said, after turning back into a dragoness. "My parents raised me among humans. They were going to take me to the dragon stronghold in a few months. My big sister is already there, waiting for me.

When I was just a hatchling they taught me how to pass myself off as a human. They said I'd be safer if people thought I was a boy, so I started dressing like one when they brought me to Aridia."

"Why did they bring you here?" asked Audun.

"My parents were King Stormclaw's representatives to the king of Aridia. Ice dragons have mined the gems under the desert for centuries. We give some to the Aridian king and take the rest to the dragon stronghold. It's a big secret among the humans. My parents said that the king tells his son on his deathbed, but no one else is supposed to know. We were good at keeping secrets. King Cadmus and my father were friends, but even the king didn't know that my father was a dragon."

Frostybreath ruffled the crest on Gem's head with his talons. "What happened to your parents, little one?"

"Everyone knew my father was a gem merchant. Soldiers broke into our house, looking for the gems, but my father had hidden them all. The soldiers killed my parents when they couldn't find what they wanted. I hid until they left, then King Dolon's men found me and brought me to the castle with all the other orphans. When the king asked us for the names of our relatives, I told him that I didn't have any in Aridia, which was true, so he made me work as a servant. I didn't mind too much. It was better than being locked in the tower like the other orphans."

Audun nodded. If any girl didn't belong at the castle,

it was Gem. "Let me guess—you rolled in muck to mask your dragon scent, didn't you?"

"It was the only thing I could think of," she said. "My parents used a lotion to cover their scent. I didn't need it when I was young and now that I do I don't know where to get it."

"You're a very clever dragoness," said Frostybreath. "Your parents would be proud of you."

"And what about you?" Audun asked the bigger dragon. "You were the new guard, weren't you?"

"Figured that out, did you? I followed Olebald here after he escaped from the stronghold. I'm supposed to take him back with me so King Stormclaw and his council can pass judgment on him. He did some nasty things to a few dragons before he left and he's going to have to answer for that."

"Did you know that he was coming to Aridia?" asked Audun.

"Not until I got here, and then I was afraid he was coming after you."

"I met Jim my first day here, but I didn't know she was a girl," Audun said, before turning back to Gem. "May I accompany you to the dragon stronghold? You said that your sister was there, waiting for you. I bet she'll be happy to see you. What is her name? If I don't know her, I'm sure Frostybreath will."

"Her name is Loolee. She was my best friend before she left."

"I know Loolee!" Audun said. "She taught me how to slide down the ice chute. You'll like the ice chute. Frosty-breath made it so little dragonesses like you could have fun."

"Would you show me how to slide down it, Audun?"

"Of course," he replied, smiling. "And then I have something very important that I have to do."

Twenty-one

$\mathcal{A}$ wide grin stretched Audun's scaly lips when he finally spotted the royal castle of Greater Greensward from high in the sky. Although the castle wasn't as big as some of those he'd visited, it was by far the most beautiful. Green pennants streamed from the tops of the slender towers, and the white stone of the walls reminded him of home. Flowers grew in profusion along both sides of the road leading up to the drawbridge where guards kept watch over the people coming and going.

It had been more than three months since Audun had seen Millie. Although he'd planned to return to Greater Greensward sooner, Prince Owen had begged him to stay to help him and his father, Cadmus, regain the Aridian throne. Because of Aridia's ties to the ice dragons, Audun had felt obliged to help them in whatever way he could. Unfortunately, the short campaign they'd planned had lasted far longer than anyone anticipated and it had been many weeks before Audun was able to leave.

Through it all, Audun had spent hours thinking about Millie. Curled up under the stars trying to rest after yet another battle, Audun often lay awake, remembering how Millie had looked when he saw her last. She'd been so happy to see him when he first arrived, and later had looked as if her heart was being ripped apart when her mother whisked her away. Sometimes Audun tried to picture what she would look like when he finally saw her again; he was sure she'd be just as excited to see him as he'd be to see her. Yet now that the time was approaching, Audun was no longer quite so certain. They'd been apart for too many months. Could time have dimmed her memory of him? Or even worse, could she have met someone else?

No, he thought, bringing his wings down with extra force so that he shot toward the castle. After all he'd gone through, he wasn't going to let doubt mar their reunion. Millie was his one true love, his soul mate and the one with whom he wanted to spend the rest of his life. He knew deep down inside that she had to feel the same way. Now that he was back, he was going to do whatever it took to make sure nothing got in their way.

Audun circled over the courtyard looking for Millie, but the only humans in sight were the guards on the towers and some servants hustling from one building to the next. Folding his wings to his sides, Audun dove toward the pavement, pulling up short beside one of the outbuildings.

He was more concerned with landing where he wouldn't frighten the horses than he was in the humans who might be there, so he didn't notice a young man dressed in a cloth-of-gold-lined cape run down the steps, grab a spear from a nearby guard, and prepare to throw it.

Audun had barely set his feet on the ground when a voice shouted, "Don't worry, Princess! I'll save you!"

Audun's head snapped around just as the young man hurled the spear. After having spent so many days in battle in Aridia, the dragon sidestepped it easily.

"Beware, foul lizard," shouted the man, as he pulled his sword from its scabbard. "I, Prince Rudolfo, am about to slay you and rip your evil heart from your chest and—"

"Oh, for the love of fish!" Audun cursed. Although instinct told him to stand and fight, the last thing he wanted to do was hurt someone who might be a friend of Millie's. He wanted to make the best impression he could when he met her family again, and was sure they wouldn't take kindly to the sight of human blood on his talons.

A shadow moved in the open doorway, but before Audun could see who was there, the prince's sword came whistling through the air, and the dragon had to jump out of the way. Wondering if things had changed so drastically that dragons were no longer welcome in Greater Greensward, Audun turned and hid behind the outbuilding.

"Rudolfo!" shouted a familiar voice, but Audun was already changing and wasn't sure he'd heard correctly.

"Did you see that, Princess?" called the prince. "I sent the beast scurrying away with its tail between its legs! Wait here while I go finish it off."

"You'll do no such thing!" Millie shouted, as Audun came around the corner, now in his human form and dressed in the blue and white tunic that he'd chosen specially for their reunion. He looked up as Millie dashed down the stairs, saying, "If you've hurt him . . ." with a worried look on her face.

"Millie!" Audun said, reaching out his hand, but she ran right past him, stopping suddenly when she saw that there was nothing behind him between the back of the outbuilding and the castle wall.

"What happened to the dragon?" demanded the prince, who had also come running. He shot a glance at Audun and frowned. "Who are you?"

Audun nodded in Millie's direction. "I'm a friend of the princess's."

Millie gave him an odd look. "The dragon is gone. He must have flown off when we couldn't see him. But that's beside the point," she said, turning to glare at Rudolfo. "How dare you attack a dragon at my very door!"

"I was protecting you!" said the prince, falling to one knee before her. "I was going to slay him and lay his head at your feet and serve you his heart on a—"

Millie looked a little queasy as she shook her head. "That's enough, Rudolfo. I don't want to hear any more.

I don't need your help. I can take care of myself. As I said before, I appreciate your request for my hand, but we really aren't suited to each other. Please go before you embarrass us both."

"Embarrass!" said the prince, his brow creasing and his mouth turning down into a frown. He stood and gave her a stiff bow. "I have done nothing to embarrass myself. However, I do think it is time that I take my leave. Good-bye for now, Princess."

Both Millie and Audun watched Prince Rudolfo stalk to the horse that a stable hand had just brought out. They waited until he was riding under the portcullis and onto the drawbridge before turning to each other again. "All right," said Millie, "tell me what happened."

"I don't know what you—" Audun began.

"Don't act all innocent with me! Rudolfo may not have seen you change, but I could see it all from the top of the stairs. How is it that you're a human? Why didn't you tell me you could do this before? I can't believe you deceived me!"

"I didn't deceive you. I spent months learning how to—"

"There you are, Millie," said the older woman with the fading blond hair who had been so rude to Audun the last time they'd met.

Audun bowed to her, having remembered that this was Queen Chartreuse, one of Millie's grandmothers.

"So Prince Rudolfo has gone," she said. "I was hoping you had changed your mind, Millie. But I see another suitor has arrived. How delightful!" Leaning closer to her grand-daughter, she added in a loud whisper, "You've already rejected most of the eligible princes in the known king-doms. Try hard not to chase this one away as well!" Smiling a little too brightly at Millie, the queen nodded to Audun. "Welcome to Greater Greensward. May your stay be a pleasant one."

Millie frowned at Audun as her grandmother climbed the stairs. "I suppose I'll have to let you in now, although don't think I'm happy to see you. I hate being lied to, espe-cially by someone I trusted."

"But that's just it," said Audun. "I've never lied to you and I never would! If you'd only let me explain—"

"Explain what?" asked Emma, Millie's mother, coming down the stairs. "I just saw my mother and she said Millie had a new suitor. Who are you, anyway?" she asked, eyeing Audun with suspicion. "I feel as if we've met before."

"This is Audun," said Millie.

"But I thought Audun was a dragon."

"Exactly!" said Millie, her eyes flashing. "Apparently he had hidden talents that he didn't bother to tell me about. I can't believe I was so gullible!"

Confused, Audun watched as Millie turned on her heels and stalked up the stairs, leaving him alone with her mother.

"Would you mind telling me what is going on?" Emma asked.

"I'm not sure I know, but I'll tell you what I can, Your Highness," said Audun, bowing. "The last time we met, I was a dragon. After I left here, I went to see King Storm-claw, as you know. Thank you for going to see him, by the way. I think your visit helped him decide to let me court Millie. Anyway, I asked the king and his council to teach me how to turn myself into a human. They did, after I performed several difficult tasks for them. I came back to see Millie as soon as I could."

"You mean you couldn't change into a human before?" asked Emma.

Audun sighed. "Don't you think I would have if I could have?"

"Then why didn't you tell Millie?"

"I was trying to! I wanted to come back sooner, but I had to help the king, and then they needed me in Aridia."

"I see," said Emma. "Millie was upset when you didn't come sooner. She was afraid you'd forgotten all about her. Explain to her what you've been doing and I'm sure she'll understand . . . eventually. It may take a while for her to calm down, though. She can be awfully stubborn at times."

"I know," said Audun, "but then, so can I."

Twenty-two

A udun wasn't nearly as confident when he woke the next day. All the previous afternoon and evening he had tried to explain what had happened, but each time he broached the topic Millie had invited someone to join their conversation or remembered a suddenly important errand that she had to see to right then. They hadn't been alone for a minute, and after a big, formal supper, Millie had slipped off to bed without even saying good night. He'd found it frustrating, but he had no intention of telling her all he wanted to say where anyone else could hear him.

Audun had spent much of the night trying to think of something he could do to get Millie to talk to him in private. He had a few ideas, but nothing he really liked, so he was still pondering the problem when he stepped through the door of the chamber where he'd slept. A page carrying a knight's sword and helmet almost knocked him over.

"What's the hurry, child?" Audun asked, as he helped the boy collect the gauntlet that he'd dropped.

"Haven't you heard?" asked the boy. "An army is advancing on the castle. The knights are preparing to defend it. They'd already lowered the drawbridge this morning, so they had to raise it in a hurry when soldiers appeared out of nowhere."

A passing serving man carrying a knife and an old-fashioned helmet stopped long enough to say, "The call has gone out for all able-bodied men. We're to bring whatever weapons and armor we have and meet in the courtyard. With the Green Witch protecting the kingdom they probably won't need us, but they're having us get ready just in case."

"Whose army is it?" asked Audun.

The boy shrugged, but the man smiled wryly and said, "Some fool who thinks he can best the Green Witch with an ordinary fighting force. You'd think everyone would know better, considering our Princess Emma's reputation."

Audun nodded as the boy and the man went on their way. Even in far-off Aridia, Audun had heard rumors about the might of Princess Emma and the fire-breathing dragons that defended Greater Greensward. He'd never once mentioned that he'd met her or that she was the mother of his one true love. From everything he'd heard, anyone who would attack Greater Greensward would have to either be crazy or think he had some very special advantage that would allow him to defeat dragons and the magic of the Green Witch. If the latter were true, it was possible that the Green Witch might just need Audun's help, even if he couldn't breathe fire. Besides, with the alliance agreement between the Green Witch and King Stormclaw signed and sealed, he felt duty-bound to help her just as he had helped Prince Owen in Aridia.

Audun learned from a passing servant girl that Princess Emma had a tower of her own. He ran up the stairs, hoping Emma hadn't already left the castle, and didn't stop until he reached the door at the top. Hearing voices inside, he knocked and was relieved when someone called out for him to come in.

Although the room was fairly large, the end near the door seemed crowded. Millie and Emma were seated on a bench by the window while two men stood only an arm's reach away. Audun had met the men at supper the night before. The younger one had curly brown hair and a pleasant face. He was Prince Eadric, Millie's father and the crown prince of Upper Montevista, the northern kingdom where Audun had encountered the witches Klorine and Ratinki. The older man was King Limelyn, Emma's father and the ruler of Greater Greensward. His hair was graying and his skin was lined from years of worry, but he still had the commanding presence of a king who had seen many battles. Audun had liked both Prince Eadric and King Limelyn right away and had had the feeling that they liked him as well. Right now, however, they scarcely glanced at

Audun before turning back to examine a ball made of crystal that Millie's mother held cupped in her hands.

Audun ducked as a brightly colored bird the size of a chicken with long, trailing feathers and a curved beak swooped past his head to land on the table on the other side of the room. "Lover boy is here!" screeched the bird in a grating voice. "It's Millie's next suitor, come to spy on her and learn all her secrets! He wants to know why none of her other suitors have—"

"Be quiet, You-too," snapped Millie. "I don't have any secrets from Audun."

"Really?" said the bird. "Does he know that you—"

"I don't know why you keep this bird around, Emma," King Limelyn said, making a grab for You-too, who lurched off the table and fluttered out of reach.

Emma shrugged. "He was a wedding gift to Eadric and me."

"I'd say he was more of a curse," said her father.

"Look, that must be the one in charge," Emma said, pointing at something in the ball that Audun couldn't see from where he was standing.

Millie bent closer to the crystal ball. "Can you see his face?" she asked, frowning in concentration.

"Give it a moment," said Emma.

"There, he's turning this way," Eadric said, "and it's . . ."

"Prince Rudolfo!" they all exclaimed in unison.

"He must have had his soldiers waiting for him on the other side of the border," King Limelyn said. "And went to fetch them when Millie turned him down."

"I told you I didn't like him," muttered You-too. "He had shifty eyes."

"You never said any such thing!" Millie said.

The bird shuffled sideways on the back of the chair where he had perched. "Yes, I did. You just didn't hear me!"

Emma shook her head. "I wish I had seen those men sooner. The first thing I do every morning is check our borders with this," she said, tapping the farseeing ball, "but I didn't see anything out of the ordinary today. I can't believe so many men made it all the way through the forest before anyone noticed them. If we hadn't heard their horses we wouldn't have known they were here until it was too late. Even then I had to cast a spell to make them visible. They must have a magic user of their own, but I can't seem to find him."

"My friend Frostybreath froze Olebald, but the wizard was able to use his magic to escape after he'd thawed just a little," said Audun. "He fled into the desert, where he gathered a group of soldiers and used a spell to hide them right beneath our noses by changing the color of their skin and clothes to match the colors of their surroundings."

Millie gave him a quizzical look. "How did you see the soldiers to fight them?"

"We didn't, at least not at first. But I sent a small puff of poison gas their way. Smaller doses of an ice dragon's poison gas makes humans ill without doing permanent harm. Soldiers who are violently sick to their stomachs aren't effective fighters."

"Poison gas?" screeched You-too. "I thought there was something odd about you. There," he said, turning to Millie. "Did I say it loudly enough for you this time?"

Eadric strode to the window and looked out. "Rudolfo's men are drawing closer to the moat. I don't think they've spotted your moat monster yet, Emma."

"Do you see anyone who might be a magic user?" asked Millie.

"Not from here," her father said, craning his neck.

"I'll try again," said Emma, turning back to the ball. Audun noticed for the first time that it was attached to a gold chain that she wore around her neck. He took a step closer, taking the place of Prince Eadric, who was still looking out the window. Audun could just make out a swirling light before the Green Witch touched the ball and the light disappeared. Even with his dragon hearing, he couldn't make out what she said as she whispered under her breath and tapped the ball again. A faint image appeared. It blurred and shifted and looked like it was about to become a face when it dissolved in a blue fog. Suddenly, the ball went blank.

Emma shook the farseeing ball, but nothing happened.

"There must be a magic user out there, but I can't tell you who it is. Whoever it is has done something to my farseeing ball. It's not working anymore."

"I need more information," said her father.

Emma nodded. "I could turn myself into a bird and go look for the magic user. It would be easy to gather information without anyone noticing."

"Just as easy as it would be for a magic user to find you, or for an archer to shoot you down," said her father. "No, there has to be another way."

"I'll go through the secret tunnel to look around," said Eadric. "I'm glad we put it in. I knew it would come in handy someday."

"What secret tunnel?" squawked You-too.

"You think we'd tell you?" Eadric asked. "You have the biggest beak in the kingdom."

"I'll go with you, Eadric," Emma said. "Just give me a moment while I change."

Audun glanced at the door. "Perhaps I should leave."

"Why?" said Millie. "She's not going to change her clothes."

"While you see what you can learn outside the wall, I'll go to the parapet," King Limelyn said. "Perhaps I'll be able to find out what Rudolfo wants."

A pale, green light had begun to shimmer around Emma, but it faded away when her father said he was leaving. "I need to renew your protection spell if you're going outside," she said, taking her father's hand in hers. "I know I put one on you just a few months ago, but they don't generally last very long. This should do the job."

> Keep him safe from point or blade,
> From all that's magic or man-made.
> Deflect their aim, repel their blows,
> Let him be well where'er he goes.

Bright green sparkles dusted the air around the king, melting on his head and shoulders as if they were tiny, colored snowflakes. King Limelyn smiled and patted her hand. "You're a good daughter, Emma."

Audun watched as she kissed the king on the cheek, something that made them both smile. The young dragon was surprised by the feelings the sight of such a simple sign of affection stirred inside him. Millie had kissed him twice before, once as she was about to enter the Blue Witch's castle, and again when she was leaving the mountain range. They were the only kisses he'd ever received and they'd given him a warm feeling inside, which was unusual for an ice dragon.

"Emma, perhaps you should change in the dungeon," Eadric suggested. "You always complain that the stairwell is too small when you're a dragon."

"Good thinking," Emma replied. Something heavy hit

an exterior wall, making the castle shake. "We'd better go. It sounds as if someone is trying to get our attention."

Emma and Eadric were already out the door when Millie started after them saying, "I'm going, too. I'm sure you'll need my help."

"Not so fast, Millie," said King Limelyn. "I want to ask your young man about the poison gas he mentioned."

"Yeah," said You-too. "Do you have it in a bottle, or do you make it yourself? And if you make it, does it come out your mouth or your—"

"That's enough from you!" declared the king. In two strides he crossed the room, snatched up the bird, tossed him into Emma's storage room, and slammed the door. Turning to Audun he gave him an apologetic smile and said, "I understand you have the same ability as my daughter and granddaughter."

"That's true, sir, although I breathe poison gas instead of fire."

"Ah," said the king. "And that's because you become an ice dragon."

"Actually, sir, I'm an ice dragon who can become a human. After I last saw Millie, I spent my time earning the right to learn how to make the change."

Millie inhaled sharply, but Audun kept his eyes on her grandfather.

King Limelyn rubbed his chin and looked at Audun

speculatively. "I didn't know that such a thing was possible. Either way, we can use a man like you in the family."

"Grandfather!" exclaimed Millie. "He hasn't even asked me yet!"

"You go with Millie and keep her safe," the king told Audun. "She's very dear to me."

"To me as well," Audun replied, turning his gaze to Millie.

Twenty-three

Millie and Audun accompanied King Limelyn down the tower stairs, separating when the king headed for the parapet while they descended the stairs to the dungeon. "Did you tell my grandfather the truth?" Millie asked. "Did you have to earn the right to learn how to become a human?"

"Of course it's true. Dragons don't lie!" Audun said.

"And you did it for me?" asked Millie.

Audun nodded. "Your grandmother made it clear that we couldn't be together as long as I was a dragon. Since you'd become the most important person in my life, I had to find a way to be with you."

"You really feel that way?" Millie breathed.

"Dragons don't—"

"Lie. I know. You already told me."

"When your mother told King Stormclaw that you were pining for me, I knew that you truly did feel the same way about me that I feel about you. I meant to come to you sooner, but I had to perform tasks for the ice dragon king, and then there was the war in Aridia . . ."

"So you came as soon as you could. I believe you, Audun." Giving him a smile that made his heart miss a beat, Millie took Audun's hand in hers and led him down the last of the stairs.

They had just reached the dungeon when Audun heard voices up ahead. Two of them sounded like Emma and Eadric, but the others were too faint to make out. As they walked deeper into the gloom broken only by the light of flickering torches, the voices grew louder. Millie smiled. "You're about to meet my great-grandparents. I can hear my parents talking to them."

"Why didn't I meet them last night when I met everyone else?" asked Audun.

"They rarely leave the dungeon. You see," she said, as they turned a corner and saw two hazy figures facing Emma and Eadric, "they're ghosts."

"I didn't know ghosts were real," breathed Audun. "I've never seen one before." He peered at the figures, trying to see them better in the dim light, but their wavery forms seemed to fade away at the edges as he and Millie approached. The ghosts were gone altogether by the time the two young people stood before Emma and Eadric.

Sometime after leaving the tower, Eadric had acquired a sword and tarnished armor, which Emma was now helping him put on. "Wasn't this Great-grandfather's?" Millie asked, running her finger over the scabbard leaning against the wall.

Emma nodded as she helped her husband pull up one of the jointed metal gloves. "Grandfather insisted that Eadric use it. My grandmother put so many protection spells on it over the years that some of them became permanent and now it's virtually impenetrable. There, that ought to do it," she said, setting the helmet on Eadric's head.

"You forgot one thing," said Eadric. Lifting the visor, he gently touched her chin with one hand and raised her face so that he could give her a tender kiss on the lips. Emma ignored the hard metal encasing his body and wrapped her arms around him, deepening the kiss. When she stepped back a moment later, Audun saw the way they looked at each other, as if nothing else in the world mattered at that moment. He wondered what it would be like to kiss someone on the lips—something most dragons would find distasteful.

"We need to go," Emma said softly, as the air began to shimmer around her. A heartbeat later a lovely green female dragon swung her tail out of the way and started down the corridor behind a knight in not-quite-shining armor.

"We should change now, too," Millie told Audun, as she stepped back to give him room.

It had never occurred to Audun that he would have to

change in front of Millie, at least not quite so soon. Not knowing how he looked when he did it, he was reluctant at first, but when she gave him a brilliant smile and started her own change into dragon form, he began his change as well. Although he had changed back and forth many times over the last few months, this time he was left feeling breathless and exhilarated. He was gazing at Millie when she glanced toward the ceiling and he became aware of the sounds coming from above. Fighting had started in earnest.

"The tunnel is this way," Millie said, hurrying in the direction her parents had gone. The corridor that had seemed wide just moments before now seemed cramped with two dragons in it. He could hear Millie's scales scraping the wall each time she bumped it and knew that it wasn't any more comfortable for her than it was for him.

When they reached what appeared to be the end of the corridor, Millie reached out and deftly pulled one of the blocks in the wall out part of the way. Audun heard a groaning sound before he saw that the wall had actually begun to move. Millie backed into him as the wall swung out, revealing a dank, lightless space. Although Audun couldn't see anything past the opening in the wall, he noticed that Millie ducked and lowered her tail before stepping into the tunnel.

"Hurry," Millie said, her voice loud in the confined space. "The door doesn't stay open for long."

Audun grunted and began to walk faster, but he was only partway through when he heard the door groaning shut. Not wanting to lose his tail, he pulled it as close to his body as he could and scurried forward until he finally bumped into Millie.

"We're almost there," Millie said. "See that light up ahead?"

Audun couldn't see anything with her body blocking the light, but he could smell fresh air and felt a hint of a breeze when he raised his head. With the next step he bumped his crest on a dangling root, and dirt showered around him. Audun jerked his head down, and was still walking hunched over when Millie pushed aside the canopy of leaves that hid the tunnel and they emerged into bright sunlight.

"Where are your parents?" Audun asked, blinking as his eyes adjusted to the light.

"Up there." Millie pointed to where a knight sat astride a flying green dragon as easily as he might a horse.

Stepping out from under the branches of the overhanging tree, Millie and Audun took to the sky. Once above the tops of the trees, Audun could see for miles and easily spotted the soldiers surrounding the castle. He saw King Limelyn as well, standing on the parapet above the drawbridge, looking down at the group of men clustered on the other side of the moat.

"Your demands are unreasonable!" shouted the king. "I'm not giving up my granddaughter or my castle."

"Be sensible! I'll let you and your queen depart unharmed if you lower your drawbridge now."

"Why should we go when we're perfectly happy where we are?" answered the king.

"Then you leave me no choice!" Prince Rudolfo shouted back.

At a gesture from the prince, the men who had been standing beside the moat opened sacks that they had hauled across the fields and began dumping rocks into the water. "What are they doing?" Audun asked Millie, who was flying only a wing tip away.

"They're trying to fill in the moat so they can use that," she said, gesturing to the tall wooden structure that another group of men were hauling out from under a copse of sheltering trees. "It's called a siege tower. They hope to push it up to the castle wall and climb onto the parapet."

"Shouldn't we stop them?" asked Audun. "You or your mother could burn that down with one puff of flame."

"The magic user has probably made it flameproof. But that won't make any difference," Millie replied. "Watch."

Audun glanced back just as two men shoved an extra-large rock into the moat and water shot up in a geyser. When the geyser failed to die down, the young dragon watched more closely. A tentacle rose from the center of the waterspout. It reached toward the edge of the moat, forcing the soldiers to back away. Two of the men weren't quick enough: the tentacle slapped the ground beside them and knocked them into the moat where they flailed about, struggling to reach the edge. The rock that they had just dumped in shot out of the water, hitting the siege tower with a thunderous *boom!* Soon the other rocks were hurtling out in a steady stream, demolishing the siege tower and chasing the soldiers across the fields and down the road.

The two soldiers still hadn't dragged themselves from the water when the last rock hit the ground and bounced across the field. Suddenly, the tentacle plucked the men from the moat and sent them screaming through the air only to land halfway across the field in a stack of freshly baled hay. Whimpering, they scrambled out of the hay and limped as fast as they could across the field.

At first, when Audun saw the prince riding away, he thought that Rudolfo had given up, but then more soldiers came out of the woods carrying bows and full quivers. The archers had assembled only a short distance from the castle when the prince gave a signal and they opened fire, raining arrows down on the parapet where King Limelyn was retreating into the shelter of one of the castle towers. Seeing the approaching cloud of arrows, the soldiers around the king held up their shields to protect him, but Emma's spell was already working. Although the arrows rushed at them with frightening speed like a cloud of deadly hornets, when they were a dozen yards from the king, they bounced suddenly as if hitting stone and fell to the ground, broken and useless.

"Now what?" Audun asked, as the archers reached for more arrows.

"Since they're being so persistent, Mother will probably want to chase them off. See, I was right. There she goes now."

Audun glanced up to see Emma come roaring out of the sky with Eadric bent low across her back, his sword in his hand. With an answering roar, Millie joined them as they plummeted toward the now-scattering soldiers, who were running before even a hint of flame left the dragons' mouths. Prince Rudolfo had already disappeared into the forest.

Audun was tempted to fly with Millie and her parents, but they didn't seem to need his help. He was circling overhead, watching the fleeing soldiers, when he noticed one figure heading in a different direction. Instead of running away from the castle, he was moving furtively around the side, stopping every now and then as if to see if he was being watched. The figure was already close to the entrance to the secret tunnel. Audun was about to follow him to see what he was up to when a dark shadow blotted out the sun. Even before he raised his head, Audun knew what was up there. Only one thing could cast a shadow big enough to darken an area that size. A roc had come to Greater Greensward.

Cupping the air with its wings, the great bird screamed as it approached the castle. The soldiers who hadn't already run away did so now, shedding heavy armor as they tried to outrun their friends. The roc wasn't after them, however. Bellowing so loudly that it hurt Audun's ears, the bird landed on the top of Emma's tower and began to rip at the roof with its massive beak. The tower sagged under the weight of the roc even as chunks of the roof fell into the courtyard below.

A green dragon swooped out of the sky, exhaling long tongues of flame at the roc. Eadric swung his sword and hacked at the bird as Emma flew past. They turned and were heading back for a second run when Millie joined them. As Emma and Eadric flew past the roc once again, Audun dipped his wing and headed back to the castle, arriving in time to breathe his poison gas into Millie's flame, making the air around the roc explode. Its feathers singed, the bird screamed and raised its head to lash at them with its beak. Millie and Audun dodged the blow and flew safely away.

On her next pass, Emma swung around to the other side of the bird. She had just started to exhale her flame when the bird turned and, with a powerful swipe of its head, knocked Emma and Eadric tumbling through the sky. Millie screamed and flew after them with Audun close behind. He was nearly even with Millie when Eadric fell from Emma's back. While Emma fought to right herself and Millie struggled to reach her father before he hit the ground, Audun pulled his wings to his sides and dove. Pulling up just below Eadric, he positioned himself so that he could lash out with his tail to catch the falling prince. With his tail securely wrapped around Eadric, he landed on the ground and gently laid the limp man on the grass.

Both Millie and Emma were there an instant later, their concern for Eadric plain on their faces. While Millie crouched by her father's side, Emma changed back into a human. Kneeling next to her husband, she placed her fingers on his throat. "He's alive," she breathed.

"Of course I'm alive," Eadric groaned, his eyes fluttering open. "I just had the wind knocked out of me, that's all."

Audun thought the prince might have protested when his wife fell on him and covered his face with kisses, but instead Eadric reached up with both hands and held her still so that he could kiss her.

"Your father is fine," Audun said, glancing at the young dragoness.

Millie smiled. "I can see that." Raising her eyes to the roc, she added, "But that overgrown crow isn't going to be if I can help it."

She was stretching her wings, preparing to leap into the sky when Audun barked, "No! You can't take on a roc all alone. You'll just get yourself killed if you try. If I thought I could get them here in time, I'd try to get ice dragons to

267

help, but it would take a dozen dragons to challenge a roc and even then they probably wouldn't win. There must be a reason the roc is here and behaving that way," he said, gesturing to the bird that was clawing at the stones of the tower walls. Another huge piece broke away, making a tremendous racket as it crashed to the ground below.

"And how would we ever find out why that stupid bird does anything?" Millie asked. "You're not proposing that we go ask it, are you?"

"Not at all, but there might be someone we can ask. Let's see if we can find him." Spreading their wings, the dragon and the dragoness took to the air and circled once above the castle while Audun told Millie about the figure he'd seen sneaking toward the entrance to the tunnel. Together they landed beside the concealing tree and peered under the branches. There was no one in sight, so Audun pushed aside the leaves and entered the tunnel, not wanting Millie to be the first to confront whoever might be inside.

It took Audun a few minutes to find the block that opened the door. Even as the stone door groaned open, he could hear a man talking nearby. "Shh!" he whispered to Millie when she started to speak. "I recognize that voice."

Moving as silently as a dragon could in a stone-walled corridor, Audun and Millie crept toward the sound. Rounding the corner, they saw a man outlined in torchlight. He wasn't very tall in his long, flowing robes and his back was curved with age, but it was his distinctively shiny scalp that affirmed Audun's first guess. Olebald Wizard was standing with his back to them, trying to get past the ghosts who blocked his way down the corridor.

"I don't know why you keep trying, you old coot," said a wild-haired ghost dressed in rags. He brandished a long chain with manacles attached to the end. Judging by the grating sound they made on the floor, they were far more substantial than the ghost. "My friend and I aren't letting you by, no matter how much you wheedle and whine."

"Quite right, Hubert," a well-dressed ghost pointing a rapier declared. "Imagine, thinking he can sneak in here and infiltrate our castle right under our noses. As if we wouldn't notice a buffoon sneaking around with a sack of rocks. We're not letting you go anywhere until someone in authority . . . Ah, here are Millie and her friend now. We found this scalawag sneaking into the castle. What would you like us to do with him?"

Olebald turned with a start and noticed Audun for the first time. "It's you," he said. "Well, you're too late. This castle is going to be destroyed and you can't do a thing about it."

"Is that so?" said Audun. He leaned toward the old wizard and exhaled a small puff of poison gas directly at his face. Olebald coughed and swallowed hard. Even in the wavering light of the torches, Audun could see the old man's face turn pale. The dragon stepped back as Olebald lost his breakfast onto the floor. The wizard looked awful as he straightened up and gave Audun a baleful glare.

"The next time I breathe on you like that, you won't be able to stand up again," Audun warned him, his voice a deep growl. "Now, tell me, how did you lure that roc here?"

Olebald tried to laugh, but the effort made his face green. Even so, he gave Audun a defiant look and kept his lips pressed tightly closed.

Audun shrugged. "It's your decision," the dragon said, taking a deep breath.

"No, wait!" Olebald rushed to say. "I made the roc think its baby had been stolen and locked away in that tower. It won't stop until it's torn apart the entire castle looking for its chick."

"Very clever," Emma said, as she and Eadric squeezed past Millie. "So this is how you'll get your revenge for the day I sent you to that island."

Olebald smirked. "This isn't about you—at least, not entirely. I wouldn't even have thought of coming here if I hadn't heard that the ice dragon was in love with your daughter. Just because King Stormclaw kept me frozen in his stronghold after I followed you from the magic market-place didn't mean I couldn't hear everything said around me. Those dragon guards were terrible gossips, but they couldn't keep me locked away forever. After I escaped and learned that Audun had helped the old king run my protégé out of Aridia, I couldn't resist coming back here and killing two dragons with one sack of stones, so to speak.

"I'm sure you recognize these, Audun," the old wizard said, kicking the sack that rested beside him so that a pile of green stones tumbled out. "But you wouldn't, would you, Emma? I had Rudolfo scatter stones like these throughout your castle while he was here pretending to court your lovely Millie. When I saw all of you come out of that hidden entrance, I couldn't resist bringing in more stones." Turning to Emma and Eadric, Olebald grinned. "You never did figure out that Rudolfo is Prince Jorge's nephew. The entire royal family of East Aridia hates you for defeating us when we invaded Greater Greensward and for making Jorge marry the troll queen."

There was another loud crash and the castle shook so that dust filtered down around their heads.

Olebald Wizard chortled. "That roc will have your entire castle down around your ears, and the stones Rudolfo planted will keep you from doing anything about it!"

Emma gave Audun an inquiring look.

"I don't know what the stones are exactly," he told her. "I just know that they keep magic from working in their presence."

"He may have planted some," said Emma, "but he

couldn't have put them everywhere. No one can get in my tower rooms when I'm not there."

"And that protection spell you put on Grandfather worked just fine," said Millie.

"Rudolfo couldn't have put them down here, either," Emma added. "Or you wouldn't be trying to do it now, old man."

"He tried to shove a stone in a crack in the wall, but Hubert and I stopped him and made him put it back in his bag. We've been watching him every minute," said the well-dressed ghost.

"In that case, I can take care of them right now," said Audun. Snagging the sack with one talon, he shuffled backward down the narrow corridor, turning when he reached the corner. He was back a minute later without the sack.

Everyone looked up as another chunk of the tower came crashing down.

"That roc isn't going to give up until it finds its baby," said Audun. "And since there is no baby to find . . ."

"We have to do something!" said Millie. "Mother, do you have a spell that could turn it into something else? A butterfly, perhaps, or a hummingbird?"

Olebald's eyes were bright with glee when he said, "Regular magic won't do anything to a roc. Even if she could change the bird, it could just become something worse."

"I'm afraid he's right," said Emma. "I tried to change a troll once. All I did was make him odder looking and give him a love of cheese."

"Then I say we should give the roc exactly what it wants," said Audun. "I know where there's a roc nest and there were chicks in it the last time I looked. For all I know, this might even be the parent of those very same chicks. We could go get one of those babies and bring it back here. The problem is that the nest is days away."

"My magic can take care of that," said Emma. "I can get us there in an instant, as long as you can give me a good description of the nest and the area around it."

"That won't be a problem," Audun said, remembering the distinctive stone formations that surrounded the nest.

"I'll have to go with you to bring you back," Emma added.

"I'll go, too," said Millie. "You might need my help."

"And mine," said Eadric.

"No!" protested his wife. "You're staying here. You've already fallen off my back once today."

"I wouldn't bother going if I were you," Olebald said, looking smug. "Magic won't do you a bit of good once you get there."

"You know, old man," Emma said, turning on the wizard with her eyes flashing, "I'm sick and tired of you and your pronouncements. I think you need to leave, and this time I want your banishment more permanent. Let me see . . . How did that spell start? Ah, yes . . ."

> Go to the isle of sun-warmed sand
> Where I sent you once before.
> Stay there 'til your life is spent
> On that far and distant shore.

"Not again!" wailed Olebald, as a tiny whirlwind rose beneath his feet. "I hate getting sand in my clothes! And I think I'm allergic to shellfish! Don't do this to me . . ." The old man's voice trailed off as the swirling wind engulfed him and carried him down the corridor and out of sight.

"And now," said Emma. "About that nest . . ."

❧

Not knowing what they would encounter at the roc's nest, Emma turned back into a dragon before saying the spell that would carry them to Aridia. Audun's description of the nest and the stone formations around it were very complete, so it didn't take her long to find it. Her magic took them to a spot just above the nest so that they were looking down on it from the sky. Even at a distance, the two chicks looked enormous. Seeing that neither of the adult rocs was present, Audun and Emma decided to take the chance and assume that the roc destroying the castle was one of the parents.

"So," said Emma, eyeing the two chicks, "which one should we take?"

"They're both so big," breathed Millie.

Audun shook his head. The last time he had seen these babies they had been the size of large horses; they were now the size of full-grown male dragons. Even Emma, the oldest dragon there, was smaller than either of the chicks. "We should take that one," he said, pointing to the smaller of the two.

"Audun and I can distract the other chick while you take that one back, Mother," said Millie.

"I shouldn't be long," said Emma. "I already know what I'm going to say."

While Emma descended to the edge of the nest closest to the smallest chick, Audun and Millie began harrying the larger of the two babies. Millie dove past and the baby snapped at her with its wicked-looking beak, but didn't come anywhere near her. It was ready, however, when Audun flew close, because it hopped into the air three times higher than he would have thought possible and almost caught him. After that, Millie and Audun were more cautious and tried to keep its attention from a distance.

"Is everything all right?" Audun called to Emma when more than enough time had passed for her to have taken the baby back.

"No, it's not," she replied, sounding exasperated. "My

magic isn't working. I've tried and tried, but I can't move this bird."

"I was afraid of that," said Audun. "You heard what Olebald said about magic not working here? He probably planted some of those stones in this nest."

"You mean like that one?" Millie asked, pointing at a stone buried so deep among the intertwined branches that it would have been impossible to remove.

"And those," Emma said, gesturing toward a scattering of smaller stones in the bottom of the nest.

Seeing how many stones there were, Audun wondered why he hadn't noticed them before, even if he had been kept occupied with the baby bird. "We won't be able to move the chick with magic, at least not from the nest. We'll have to get it far enough away from here that your magic will work again, Emma."

"It looks awfully heavy," said Millie.

"I'm sure it is, but we can lift it if we all work together. I've done something like this before," he said, failing to tell them that that time it had been in water.

Pulling out some of the enormous vines that held the nest together wasn't easy. It was even harder to tether the larger chick to the opposite side of the nest to keep it away while they wrapped more vines around the smaller of the birds, pinning its wings to its sides and securing its lethal beak and talons. Once the baby roc was trussed up like a chicken, Audun took a loop of vines in his own talons and beat his wings, struggling to lift the chick high enough that Millie and Emma could get underneath. With the two dragonesses pushing from below, they were able to raise the bird to one of the neighboring pinnacles, where it struggled to get free while they caught their breath.

"Where are you going . . . to put the baby?" Millie asked her mother.

"The base of . . . the tower," Emma replied. "If it's still there."

Audun held his breath as once again Emma tried to take the chick back with her magic, exhaling loudly when both dragon and chick disappeared. He'd scarcely had time to wonder if he and Millie would have to fly back when Emma reappeared and touched her wings to theirs and then all three of them were perched on the parapet where King Limelyn had been standing only hours—or was it minutes—before.

"Look!" Millie said, gazing down at the rubble where the tower had stood for hundreds of years. After screaming her rage for so long, the mother bird's cry was a hoarse bleat, but even those unused to the sound of a roc's voice could tell when it changed from anguish to delight. Peering down through a gap in the floor below her, the roc cooed to her chick, ripped up the floor with her beak, and plucked the hefty youngster into the air with her massive talons. Screaming in triumph, the enormous bird beat her wings and rose into the clouds, heading west toward Aridia.

Although most of the castle's inhabitants had fled into the surrounding fields and forest as the roc demolished the tower, they returned now, singly and in groups, laughing aloud in their relief that the attack was over. "Do you see your father or your grandparents?" Emma asked, looking worried.

The three dragons sat side by side, watching for members of the royal family. Audun was turned around when he heard a small sound behind him. Something moved beneath a patch of crushed stone, which shuddered and fell in a small avalanche down the side of the wreckage. A moment later, You-too emerged, fluffing his feathers and preening with his beak.

Noting the dragons perched on the parapet, You-too flew up to join them. "Look at you three, sitting up here like you own the place! Well, I guess you do, sort of. I could have used your help, though! I was locked in this little, bitty room while a horrible monster tore it down around me! I'm going to have nightmares for weeks!"

"It wasn't a monster," said Millie. "It was a roc."

"That thing was a bird?" You-too said, sounding incredulous. "I knew rocs were big, but, wow! Say, you know what this means, don't you? Your father was wrong when he said that I have the biggest beak in the castle. Speaking of your father, isn't that him now?"

Everyone turned as Eadric emerged through the castle door. With a whoop of glee, Emma spread her wings and swooped down to join him, turning into a human again even as her feet hit the ground. She stumbled and almost fell, but her husband caught her, wrapping her in an embrace that looked as if it would never end. When Emma raised her face and Eadric began to kiss her, You-too turned away in disgust. "Ick!" he said. "I can't watch this!"

Audun didn't notice the bird fly away; he was too busy looking at Millie. "Your parents do seem to kiss a lot."

Millie shrugged. "They've always been like that. I guess they do it because they love each other so much."

"Do all married humans kiss like that?"

"No," said Millie. "My grandmother and grandfather hardly ever kiss. But then, they don't talk to each other much, either."

"When we're married, we'll kiss all the time, too," Audun announced.

"Is that your way of asking me to marry you?"

"Only if you'll say yes."

"Well, then, here's my answer," Millie replied. Sidling closer so that her scales touched his, Millie, the fire-breathing dragon, kissed Audun, the ice dragon, full on the lips. And he liked it.

Princess Millie is about to get her happily-ever-after—right?

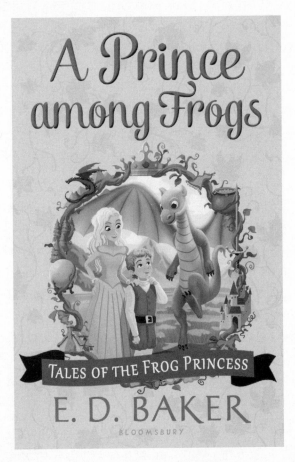

Read on for an excerpt from **A Prince among Frogs**, the eighth book in E. D. Baker's delightful Tales of the Frog Princess series.

illie leaned back against the dragon's side, enjoying the coolness of his bluish white scales on the hot summer day. The dragon, Audun, was curled around her with his head resting on the grass near her feet while Felix, her baby brother, lay on the blanket beside her, cooing at the tip of the dragon's tail that dangled over his head. Millie glanced down when the baby batted at the tail with his chubby hands.

"As far as I'm concerned, the smaller the wedding the better," she said to Audun as she reached out to stroke the baby's red gold curls. "I want it to be intimate, with just us and our immediate families."

"Don't you want our friends there, too?" Audun asked.

"Well, yes, of course, at least our closest friends, like Zoë and her parents and Ralf and his parents and your friends Frostybreath and—"

"Do you see what I mean? It's going to be nearly impossible to have a small wedding. I don't have a lot of relatives, but I do have lots of friends I want to invite."

"Speaking of relatives," said Millie, "I'm not sure what to do about my father's side of the family. My uncle, Bradston, is all right, but I've told you how much my grandparents hate dragons. They can't even accept the fact that *I* turn into a dragon. I can only imagine what they'll say when I tell them about you!"

"Millie!" called her mother, Emma, from where she was kneeling in the garden, supervising the weeds that were pulling themselves out of the ground. "Don't let the baby put that thing in his mouth! You have no idea where it's been. No offense, Audun."

"None taken," the dragon replied, moving his tail out of the baby's reach. Felix began to fuss, so Audun pulled a golden chain from around his neck and held the dangling amulet over the baby. "Here, you can play with this instead." The ice dragon council had given the amulet to Audun to allow him to breathe underwater, and the rolling waves that decorated it soon caught the baby's eye.

Millie's great-aunt, Grassina, sat back on her heels and wiped the perspiration from her forehead. "When we finish this, I'm going to add a new section to the garden. I want to have plenty of fresh flowers for the wedding," she said, smiling at Millie.

"We have to invite all the dragons who helped us, too, you know," Audun said, nudging Millie's foot with his chin.

Millie turned her head to watch Grassina gesture, making a strip of ground crumble until it was well worked and ready for seeds. The seeds flew from the witch's hand, burrowing into the soil. Another gesture, and a dozen willow wands pushed into the soil beside the seeds and wove themselves into a delicate fence.

"Like who?" Millie asked Audun.

"King Stormclaw, for one. If he hadn't given us permission to marry, we wouldn't be having this discussion."

"That's true . . . ," Millie said.

"And then there's his council . . . ," said Audun.

"His entire council?" Millie said, sitting up abruptly. A lock of her long blond hair had gotten caught around one of Audun's scales, and she winced when it yanked at her scalp.

Audun moved his back legs, and his tail twitched closer to the baby. "My grandmother is one of the members, and they all voted to let us get married."

Millie sighed as she reached back to free her hair. "I suppose we'll have to invite them, too, but we can't include everyone we know."

"I didn't say we had to. I just want—YOW! Watch it, kid. Those scales are attached, and I'd like them to stay that way!"

Millie giggled. Her baby brother was just an infant, but his tiny fingers were already strong. She adored the little boy and was still surprised and delighted that he had become part of her life. Although most royalty relegated the care of infants to nursemaids, Millie and her parents spent as much time with Felix as they could. When Emma and Eadric were busy with the demands of the kingdom,

Millie often visited the nursery on her own. Sometimes she felt almost as if she were the baby's third parent.

"Excuse me," Audun said, edging away from Millie as he got to his feet and put the golden chain back around his neck. "My back is getting stiff. I think it's about time for a change." Like the air above a sun-heated boulder on a hot afternoon, the air shimmered around Audun as he turned from a dragon into a young man with silvery white hair and vivid blue eyes. He was handsome whether he was a human or a dragon, with a strong chin and prominent cheekbones.

When Felix's smile melted away and he began to fuss, Emma looked up from the growing pile of weeds and muttered under her breath. Butterflies flitting around the garden rose above the blossoms and flew to where the baby lay. The multihued cloud descended over the baby, fluttering just out of reach of his flailing fists. Felix chortled and his smile returned even brighter than before.

Audun had just taken a seat on the blanket when the shadow of a large bird passed overhead. Millie glanced up. Her heart rate quickened when she saw that it wasn't a bird at all, but a witch with long white hair whipping behind her as she darted to a landing on her broom made of palm fronds tied to a stick.

Millie was used to visitors arriving at all hours of the day and night. Her mother was the Green Witch and in charge of dealing with the magical issues in Greater Greensward. Because Emma was married to Eadric, crown prince of

Upper Montevista, she had to watch over that kingdom as well. Witches, fairies, and normal humans were always stopping by to tell her about yet another problem. Millie wouldn't have minded if their arrival didn't usually mean that her mother was going to be called away once again, leaving Grassina and Millie to deal with whatever problems might crop up in the two kingdoms. So far Grassina had been able to deal with it all, but there was always the chance that Millie would be called upon to help, and that the small amount of magic she was able to use wouldn't be enough.

Millie tried to stay calm as the visiting witch, who appeared to be nearly ninety, hopped off her broom like a spry sixty-year-old and brushed her snarled hair back from her face. She was a pretty woman with tanned, not-too-wrinkled skin. When she spoke, her voice was unexpectedly husky. "Which one of you is Grassina?" she asked, peering at the women. "My eyesight isn't so good anymore."

Grassina stood, dusting off her hands. "I'm Grassina, and I know who you are, Cadmilla. How can I help you?"

"You can offer me a drink and a seat in the shade," said the witch. "I've been on that pitiful excuse for a broom since yesterday, and my joints ache worse than a whale with a sick belly." She sighed and shook her head. "Listen to me. I've spent so much time with those old crones on the island that I'm beginning to sound like them."

While Grassina hurried into the cottage, Emma helped Cadmilla to a bench under the spreading branches of the oak that grew at the river's edge. "I must be a sight," the old witch said, fussing with her sleeves as she made herself comfortable. "I got caught in the rain yesterday. It took forever for my clothes to dry out."

Grassina emerged from the cottage, carrying a large tankard. "Why were you looking for me?" she said, handing the woman the drink.

Cadmilla took a long sip. "I didn't want to come, and I wouldn't have if the old biddies back on the island hadn't left me the short straw. I think they cheated and used magic to make their straws longer. I would have, too, if I'd thought of it soon enough. I came because of that sea monster. Wrecked our cottages and drove us into the woods. The ugly beast won't leave us alone. It's been coming for a week and hasn't shown any sign of leaving."

"If you and your friends are witches, couldn't you have gotten rid of a sea monster on your own?" Audun asked.

Cadmilla curled her lip in exasperation. "Don't you think we tried? But either our magic is getting as feeble as we are, or the monster is stronger than all of us put together. All our spells and potions didn't affect Old Warty one bit. That's what we call it, because of its warts."

"And you came here because . . ."

"We heard that Grassina had taken it upon herself to get rid of all the monsters around that town Chancewood . . . Chanceworld . . . something like that."

"Chancewold," said Grassina. "Tell me about the monster. What does it look like?"

"It's gray and has a floppy body like a half-empty bladder covered in warts. It stays in the water most of the time, but when it does come out, it crawls around on three big flippers. It has long tentacles with leaf-shaped tips, and it smells like a slop bucket that hasn't been emptied for a month."

"That's one of mine, all right," Grassina said, frowning. "I guess I won't be able to work on the garden after all. If you'll excuse me, I need to get ready to go."

"I remember that monster," said Emma, placing her hand on her aunt's arm. "I'm the one who sent it away. If anyone should deal with this, it's me."

"Don't be absurd. I created the monster, so I'll take care of it."

Emma shook her head. "You can't go alone. I'll go with you and—"

"You'll do no such thing. Haywood will go with me. You're the Green Witch and your responsibilities are here in Greater Greensward. Don't worry. I've dealt with many monsters over the last few years. Haywood and I will be back before you know it."

Although Emma didn't look happy, Millie relaxed and gave an unconscious sigh of relief. She didn't mind helping her mother if she needed it, but then her mother very rarely needed help. All Millie wanted to do was plan her wedding; with her mother there, she just might get the chance.

$\mathcal{B}$efore she met Audun, Millie had thought she knew everything there was to know about being a dragon. But after they fell in love and Audun had had to earn the right to learn how to be a human, she discovered there were a lot of things she didn't know. Most of them, like how ice dragons differed from fire-breathing dragons, were interesting, but only a few affected her directly. Her sweet tooth was one such discovery. She'd always thought it was part of her human side, so she'd been surprised when Audun, who had been a dragon at the time, nibbled a honey-laced confection and declared that it was the best thing he'd ever tasted. It had never occurred to Millie to try anything sweet as a dragon, but when she did, she discovered that dragon taste buds amplified the flavor so that her entire mouth tingled. After that, Millie got in the habit of fetching a huge bowl of porridge in the morning, dribbling a generous serving of honey over it, and taking it back to her chamber to eat. She was sure most of the other inhabitants of the castle would find it disconcerting to see a dragon eating breakfast in the Great Hall, and she didn't want to have to explain why she turned into a dragon just to eat breakfast.

She was in her chamber eating her porridge on the second day after Grassina's departure for the tropical island when she heard a knock on her door. Thinking that it was Audun, she left the bowl on the floor and shuffled across the room, keeping her wings tucked to her sides so she wouldn't knock anything over. Opening the door, she was surprised to find her grandmother Queen Chartreuse waiting on the other side.

After one glance at her granddaughter, the queen pursed her lips in disapproval. "Can't you refrain from turning into a dragon at least for one day? And if you can't restrain yourself, I wish you wouldn't do it inside. This castle was never built for creatures with your . . . bulk."

"Are you saying I'm fat?" Millie asked, backing into the room. Unlike her mother, Millie had never balked at speaking her mind to her grandmother.

"I'm saying that I'd prefer to talk to you while you're a human. There," said the queen as Millie obliged her by changing form. "That's better. Some people have come to see your mother. If you'd been eating in the Great Hall as you should be, you would know that she was called away to speak to a herd of centaurs who have been stealing horses from local farms. They call it liberating them, which is the silliest thing I've ever heard. Your mother had just left when these people came to see her. Ordinarily, I would send them to see Grassina, but she's away, as you know. Your grandfather and your father have gone hunting, leaving me to deal with everything, but I put my foot down when it comes to dealing with something like this. You're going to have to talk to them, so wipe the porridge off your chin and come with me."

"Who are these people?" Millie asked, following Queen Chartreuse down the corridor. Her stomach was beginning to clench—not a good thing when it was full of porridge. She doubted that she'd be much help in a magical way, and she dreaded telling people that she couldn't do anything for them.

"Fairies! Young people like you have no problem talking to them because you're used to it, but when I was a girl, they never came to visit the way they do now. And I'm not like your father's mother, Frazzela, who dotes on fairies. I have no idea what to say to them. Then there's the wing issue. If they have wings, I try not to stare at them, but I know I will anyway, which is rude. And if they don't have wings, I wonder why not—I always do—and then I lose track of whatever they're saying. They shed fairy dust, too, which is so untidy. Now you go on ahead," the queen said as they reached the bottom of the stairs. "You'll find them just outside the door leading from the Great Hall into the courtyard."

"No one invited them in?" asked Millie.

"Of course not," the queen said, wrinkling her nose with distaste. "You'll see why when you meet them. Oh, and by the way, you *have* gained a few pounds lately. You really must cut back on the sweets."

Three fairies were waiting by the stairs in the court-yard, looking as if they weren't sure they should be there. They turned to face Millie as she reached the bottom step. She'd met the fairy dressed in the soft green gown and matching floppy cap before. Moss had visited her mother and even come to some of the parties at the castle, but the other two fairies were unfamiliar.

"Good day, Millie," said Moss. "Is your mother, Princess Emma, here? We have a problem and we think she's the only one who can handle it."

Millie shook her head. "She left this morning and I have no idea when she'll be back. Maybe I can help," she added, more because she thought she should than because she wanted to.

"You can if you're as powerful a witch as your mother," said the fairy with the pale skin and gown made of shiny green leaves. The nostrils of her thin, arched nose flared when she looked at Millie, giving the fairy's narrow face a scornful expression.

"I'm sorry, I should have introduced my friends to you," said Moss. "This is Poison Ivy, and this is Trillium," she added, indicating the shorter fairy with dark red hair that hung down her back almost to the ground. Her flower-petal dress was only a shade or two lighter than her hair, and it glistened as if sprinkled with dew.

"It's nice meeting you," said Millie. "But I'm not a witch."

"I knew coming here was a waste of time," Poison Ivy said, tilting her head back so that she looked down at Millie.

Taking a deep breath, Millie tried to tamp down the irritation welling up inside her at Poison Ivy's rudeness.

Trillium sighed and said in a whispery soft voice, "Perhaps we should go."

Millie started to agree with her. If the fairies thought they needed powerful magic to deal with their problem, Millie probably couldn't help. Aside from her dragon magic, she had very little magic of her own. She could find lost items, but only if they were things she used all the time and had lost recently. She could turn the pages of a book with the wave of a hand, but only one at a time. She could even blow out a candle from across the room, but she couldn't light it again unless she turned into a dragon. Millie wanted to tell the fairies that they'd have to return when her mother was home, but then she glanced at Poison Ivy again and knew from the curl of her lip that the fairy expected her to back down. The irritation she'd felt before flared into a spark of anger.

For most of her life, before Millie had learned how to control her temper, she turned into a dragon each time she got angry. Even now, controlling her temper wasn't always easy. She knew that if she let little things bother her, even the smallest spark of anger could flare into full-blown rage. Millie glared at the narrow-faced fairy, then purposefully turned toward Moss. "If you tell me what the problem is, I might be able to help."

Moss shook her head, and her cap slipped down over her eyes. She pushed it back with a rueful smile and said, "That's very nice of you to offer, but I don't see how you can possibly help us. It's a plant problem, you see, and not a nice plant, either."

"Is it one of your plants?" Millie asked, glancing from one to the next but letting her gaze linger longest on Poison Ivy.

"Don't look at me!" Poison Ivy declared. "My ivy has nothing to do with this. I only came along to help."

"There's no need to act defensive," said Moss. "I'm sure Princess Millie didn't mean anything."

"Ha!" said Poison Ivy.

"It's not one of our plants at all," whispered Trillium. "It's a plant so nasty that it doesn't *have* a fairy to watch over it."

"That's right," said Moss. "No fairy wants anything to do with it. It's new to the enchanted forest. We think some horrid person brought it here to stir up trouble. Thank goodness there's only one."

"It comes from a rain forest far away," Poison Ivy added. "Too bad it didn't stay there."

"What's so awful about this plant?" asked Millie. She was intrigued now. A plant couldn't be that bad, could it?

"What plant?" asked Audun as he descended the steps behind her.

"Are you a wizard?" Poison Ivy said, looking Audun up and down. "Because we could really use a good one."

"This is my betrothed, Audun, and he's not a wizard."

"Even so, I'm sure we can deal with a plant," Audun told them.

Poison Ivy snorted. "Not this plant!"

Trillium tugged on Poison Ivy's sleeve. "We could show it to them," she said in a voice so soft that Millie had to strain to hear it.

"I'm not sure . . . ," Moss began.

"Why not?" said Poison Ivy and sneered at Millie. "I'd suggest that you follow us on your broom, but you're not a witch, so—"

"Would a magic carpet do?" Millie asked, anger building inside her again. "I'll be right back."

She left Audun talking to the fairies while she went to her chamber to fetch the carpet her mother had given her for her last birthday. It was also an excuse to leave the fairies for a few minutes. Generally, the only people who were rude to Millie were those who didn't know either that she was a princess or that she could become a dragon at will. Moss had mentioned in Poison Ivy's presence that Millie's mother was a princess, so it couldn't be that. However, there was a good chance that Poison Ivy might not know about Millie's dragon side; Emma had been using magic for years to keep it a secret. Millie was tempted to turn into a dragon to show the fairy just whom she was dealing with— which was exactly why she couldn't let herself do it. Once she was a dragon, the temptation to fry Poison Ivy would be hard to withstand.

E. D. BAKER is the author of the Tales of the Frog Princess series, The Wide-Awake Princess series, and many other delightful books for young readers, including *Fairy Wings, Fairy Lies, A Question of Magic,* and *The Fairy-Tale Matchmaker. The Frog Princess* was the inspiration for Disney's hit movie *The Princess and the Frog.* She lives with her family and their many animals in Maryland.

www.talesofedbaker.com